THE CHARLEMAGNE CONNECTION

by
R.M. CARTMEL

The Charlemagne Connection © R.M. Cartmel

ISBN 978-0-9929486-2-7
eISBN 978-0-9929486-3-4

Published in 2015 by Crime Scene Books

The right of R.M. Cartmel to be identified as the author
of this work has been asserted by him in accordance with the
Copyright, Designs and Patents Act 1988.

A CIP record of this book is available from the British Library.

Printed in the UK by TJ International, Padstow

To David Clark

You helped me immeasurably in the creation of this and The Richebourg Affair.

You also made some sensationally good wine, even though we usually drank tea when we met. A la vôtre, [Vosne that is!].

Acknowledgements

Firstly may I thank the people involved in the creation of this book, Sarah Williams and her editing and publication team, including Kelly Mundt, Mark Hoben and Martin Sanders.

I know of no author who has been better served than by Maryglenn McCombs and Teresa Quinlan to spread the word.

Nick Marquez-Grant from the laboratory at Cranfield for his help with the forensics and Mark Spencer, forensic botanist at the Natural History Museum.

Noël de Spéville helped with the intricacies of Inheritance Law in France.

David Clark of Domaine David Clark in Morey-Saint-Denis and Pierre Vincent and Sylvie Poillot of Domaine de la Vougeraie in Prémeaux-Prissey gave immeasurable help on the viticulture side of things. La Vougeraie produces the quarterly *La Lettre* and that too provided me with viticultural wisdom.

Jasper Morris MW wrote the wonderful *Inside Burgundy*, and Hugh Johnson and Jancis Robinson conspired to create the 7th Edition of the *World Atlas of Wine*. Those books helped me find my way round the Côte-d'Or both while I was walking round, and also in my thoughts.

The Café du Centre in Nuits-Saint-Georges and the Royal Sun at Begbroke in Oxfordshire provided an 'instant office' with pleasant food, wine and ambience in which to work.

Thank you to the makers and stars of the French TV Detective series 'Les Engrenages' [UK:Spiral] for its explanation of the Police in France.

And finally, may I say a big *merci* to the non-fictitious agents at the Gendarmerie in Nuits-Saint-Georges. They tolerated this ageing English writer wandering in and asking them in his own peculiar style of French, peculiar questions like 'where can I put this corpse so that it will still remain in the jurisdiction of my fictitious Nuits-Saint-Georges' gendarmes?' And they didn't arrest me even once!

Of course there are many slips between cups and lips and I accept full responsibility for misunderstanding the words of wisdom of those whose advice I sought, any mistakes in the text are due to my personal brain fade alone.

The Côte de Nuits

To Beaune
(Premeaux-Prissey, Aloxe-Corton)

TREELINE

Nuits-St-Georges

Nuits-Nos-Georges

D974

Vosne-
Romanée

Vosne

Chambolle-
Musigny

Échezeaux

Yougeot

Clos de Vougeot

Morey-
St-Denis

Gevrey-
Chambertin

VINEYARDS

Fixin

Couchey

Marsannay
la Côte

D974

To Chenôve

N

0km   1km

Dramatis Personæ

Commander Charlemagne Truchaud. *A detective; our hero*

His team from Paris

Sergeant Natalie Dutoit, *A gorgeous Parisian detective, sharp as a tack*

His family in Nuits-Saint Georges

Dad [Philibert], *His father, not as well as he used to be, and getting worse*

Michelle, *His brother's widow, who is now running the business*

Bruno, *His brother's son, a twelve-year-old boy, who thinks his uncle [above] is wonderful, and Suzette [below], and…*

Other police officers in Paris

Divisional Commander, *Truchaud's ageing boss*

Commander Lucas, *Another Parisian team leader going places*

At the Gendarmerie in Nuits-Saint-Georges

Captain Duquesne, *The chief*

Constable Lenoir, *A policeman who is a frightening driver*

Constable Montbard, *A policewoman with strawberry blonde hair*

Constable Savioli, *Another policeman, new to Burgundy*

Civilian administration in Nuits-Saint-Georges

Monsieur le Juge de Castaigne, *An investigating magistrate*

Madame Clermont, *A ferocious crime scene investigator*

A guardianship magistrate

The Deputy Mayor of Nuits-Saint-Georges

At Maison Laforge, where the Truchauds do business

Old Mr [Émile] Laforge, *who used to be in the Maquis*

Young Mr [Jérome] Laforge, *who would be middle-aged if he were not already a corpse*

Marie-Claire Laforge, *Old Mr Laforge's granddaughter*

Jacquot Laforge, *Her son; a lad of fourteen years*

Simon Maréchale, *A master winemaker*

Celestine, *who works in the office; on the lookout for a ladder to climb*

Armand Laforge, *Emile's brother, abducted by the Boche during the War*

Other people in and around Nuits-Saint-Georges

Christine Blanchard, *Manager of the municipal campsite on the edge of Prémeaux*

Doctor Girand, *Suzette's father and the local GP*

Geneviève Girand, *Suzette's mother; a very old friend of Commander Truchaud*

Suzette Girand, *A university student, who sometimes works in Laforge's shop*

Jean Parnault, *A winemaker, Geneviève's brother, and an old friend of Bertin*

Bénigne Gauvre, *A winemaker, who had parents with a sense of humour*

Sophie Gauvre, *who responds to being addressed as 'Wife'*

Solange Gauvre, *Bénigne's teenaged daughter, who has gone missing*

Adèle Gauvre, *Bénigne's other teenaged daughter, whose only responses are monosyllabic*

Pierre LeCaillou, *A lad with a flat in Chenôve, who also had parents with a sense of humour*

German tourists from Chemnitz (which used to be known as Karl Marx Stadt)

Horst Witter, *who was the first to arrive and then wasn't there*

Dagmar Witter, *His Sister, who came to look for him*

Renate, *Her best friend, who came for the ride*

People who actually exist!

Christine Tournier, *who owns and runs the Café du Centre in Nuits-Saint-Georges*

Prologue

Nuits-Saint-Georges, sometime after last year's harvest

Captain Duquesne raised an eyebrow when the angular features of young Constable Lenoir appeared round the corner of the door without warning. He was usually expected to announce himself from his seat behind the counter in the outer office, with a quick call on the intercom. After all, you never knew quite what the *chef* might be doing. 'Can I help you, gendarme?' he asked icily.

'There's a woman out here with a problem which I think you ought to be aware of,' the constable replied carefully.

Duquesne thought for a moment, and then replied, as Lenoir looked as if he required some sort of answer. 'Well, are you going to bring her in then?'

Constable Lenoir's head disappeared from round the door, but his shoulder remained in sight, as Duquesne heard him telling someone outside to 'come on through'.

'This is Madame Blanchard,' Lenoir said, introducing the middle-aged woman. 'She runs the campsite just south of town.'

Duquesne remembered his manners and invited the woman to sit down, before asking her what appeared to be the problem.

'It's one of our campers,' she said. 'I think he's disappeared.'

'How might you mean *disappeared*?' he asked extremely politely, somewhat to Lenoir's surprise.

'Well, he always comes to the shop at the beginning of the day, to buy some fresh bread and milk for breakfast; sometimes croissants as well; sometimes not. But for the past three days, he hasn't even been into the shop at all.'

1

'Might he have found another shop to get his breakfast from?' asked Duquesne, the polite tone persisting, but with a slight overtone of dryness creeping in over the top.

'Oh, I agree,' she replied. 'We're not a monopoly, and we don't demand that our campers buy only from us. All we expect is that our campers pay up for the rentals of their pitches. And his pitch rental also became due yesterday.'

'How do you mean?'

'Well, we charge a daily fee for each day stayed. When he first arrived, he paid a week's rental up front in cash. He was quite chatty, and spoke good French for a German, and each time he's stayed, his French has improved, so he really seems to quite enjoy testing out his latest French idioms, while collecting the bread and milk.'

'You mean this isn't the first time he's stayed with you?'

'Oh no. This must be the fourth time he's stayed at the Camp Millésime.'

'And he has always got his breakfast from you?'

'Yes, without fail; every time he's stayed.'

'Go on.'

'Well, yesterday, as part of my walk round the campsite, to make sure all is well, I looked round his area, and he wasn't there, and nor was his bicycle.'

'Bicycle?'

'Yes, he has a bicycle to get about on.'

'He didn't come all this way from Germany on a bicycle, did he?' asked Duquesne, sounding slightly surprised. 'What is he: an athlete in training for the Tour de France?'

'No, captain. He comes here in an old Volkswagen Kombi campervan, which he parks up and sleeps in while he stays. He then potters about on a bicycle which he brings with him. He does appear to be quite fit, I suppose, but the Tour de France? No, I don't think so.'

'How old is he?'

'About twenty-five,' she replied.

Duquesne grinned at Lenoir. 'Do you think he has found himself a little friend to make his holiday more fun?'

'I thought that too,' said Madame Blanchard without missing a beat. 'But when I came back this morning the pan was in exactly the same place.'

'The pan, madame?' enquired the captain quizzically.

'Yes,' she replied, 'the pan. You see, when I went by yesterday there was a saucepan, of the sort you might boil water in, or cook things in perhaps, lying just outside the door of the camper. It was still in exactly the same place this morning. So, it's extremely unlikely that he came back last night, because if he had, he would have had to move it, even just slightly, to get into the camper without twisting like some sort of contortionist. And why would you do that when all you have to do is shift a little saucepan?'

'And it was in exactly the same place?'

'Yes.'

'Wasn't that rather unfair of you leaving the young man's pan outside? Anyone could have stolen it,' remarked Lenoir.

'But no one did. That's the point. Nobody moved it to get into the camper either. I did ask the young couple with the baby – who had a pitch and a tent just across from him – if they had seen him at all, and they said they haven't; not for the past three days.'

'And he owes you money?' remarked the captain.

'Well, yes, but only a couple of days' worth.'

'And if he had been fully paid-up, then you wouldn't have come round here bothering the Gendarmerie with all this?'

'Oh, captain, I don't think that's fair. I'm worried for him too. He seems a nice young man: always comes on his own; seems a solitary lad; but has always been polite and pleasant to us. He doesn't flirt with the assistants or anything.'

Captain Duquesne shrugged. The realization was dawning on him that he wasn't going to get rid of this woman without making some sort of effort to address her concerns, unless he just physically threw her out, and that simply wasn't Duquesne's way. 'What time are you going to be back at the campsite, madame?' he asked.

'I should be back there in about half an hour,' she replied.

'I shall come and have a look at the scene when you get back, or perhaps young Lenoir here will,' he added, tossing a glance at the gendarme still standing behind the woman. 'Do you know how to get to the campsite, constable?'

'Yes, sir.'

'Then you can show Madame Blanchard out. Once you have done so, will you come back in again?'

Lenoir returned almost immediately.

'Sit down,' his captain instructed him, and he did so where erstwhile Madame Blanchard had been sitting. 'Your concerns?' he asked.

'Well, sir, I was just thinking … suppose she's right? I mean, people don't just disappear, not here in Nuits-Saint-Georges.'

'You're telling me that you'd like to investigate this?'

'Yes, sir, if I may. Just to see if there really is anything to her concerns.'

'Go for it then. You'll find it good training, if nothing else.'

Lenoir left the office and walked back into the front office. The new kid, Savioli, had taken his place at the front desk, and Lenoir waved at him to stay there. He looked into the back office and there espied Montbard: stocky, strawberry blonde and female. He caught her eye, they didn't actually need to speak, and she led him out to the car park.

Duquesne watched them through his window. Montbard reached the car first and climbed in the passenger side. That was definitely her choice; to leave the driver's seat for Lenoir. She was either exceptionally brave, he thought, or had no imagination. Given the amount of tyre-squeal Lenoir got out of that poor little Mégane, sooner or later, either a tyre or the little car itself was going to surrender and explode.

'Where are we off to?' she asked.

He explained what they were up to, and headed the car out round to the D974, turning left onto it, heading south. The 'Seventy-Four', as it was originally known, when it had had Route Nationale status not that many years before, had been the main road to the south, but the motorway system had been put in place and had taken all but local traffic out of the little

4

town of Nuits-Saint-Georges. It took him no more than ten minutes to drive to the campsite in Prémeaux, and that hadn't required him to squeal any tyres. Madame Blanchard had just arrived and was unloading her car. The gendarmes helped her into the kitchen with her shopping, and then she took them into her front office, and passed the register to them.

They noticed the name, Horst Witter, was written in block capitals, but the address was in some sort of scrawl. They all agreed among themselves that the street address was Hauptstrasse 2, but none of them could make out the town. 'Do you know where he lives?' Montbard asked her.

'Well, he did tell me, but as I've never been to Germany, it didn't mean anything to me, so I'm afraid I don't remember.'

'We'll probably get some kind of hint from the number plate,' said Lenoir. 'German number plates have their town where they're registered on the plate. For example, they have 'K' for Cologne.'

'Go on,' said Montbard. 'Tell me why K means Cologne. You know you're dying to.' The light dusting of freckles over her nose crinkled slightly to accompany her grin.

'Well, Mac, the Germans call Cologne *Köln*, you see.' She was known as 'Mac' among the other gendarmes at Nuits-Saint-Georges, owing to the red hair and intense blue eyes that somewhat suggested she had some Scottish ancestry.

'You don't think he's been abducted, do you?' asked Madame Blanchard with a slight tremor creeping into her voice.

'It's far more likely he's found himself a new friend to play with,' remarked Montbard drily.

'Or he's found a casual job at one of the winemakers.'

'But why would he leave his camper here at the campsite incurring rent? It seems silly to be earning money on one side and leaking it out on the other.'

'We might know the answer to that when we find him. Mind you, if he's found a new playground in Chambolle, then there might well be nowhere for him to park it nearby, without clogging the street.'

'Okay,' she said. 'So let's wander up to his camper and play detectives. Let's see what his number plate actually tells us.'

Madame Blanchard led the two gendarmes up the campsite to the German's pitch.

She was right. The Volkswagen Kombi was distinctly old and tatty, and had been at least partly repainted by hand. However, on close inspection, both the tyres and the exhaust pipe were almost new. The machine had had money spent on it where necessary, and recently. When Lenoir leaned against the tailgate, there was no sensation of movement either.

'You're not trying to push it downhill, are you?' asked Montbard quizzically.

'Only if it will actually roll,' he replied. 'And it doesn't seem to want to,' he added after a moment. 'It's got good brakes, you see.' He also noticed the pan, which Madame Blanchard had mentioned earlier. He understood how it would have been a little ungainly trying to climb into the camper without moving it even slightly from where it was lying. Lenoir walked round to the front of the camper to look at the number plate. It didn't have two letters in the middle, it had three, and they were very strange indeed. 'MYK' did not bring any German town to mind.

'Mykonos?' enquired Montbard, crinkling her freckles again with another grin. 'That's a Greek island, and I'm sure the Boche gave it back to the Greeks when the War was over.'

'I'm sure the Greeks took it back by force long before the War was over, unless they've recently sold it back to Germany in part-payment for their EU loan,' Lenoir replied drily. He thought for a while, trying to think of another German town starting with MYK. Damn her, Mykonos was such an obviously good idea that he couldn't think of anything else. He took his notebook out of his pocket, and wrote the numbers and letters down. He flicked the book closed and back it went into his pocket. No doubt they would find out sooner or later.

He tried the doors, but they were all locked. He looked through the windows. The back was somewhat occluded by rather delicate lace curtains over the side windows, but when he looked through the back window over the engine, he could see a rather rumpled sleeping bag under the window. If he had slept in that there, he thought, he probably wasn't very tall as he would have been sleeping across the vehicle. Maybe he slept curled up. Lenoir knew that he couldn't. What it did mean was that his table was still up behind the driving seats? There didn't appear to be anything on the table, but, he asked himself, if the table was still up, why had he left his saucepan outside? He walked round to look through the quarter lights and the windscreen itself, but apart from describing the whole-sale slaughter of insects on the front of the cab, that didn't tell him very much either.

The two gendarmes both bade Madame Blanchard a polite farewell and drove back to the Gendarmerie. Lenoir tapped on the captain's door and was invited back in.

'He's certainly not there at the moment, though as Madame says, his camper certainly is.' Lenoir started.

'Any evidence where he might have got to?'

'None whatsoever. Madame wondered whether he had gone and got himself a casual job at one of the winemakers, although the season is really over now. There will still be a few jobs around cleaning out the fermentation tanks they've been using, ready for next year, I suppose. There are also last year's new barrels that will need cleaning out, as they don't put all the wine they've just made into new oak barrels; it would taste far too woody.'

'You have been studying hard, constable,' grinned the captain.

'The more you know about the locals' lives, the better you can police them,' Lenoir replied evenly.

'That sounds like a quote from one of the lectures at Police Academy,' he replied. 'Changing the subject, did you get the number plate from the camper?'

Lenoir pulled out his notebook and reeled off the number.

'MYK?' asked the captain, 'You wouldn't happen to know where that comes from?'

'Mac said she thought it came from Mykonos, but that can't be right, as it's a Greek island in the Aegean.'

Duquesne looked up at him and smiled slightly sadly, 'You do realize when you're having your leg pulled, don't you? Leave it with me. I'll take it from here.'

A couple of days later Captain Duquesne called the two gendarmes into his office. 'Know where Boppard is, team?'

'Boppard?'

'Yes.' He looked at the pair of them expectantly but they didn't reply. 'I'll put you out of your misery then. It's a small town, similar in size to Nuits-Saint-Georges, and it sits on the Rhine a few kilometres south of Koblenz. Our Helmut Witter's Volkswagen Kombi is registered to him at an address there, at 2 Hauptstrasse, just like you said.'

'Boppard,' said Montbard chewing gently on the word. 'That doesn't work; there isn't an 'M', a 'Y' or a 'K' anywhere in that word, however ethnically you spell it.'

'Ah, well,' replied the captain, 'here's the trick. I did get through to the German Traffic Registration Office to find the address to which the vehicle is registered. You know something? I asked them that very same question.'

'Go on?'

'Well, MYK is taken from the names of Mayen and Kobern-Gondorf, which are the administrative villages in that part of the Hunsruck.'

'That doesn't work either. It's MYK not MKG.'

'Well, maybe MKG had already been allocated. I don't know,' replied the captain, beginning to lose patience. 'That's simply the way it is. Maybe they selected MYK specifically to unsettle young French gendarmes with a fetish for the Aegean. What I suggest we do, to keep Madame Blanchard happy, is impound the camper here in our police pound. We can leave a message for him at the campsite so that he can come and collect his camper when he gets back. I'll also send a note to him at his home address, telling him what has happened to his camper, and we wait and see.'

'Good idea, chief. When would you like us to go and pick up the camper?'

'We'll give him a few more days. Say by the weekend? Nobody's reported him missing, apart from the campsite, and that's only because he's two days overdue with the rent. He's not wanted for any crime anywhere, and he hasn't turned up anywhere where he isn't supposed to be. He's a citizen of the EU, so he's perfectly entitled to get a job round here, or anywhere else in France for that matter, and maybe he really has outgrown that barrel of bolts we charitably call a camper. If he's the new Mayor of Bordeaux, then I could quite understand his not wanting to be seen dead in it!'

And that is exactly what happened … well, not the Mayor of Bordeaux bit obviously, but the rest of it.

After about a month, the gendarmes seemed to forget about the elderly German campervan rotting quietly in the back of the car pound, unclaimed and apparently unwanted and unloved.

Chapter 1

Paris, mid-June

The detective sat back in his chair and looked out of the window. Somehow a pleasant late spring day in Paris did not in any way echo his feelings. The sound of birdsong, the small gentle clouds scudding across a bright blue sky, the tourists in their colourful sleeveless shirts on the street below, all somehow felt out of place. He had been back in Paris on active duty for a fortnight, and on the first day of that fortnight, a new case had been deposited on his desk; that of a child, abused and abandoned, burnt to a cinder in the boot of a car. The welter of deprivation and depravity they had uncovered was something he never wished to see again. The smell, and somehow the taste, of cooked meat still lingered unpleasantly in his mouth, however much of the unpleasantly strong and strongly unpleasant Quai des Orfèvres instant coffee he swirled around his tongue. It was almost enough to turn him vegetarian, and him a Burgundian! He was beginning to think he should be finding something different to do with his life; he didn't want to face that sort of stuff for much longer. He reflected back to a few weeks before when he was in ensconced in his family home in Nuits-Saint-Georges; he had rather enjoyed the bucolic flavour of that sort of police work.

His phone rang, or rather bleeped. He glared balefully at it. That was something else he didn't care for much; the sound of an electronic telephone bell. He was as disposed to like it as to enjoy a record of electronic music. He picked up the phone. 'Truchaud?' he answered.

'Lucas here. Have you got a moment? I think I might have someone with a solution to your barbecued kid case down here in the interrogation room. Interested in sending someone down

11

to meet him?' Truchaud would describe Commander Lucas as a colleague, not a friend. Lucas was taller than Truchaud, but that wasn't the reason why Truchaud always felt Lucas was looking down on him. Truchaud felt that all pure-bred Parisians looked down on him, even his own lieutenant Leclerc, but no one made him feel more inferior than Lucas. Once upon a time he had outranked Lucas, but over the fullness of time, Lucas had caught him up, and sooner or later, he knew that Lucas would be promoted beyond him. Truchaud found being despised by a colleague an unpleasant experience, and particularly so, as in this case, when that colleague was being 'helpful'.

'He's a suspect in my case, but he keeps talking about yours,' said Lucas. 'I think he's trying to grass his way out of trouble.'

Truchaud glared at the phone, but replied amiably into it. 'We'll be right down.'

He looked across the squad room and said loudly, 'Constable, you're with me.'

He stood up and walked out of the door, not bothering to check which constable was following him; he knew one of them would.

Three floors below, in the interview suite, Lucas stood in the corridor, his hands clasped behind his back, looking just like a good schoolboy.

'Truchaud, old friend, come on in,' said Lucas with false affability. 'Our man's in number 3. Be my guest. Mind if I watch?'

Lucas pointed at the one-way mirrors. Truchaud looked round to see who had actually followed him from the squad room. Constable Dutoit was a young woman who had been allocated to his squad last year. Most of the other officers drooled quietly over her astonishing good looks, but fortunately for both of them, Truchaud was not of the drooling variety, even if he was utterly impressed by a girl's appearance … which in this case, he wasn't. He was far more impressed with her razor-sharp mind and the way she could instantly get to the root of an issue. In some ways, Truchaud considered, she was quite lucky to have been allocated to his team. He felt that he treated them like a good father should treat their children. With a raised eyebrow and a shrug of the opposite shoulder Truchaud indicated that Dutoit should do the interrogation, and parked himself on a chair alongside Commander Lucas behind the one-way mirror.

'That's most unfair. Not a cat's chance in hell.' Lucas remarked. 'You know the fellow's a paedo, don't you?'

Truchaud left his reply to that in the air. At least he knew which one of them beyond that window was at a disadvantage. The suspect looked up at Dutoit as she walked through the door. Her skin had the colour and sheen of freshly churned cream. Her fair hair was tied at the back of her head in a pigtail. She was dressed in a loose shirt and blue denim jeans, which just hinted at lithe curves beneath, but didn't leave them in any doubt. Her steel-blue eyes looked at the soft-looking middle-aged man in front of her with faintly disguised contempt, and he looked up at her and knew he had made at least one bad decision in his life.

Clicking on the standard issue tape deck to record, Dutoit clearly announced her own name, that of the accused, and the time.

'I understand you have some information to give us, which may, in turn, help how your own case turns out,' she said. 'I've been sent down to collect that information.'

Both officers on the far side of the window couldn't help being impressed by the way and how quickly she got the suspect eating out of her hand, despite the fact that the man was allegedly unimpressed by her femininity. Moreover, she also got him talking on other issues apart from her own case, and that got a great deal more of Lucas' attention and had him scribbling furiously in his notebook. It took less than ten minutes in total before she told the tape recorder she was concluding the interview, and turned it off. She turned to face the one-way mirror, and raised both her eyebrows. She then thanked the man in front of her, and suggested that someone else would be with him in a moment or so. Lucas was up very rapidly and bolting towards the interview room.

'You told me she was good,' he tossed at Truchaud. 'I thought you just meant she looks good. She thinks good too.'

Dutoit came out of the room grinning, especially at Lucas as he barged past her.

'Well, chief,' she said to Truchaud, 'what did you think?'

'Nice work,' he replied. 'You can be very persuasive, you know.'

'With whom? The suspect or Commander Lucas?' She beamed.

'In this case, I think both, and more or less equally. It takes most people a lot longer than you to acquire those skills.'

'I started learning unpleasantly young,' she replied ruefully, 'so I was left with the choice of getting involved in some form of entertainment, or joining the police when I grew up.'

'And which did you choose?' said Truchaud, and felt immediately stupid. It was blindingly obvious which she had chosen; she was standing there in front of him, wasn't she?

'The stage, of course,' she replied with a grin. 'I'm still waiting for that chance-in-a-lifetime audition, so I thought I'd do a little police work to keep me in lippy, and pay the rent. It also helps to occupy my time.' Truchaud had no idea whether she was just joking. He hoped that was all.

It didn't take the team very long to make the arrests, and Georges Delacroix took the point on that one; the first time he had been fully back in action since his accident in the spring. He was a little thinner and paler now than he had been before the accident, but everyone was pleased to see he was back, from the Divisional Commander downwards.

With the arrests made, Truchaud passed the case on to the Investigating Magistrate, who having discussed it with the team in general, took Delacroix and Dutoit off with him to interrogate the sleazy apology for a human being they had arrested. They all knew he was close to the leader, and before very long they would have the whole gang of perverts behind bars. What had he said when asked about the child? 'Disposing of the evidence'. Just how cold and brutal and beastly could you get? But Truchaud knew all too well that although you locked one rat gang up, almost immediately another one's nose appeared from beneath the skirting board to take its place. *Paris, what have they done to you?*

Chapter 2

Paris, a few days later

Truchaud was once again sitting back in the chair in his office. If you were to ask him, he would have said he was thinking about his team working with the Examining Magistrate, though in reality, he probably wasn't thinking about anything at all. His phone rang. Vaguely annoyed, as ever, with the timbre of his phone's ring, he picked up the receiver to prevent it from continuing with its pathetic bleeping. Maybe that was the point of the noise. 'Truchaud!' he said into it.

'Simon Maréchale here. Do you have a moment?' Maréchale was the master vintner of his family's wine business in Nuits-Saint-Georges. He had been taken on to replace the detective's brother, who had died a few months previously under circumstances he would rather not think about. Maréchale was a shrewd, possibly shifty, but undoubtedly clever, grower of the vine, charmer of the grape, fermenter of its juice, and blender of wines. Not that he really needed that particular skill in Burgundy; perish the thought.

'Simon, I always have time for news from home,' he replied cheerily.

'Not this news, you won't,' the winemaker replied drily. 'Your father's been making a right nuisance of himself, and I've been told in no uncertain terms by the cops that if the family doesn't sort him out forthwith, then they will.'

'That doesn't sound like Captain Duquesne's view on life.' The detective had got on famously with the local Captain of Gendarmes the last time they had met.

'That wasn't the gendarmes; that came from your lot's head office in Dijon. Apparently, the bloke who caught your father relieving the call of nature all over his vines in flower has friends in very high places.'

'Oh dear god! I'll be right down. See you later today.' That sort of news did worry him. His father's Alzheimer's seemed to be of the rapidly progressive variety.

The next stop was a quick visit to the Divisional Commander's office. It appeared he had already received a telephone call from his opposite number in Dijon, and it had been apparently the old man's intervention that had caused the temporary stay of execution, so to speak. If Truchaud hadn't been in the process of asking for leave to go and sort out his father, the Divisional Commander would have sent him there, with a missile in a fairly painful location. 'Go and sort him out, young man. We can't be having all this. Do you want to bring him up here?'

'I think there would be little point. If he's already seriously confused in a location he knows, he wouldn't stand a chance in Paris.'

'Yes, I understand that. How long do you think you're going to be?'

'I have no idea how long this will take.'

'Well, we still owe you a great deal of holiday, but I'm not sure we'll be able to put your whole squad on standby until you get back this time.'

'I understand that. What're you thinking of doing with them?'

'That rather depends how long you're going to be. You know, Commander Lucas is rather taken with your exceptionally brainy Detective Constable Dutoit.'

'I don't think it's her brains that he's particularly taken with,' Truchaud replied tersely.

The old man grinned. 'Well, that may well be true; you can always tell a skilled copper by the effectiveness of their leg work; and her legs work ... you only have to look at them once to see that.'

'Are you being deliberately politically incorrect, sir? She's a very competent police officer, not just a piece of fluffy eye-candy,' the Commander replied, well aware he sounded very blue-rinsed and middle-aged.

'If there were anyone else in the room, or I had the faintest inkling that you would pass that comment on, especially to Lucas or indeed Constable Dutoit herself, I'd have never said it in the first place. However, if you're going to be away for a while, I'm thinking about some internal promotions within your squad.' He paused for a moment. 'But I'm sure that if I arrange for Inspector Leclerc's promotion to Commander, he'd never accept being demoted back to Inspector again if you were to come back a week later. I accept also that if you were not here, Detective Constable Dutoit wouldn't feel in the least bit threatened in a squad led by him, and anyway, she'd make a good sergeant. I know you think Leclerc's a bumptious Parisian, but he would support the squad as far as they needed, and they've all passed their required exams. You know something, I think he's more than just a competent detective, and we both know she is.'

'I'm not sure that Natalie needs any protection from anyone within the force, or outside the force for that matter. Have you seen her handle a pistol? She's a far better shot than I am.'

'Well it was you who finished off that incident in Burgundy with a pistol shot,' the Divisional Commander reminded him.

'And wasn't I the lucky one then?' he replied. 'She wasn't even in Nuits-Saint-Georges to help.' He paused for a moment and then continued. 'Anyway, I need to get off to sort my father out, and if you're okay with it, today was what I promised.'

The Divisional Commander duly sent him on his way. He quickly explained to his team that he was off, and that they would see him again soon. He didn't explain that he had no idea how soon, but Constable Dutoit, looking up slightly wistfully from her desk, obviously had some inkling that it wouldn't be immediately, as she said, '*À bientôt, chef,*' as her au revoir.

His landlady also appeared to have some idea that he might not be back in the immediate future, owing to her question about forwarding his mail, which he agreed should go to the family domaine in Nuits-Saint-Georges. And yes, the deliveries should be cancelled until he got back. He packed the required essentials and threw them into the back of his car, once again making sure his trench coat was where he would expect to find it, on the back seat. He set off and headed south.

The drive south down the 'Motorway to the Sun' was much as it always was, though he didn't usually travel to Burgundy in the height of the summer. He was always willing to demur to the officers with children as far as holidays were concerned. If they'd got kids, let them suffer them on holiday; that was one responsibility he was glad he didn't have. But even as he had those thoughts, the thought about his father entering what was sometimes politely known as his 'second childhood' crossed his mind, and didn't make him feel any happier at all.

Reaching Beaune, he turned off at his favourite motorway junction, and as he always did, reached for his identity card, and – as was always the case – there was no one at the tollbooth to share the joke with. He stuck his credit card in the payment machine's ear, wondering why it didn't require a code like everything else as he watched the barrier lift. Having removed his card, he drove the fifty yards to the roundabout and turned right for the last bit of the journey north, past Corton Hill with its tufts of woodland on top. It took him no more than fifteen minutes until he got to the edge of Nuits-Saint-Georges, and, on reaching the traffic lights, he turned left into the small town itself.

Michelle greeted him as he pulled into the courtyard of the family home. She was a roly-poly woman in her early forties, the widow of his older brother, and mother to his favourite, and come to think of it, *only* nephew Bruno. She didn't look quite as miserable as she had done on his last arrival in Nuits, but that was understandable; on that occasion, his brother had died during the previous night.

They kissed each other on each cheek, and then he asked, 'How are they all?'

She looked at him slightly askance. 'You know the answer to that, otherwise you wouldn't be back down here again so soon,' she replied, slightly acidly. 'Oh Shammang, he's really not well at all. He's also got so very disagreeable, as if it's everyone else's fault. Bruno's trying, wherever possible, not to be at home. He's got lots of friends, as you know, and he spends most of the time when he's not at school around at a friend's house. He always says that their parents don't mind, but sometimes I feel so guilty that someone else's parents are paying to feed him.' It all came out in a rush as if she'd been bottling it up, and his arrival had just opened the floodgates. 'What are we going to do?'

'Well, tomorrow,' he said, 'I'm going to have to find the right magistrate to take out some sort of power of attorney order on him.'

'Then what?'

'I really don't know. Hopefully, the magistrate himself will have an idea.'

'Michelle, who's that?' came a bark from the doorway.

Truchaud looked round. His father looked considerably older than he had less than a month ago, and yet much more savage.

'It's your son, Charlemagne. He's come to see you. Isn't that nice?'

'Don't be stupid, woman. I haven't got a son called Charlemagne. I used to have a son called Bertin, but he's dead now, so what would I be wanting another son for at my time of life?'

'Yes, you have,' she replied soft-voiced and seemingly unabashed, 'and here he is; Charlemagne. Only we call him Shammang, because that's what Bruno called him when he was little.'

'Bruno? Who's that?'

'Bruno, your grandson, who lives here too. My son, Bruno.'

The old man looked bewildered for a moment and then replied, 'I can't see any Brunos in here.'

'Well, no, he's not in here at the moment. He's out with his friends.'

'So who's this?' he started all over again, waving a hand at the detective.

21

'Your son, Charlemagne,' she replied in exactly the same patient tone as before. Truchaud looked at her in disbelief; the woman was a saint, coping with all this without losing her temper. He would have probably lost his already if he were in her shoes. The conversation took its continuing repetitive path for a while and then unexpectedly the old man walked out. Michelle watched him shamble through the door to his annex, and then walked back to the table and sat down. 'It's so exhausting,' she said letting out a long steady sigh.

'Has Dr Girand seen him when he's like this?' the detective asked. 'Surely the GP should be able to do something for him?'

'Not a lot,' she replied. 'Your father would have to be willing to swallow any medications he was prescribed, and right now he's so paranoid he won't swallow anything at all. I suppose I could crush it up and serve it to him in his food, but if he realizes that I've done that, he might refuse to eat altogether.'

'I think, before I go and find a magistrate, I need to have a word with Girand. Surely there isn't a rule about patient confidentiality now?' He picked up the phone and dialled the surgery. 'Truchaud here. Any chance I could have an appointment with the doctor tomorrow, about my father?'

'Hang on a moment,' came the reply. 'I'll see.'

There was a pause, and then the doctor came on the phone himself. Truchaud replied immediately. 'Oh, I'm so pleased to speak to you. I've got to go and see a magistrate for care about Dad as soon as possible, and I thought I ought to be fully briefed before I did so.'

'I've got a gap in my appointment book in about twenty minutes, if that's better for you,' came the reply back down the phone.

'Terrific!' Truchaud replied. 'I'll be there on the double.'

That evening it was a sad little family gathering over supper. Dad was present and, for the time being, quiet. Bruno had come home for supper, but was planning to go out immediately after. Michelle had pulled together some salad with some baked beef. After dinner, Bruno went out to join up with Jacquot, his new best friend and shirt-tail cousin from the Laforge family. Michelle didn't seem unduly alarmed despite the two-year age gap and Jacquot's breaking voice. Maréchale came by to talk wine business briefly with Michelle. Dad didn't take any notice of any of them. Truchaud poured himself a little Marc, and decided not to offer one to his father. One thing he had forgotten to ask the doctor was the effect spirits would have on his father, and this very old Marc was a very strong rather nutty spirit made from the pressings; the skins, pips and pulp of the grapes before fermentation really began. The tragedy of it was that his dad had always really liked this brand of Marc at the end of a meal as a digestif, when he had been well.

On his way out, Maréchale acknowledged him again. 'Thanks for coming down so fast,' he said. 'Those of us who really care about him are getting really worried, and those who don't, I think, just want him locked up, and the key thrown deep into the Saône.'

'Thanks for calling me,' he replied. 'I'll do what I can.'

Chapter 3

Nuits-Saint-Georges, Friday morning

Truchaud headed north to Dijon. He had made an appointment with the Guardianship Magistrate whose office, he was informed, was in a grand building on the Boulevard Clemenceau. The magistrate's office on the first floor was lined with books, many of which had a leather binding and looked rather too frail to be in everyday use. The office had a grand oak desk and behind it sat the magistrate himself. He was a fairly elderly man with salt and pepper hair and half-moon spectacles, over the top of which he looked at Truchaud as he came in. He did, however, look friendly, and was suitably prepared for the meeting.

'Yes,' he said, 'they explained why you're here, and I think I understand what is happening. I am sorry to hear about this.'

'So are we, and really we have no idea what to do about it. He is becoming very difficult to manage at home at the moment, and if someone isn't there all the time looking after him, then who knows where he will roam, or what he will do.'

'And who's there to look after him at the moment?'

'There's my sister-in-law, and my twelve-year-old nephew permanently resident with him in the house.'

'And you?' asked the magistrate fairly pointedly.

'I'm on leave at the moment from my job in Paris.'

'Which is?'

'I'm a Commander in the National Police.'

'I see your problem. Are there any other relations nearby? You said *sister-in-law*, so presumably you've a brother around?'

'He died a couple of months ago. If he was still alive, no doubt it would be him sitting here, instead of me.'

'So, what is it exactly you want from me?'

25

'Well, from what I understand, he was caught urinating over someone's vines the other day, and the owner of those vines wanted him locked up. We really don't want that, nor, I gather, do the gendarmes.'

'Nor, I suspect, would the Municipal Police,' added the magistrate thoughtfully.

'What we also want is some sort of power of attorney, as at the moment he still owns the family business, and if the mood took him, he could destroy it, and possibly also the other business with which it is partnered.'

'How do you mean?'

'Our family business is a small independent winery in Nuits-Saint-Georges. We have a plot of Grand Cru Vougeot, and some very nice village crus as well. We also have quite a lot of vines on the east side of the 74, which the other winery buys off us each year to upgrade their basic Bourgogne. We work very closely with that firm, and they probably need our cooperation for their own survival.' He paused for a moment, and then continued. 'That's my feeling anyway.'

'Were you to be awarded power of attorney, how would you manage it?'

'At this moment in time, I'm on leave from Paris, so I would be here to take advice, or more likely orders, from my sister-in-law, who right now runs our domaine, in conjunction with a manager we share with the other firm.'

'And Paris is happy you're here rather than there?'

'I don't know whether 'happy' is a word they'd use, but they're tolerating it because they owe me a lot of holiday, and my sidekick is ready for promotion, and therefore the hole my absence leaves there is ready to be filled.'

'So what happens when you go back?'

'That is a good question, which I don't really want to answer until I have to. Does that sound a little irresponsible?'

'Perhaps a little, but at least you recognise it, and after all, less than twenty-four hours ago, you were sitting in your office in Paris unaware that this was all going to blow up in your face. In the long term, where do you see the future of your domaine?'

'My nephew Bruno, who is twelve at the moment, will take it on, and run it and make wonderful wine.'

'Suppose he doesn't want to? After all, you didn't.'

'If he decides he doesn't want to, then that is a bridge we will have to cross when he makes that decision. As far as I was concerned, there was only enough room for one brother, plus my father, in the family business. The spare brother, being the younger one, me, had to go off and make his own way in the world. If my brother had decided he didn't want to make wine, then I would probably have been up for it. Whether I would have been as good as he was, I have no idea. Let's hope his talent, which he inherited from Dad, continues down the line to Bruno.'

'So, it is at least in part to protect Bruno's interests that you want this power of attorney?'

'Completely.'

'Are you married?'

'I was once. It didn't work out, so we went our separate ways.'

'Children?'

'None, we didn't get that far, I'm glad to say.'

'Current relationship?'

'Only with the law. I'm a jobbing policeman, who gets on with his life and listens to music on the rare occasions that he's not involved with a case.'

The magistrate leaned back in his chair. He made a steeple with his index fingers and thought for a moment. 'I think we can do something here,' he said. 'Leave it with me for a couple of days, and we'll see if we can get something sorted. Meanwhile, I think the Deputy Mayor of Nuits-Saint-Georges has an idea he wants to put to you, if you wouldn't mind hanging on for a moment. I'll see if we can find him.'

Truchaud raised his eyebrows, but he wasn't going to be drawn further. The magistrate picked up the phone, had a short conversation, and then put the receiver back on the rest.

27

He caught Truchaud's eye. 'If you hang on here, I gather he won't be a moment.' And picking up the folder with the papers in it, he left the room.

There was a tap on the door, and in walked a woman aged about forty, certainly no more, but was certainly dressed in a middle-aged manner, with her hair quite severely permed.

'Commander Truchaud,' she said, very affably, 'Thank you for waiting to see me.'

'Very pleasant to see you too,' said Truchaud nonplussed, uncertain what the Deputy Mayor had to contribute to the care of his father, or why she'd come all the way up to Dijon to talk to him about it. 'My father–' he started.

'In a moment,' she interrupted. 'Tell me, does the name Molleau mean anything to you?'

'Yes,' said Truchaud slowly. There was only one Molleau who had ever crossed his path.

'You shot him,' she said abruptly. Yes, that was the one he'd been thinking of too.

'Yes, I did.'

'He was our Municipal Police Chief.'

'I was aware of that,' said Truchaud carefully, but added, 'I don't suppose he was being a Municipal Police Chief when he tried to kill me?'

'No, no. I quite agree. The problem is that we haven't been able to find a replacement for him yet, and I understand that you're going to be down here for a while. So, we had a word with your Divisional Commander in Paris, and he said that you might as well be making yourself useful down here doing something productive if you're going to be drawing your pay.'

'Damn cheek!' spluttered Truchaud. 'I'm on leave.'

'He said you'd say that, but he also said that you'd undoubtedly find some crime to unravel while you were down here, and that if we didn't actually want there to be a crime wave in Nuits-Saint-Georges over the next few weeks, we had better find something for you to do … apart from just looking after your father. It's rather good actually. We've never had a

Municipal Police Chief that outranks the local Captain of Gendarmes before.'

'Do I have a choice?' asked Truchaud, feeling his soul falling through his boots. The Municipal Police? He'd never live it down in Paris: parking tickets and speeding fines; dangerous dogs and building regulations! He was a serious crimes flic, for goodness sake.

The Deputy Mayor smiled at him and said nothing more. Truchaud stomped out and his heavy footfall would have told anyone it would have been dangerous to argue with him. He was still seething while he drove back to Nuits-Saint-Georges. He turned left at the traffic lights, past the sign that had said that the road was barred for as long as he could remember, and immediately hung right into Argentina Square. He stormed into the town hall, not really sure who he was looking for, when he realized that the girl at the reception desk, who usually looked constipated and cross, was actually smiling. He stopped in surprise. He had never seen anyone sitting at that desk wearing a smile before.

'Commander Truchaud?' she asked, still smiling, and it really was friendly, not just painted on her face.

'Yes?' he asked quizzically.

'I understand that you're going to be working with us for a while.'

Truchaud looked at her incredulously. It seemed that everyone had been planning this for weeks. He wondered whether his father was part of it too. He could just imagine the conversation, 'Okay, old man, it's all set up. Now just go and relieve yourself all over whoever's Grand Cru vines, making sure that someone influential is watching, and we're up and running!'

'Yes,' he replied, 'so I understand.' He thought about asking her how long she had known about it, but then decided against it. That sort of information might have been too much for him to handle at this moment in time.

'I wondered if I might have your mobile phone number in case someone needs to get in touch with you in a hurry,' she said. 'You do carry it on you, don't you?'

'Yes,' he said, admitting defeat, and gave her his number. He would be giving the old man in Paris a bit of a mouthful shortly too. However, probably the first person he ought to see, before he actually went home to explain to Michelle that the domaine might become a police office, was the Chief Gendarme.

Captain Duquesne was a big, bluff man around forty years old, who had been born and brought up in Touraine. His father had been employed as a stonemason there, so there had been no family business to require his services. He had joined the Gendarmerie and risen in the ranks by dint of sheer competence, and the passing of required exams. He felt that his current posting to Nuits-Saint-Georges was a reward for good work, either in this lifetime or a previous one. He enjoyed the life, and he got on well with his team. Fairly recently, he had been involved in a complex case of wine fraud, and had teamed up with an off-duty detective from Paris to solve it. They had become very good friends. Truchaud was not sure that that friendship would necessarily survive his becoming the Municipal Chief of Police. Dammit, he didn't want to outrank Duquesne. He wanted to be able to sit in the Café du Centre and share a cup of coffee with him, putting the world at large to rights, not sorting out speeding tickets. Besides, the streets of Nuits-Saint-Georges were so narrow and difficult to drive round that the only driver who was likely to exceed the speed limit was the irrepressible Gendarme Lenoir, who invariably made his poor little Mégane's tyres squeal. He was really not keen on sticking a traffic ticket on a gendarme.

He pressed the sonette outside the front door of the Gendarmerie, and walked through the door, hoping to catch Lenoir asleep at the desk. If he wasn't bullying the official police car, Lenoir was often to be found asleep at the front desk. This time he wasn't. The young face of Constable Savioli smiled alertly up at him, and brightened up even more when he realized who had just come in. 'Commander!' he said. 'Come in. I'll get some coffee on and tell the captain you're here.' He leapt up and went round to let Truchaud into the building.

Before he knew he had arrived he was sitting in the captain's office, while the captain was shouting, 'The Commander likes his with cream in it.' Duquesne turned to Truchaud. 'I've just been told you're coming to work with us for a while,' he said.

'Yes, I've just been told that too. I'm trying to work it out as well. It seems that nature abhors a vacuum, and that a senior police officer without a job or a bullet hole constitutes a vacuum. Is this going to be a problem?' he asked.

Duquesne looked at him for a moment 'I don't see why,' he said. 'It means that my lads won't have to worry about the municipal issues any more. I have a feeling that you may find it a little tedious, but the municipal lads are all right. There are one or two rather dodgy dogs around, and I'll let you know where you might find them if you were minded to look. On the other hand, you might just not be minded.' Truchaud looked at him, quietly impressed with Duquesne's ability to keep a straight face.

'So what's going on in Nuits?' he asked.

'Well, we had a bit of a fracas with an old man relieving himself over some Grand Cru vines in flower the other day, but I gather you've got that under control too,' he grinned. The coffee arrived.

The conversation continued over the coffee, amiably touching on this, that and the other, as happens between men who find they have a lot in common, without going into specifics of exactly what those commonalities might be.

The next person Truchaud felt that he needed to talk to about the happenings of the day was his sister-in-law.

He left the Gendarmerie, and set off again across town.

Chapter 4

Nuits-Saint-Georges, Friday night and Saturday morning

'Well?' she asked. 'How did it go?' Her eyes opened slowly wider as he told her exactly how it had gone. 'They can't do that, surely?'

'They probably couldn't if I were to really object,' he said. 'But if I were to really, really, object they would probably require me to report for duty in Paris next Monday morning. Then where would we be?'

She looked at him. 'So what does that mean?'

'The way I understand it is that I'm on call if they need me, and when Old Mr Laforge is summoned to explain himself to the Heavenly Host, I have to arrange a state funeral as befits a hero of the Maquis. Meanwhile, my officers stick parking tickets on windscreens, arrest dangerous dogs, and call me in if somebody's thinking of erecting a building that someone else objects to their erecting. I think if Dad pees on someone else's vines, it's probably too big a case for me, and Captain Duquesne has to sort it.'

Michelle smiled. 'In other words, you're to be the responsible adult.'

'I think that's about how it is.' He went on to talk about the first half of his discussion with the magistrate. He reported that there was no definite decision made as yet, but at least discussions had been opened. She wasn't particularly keen that her house should become an office for the Municipal Police, and he agreed that wherever possible that would not happen.

Meanwhile, he wondered how the season was coming along. 'Well, the flowers are looking promising enough at the moment. Tomorrow you should get Bruno to take you round and show you. Better not take Dad in case he relieves himself on our vines this time.' She shrugged. Maybe it wasn't funny, but with all the stress she was under, he would allow that one through. He didn't remember seeing grape flowers. He must have done when he was a child, but he couldn't remember them. He knew the little flowers that created a blaze of royal blue at the base of the vines, which you saw as you drove past, were nothing to do with the vines themselves, they just grew in the same soil.

Simon Maréchale pushed his nose round the door. 'Smells good,' he said. 'I think I'll invite myself to supper here tonight. Suzette's busy working for her exams, and doesn't want to be disturbed.' Truchaud had tried to conjure up a domestic scene with Maréchale and Suzette, but had never succeeded. Suzette was the daughter of the local doctor and the girl he had adored when he was on the cusp of adulthood. Suzette and Maréchale had a thing going, which if he had been her father, he wasn't sure he would have been happy about. Mind you, if he had ever had a daughter, he doubted that anyone would have ever been good enough for her, whoever he was. He had first become aware of Suzette only a couple of months ago over a dead body. Whether that had triggered a parental instinct in him, he couldn't fathom. Or was the concept of parental feelings already being triggered in him at the same time by coming home for his brother's death, and there was Bruno, twelve years old and very brittle.

Bruno was learning for the first time, from within, all about hormones and emotions. Then he'd had to understand that there was something terribly wrong with his grandfather and the contents of his head, and then to cap it all, his father had upped and died. He obviously had a very soft spot for his Uncle Shammang, the detective in Paris, as indeed did the detective for him. Truchaud had never felt parental feelings for anyone before, but suddenly he had found them for two growing kids, one at the early stage of his second decade, and one at the far end of hers. This he found bizarre. He would never tell either of them, of course, but then he really wouldn't understand how to tell them anyway, especially Suzette. He had been around all of Bruno's life if not very near at hand. Suzette had known him for a couple of months, tops. He had heard from Suzette's Uncle Jean that Geneviève, her mother, had reciprocated his feelings when they were kids, but he'd only found that out a couple of months ago too. This year's spring had been a season of great learning for Truchaud, but it had all come far too late.

Truchaud looked up at the winemaker, 'How are you, Simon?' he asked.

'Fine,' came the reply. Maréchale was the winemaker both for Truchaud's and Laforge's vineyards and kept a close eye on both sets of vineyards together. Each family had a parcel of Grand Cru vineyard: Truchaud's was a rather good strip in the Clos de Vougeot; and Laforge's was a piece of Echézeaux, a few hundred yards further south. Truchaud's, on the west side of the Seventy-Four, also had a rather good patch of village cru in Vosne-Romanée, and both families had vineyards in Nuits-Saint-Georges itself. Both families were justifiably proud of the wine that came out of those vineyards. The detective was particularly fond of the Vosne.

'We've been watching the flowering closely of course, and trimming off any branches that don't have flowers on. We also prune off any rather excessive leaf formation. If there's too much foliage, then the grapes don't get enough of nature's bounty, and it's all about the grapes.'

'It sounds like hard work.'

'It all has to be done by hand, especially at this moment in time. We've got to be very careful with the flowering in process. If the flowers get knocked off the plants, there won't be any grapes.'

'I don't remember these flowers,' said Truchaud. 'I must have seen them when I was a child, but I haven't seen any recently, and I'm darned if I can remember what they look like.'

'Well, come along with me and Bruno tomorrow morning, and we'll show you. He's not at school tomorrow, so he always

35

comes out on the vines with me. I think he finds it easier than being at home, at the moment.'

Truchaud shrugged. 'I can understand that,' he said. 'Will you come and collect us after breakfast tomorrow?'

'Certainly will, but remember … I've already invited myself to supper this evening, so I'm not going anywhere fast.' He delved into a hessian sack he had slung over a shoulder, and produced a very fresh baguette, an Époisses cheese, and a bottle of Nuits-Saint-Georges of a very nice ripe vintage. 'My contribution to the feast,' he added, smiling.

The following morning was bright and dry. There was a light zephyr of a breeze, and Truchaud could almost imagine Maréchale whistling as he arrived at the house. 'I'd like to check the Vosne this morning first,' said the winemaker when he actually did arrive, 'and from there, we can wander up to have a look at the Grands Crus. Sylvain has been working those for the last couple of days, but as I haven't actually seen him to speak to, I thought I'd just pop in and see how he's doing.'

The village cru vineyards lay between the buildings of the village of Vosne-Romanée and the main road, which used to be called the N74, but was now declassified as a Departmental Road only. Alongside the village and uphill to the west of it lay the Premiers Crus and the Grandest Crus of all Burgundy, which most people who weren't Russian oligarchs could only dream of ever tasting, with names such as Romanée-Conti and La Tâche. Truchaud wondered whether the Russian oligarchs in question really appreciated what it was they were drinking. He didn't know; he had never met one.

They walked towards the rows of the Domaine Truchaud vines. There was no delimiting mark in the land between their plot and the plot which belonged to the next vintner along, but one just knew. The grapes were slightly differently tended perhaps? The vines themselves appeared to acknowledge Maréchale, and especially Bruno. They appeared aware of the boy and his affection for them. They were also aware that, in the years to come, he was going to look after them and nurture them, and in exchange, they were going to give him their gorgeous red juice to turn into wine.

'There they are, Uncle Shammang,' said Bruno, lifting a leaf on the plant he was crouching beside. And there they were. The flowers were tiny dry green balls about a millimetre in diameter, hanging in a bunch from the stem. 'Now, these haven't pollenated yet,' he went on. 'As you can see, these are still intact.' He walked down the row and checked another couple of plants, and then stopped, 'This plant has done its duty. Look!' The little balls had a hole in them. 'Have a sniff,' Bruno continued. Truchaud bent down to sniff. So that was what the smell of citrus was that he had smelled in the air last night. 'Those pollens will have blown and fertilized some other plant nearby. Hopefully, they will have fertilized ours, but maybe not. Maybe the wind was blowing in just the right direction for them to fertilize the grapes on the Richebourg vineyard.'

He stood up and pointed, just past the village buildings uphill. They grinned at each other.

'Maybe, of course, the wind was coming in from the west,' said Truchaud, 'and the Richebourg pollens pollenated our plants here, and that one pollenated our vines on the other side of the Seventy-Four.' Both Truchauds looked at each other. 'How do these look?' he asked Maréchale.

'Just fine,' the winemaker replied. 'Sylvain's got these well under control. Next stop our Échezeaux?' They all clambered back into the little car, and drove to the next village north, called simply Vougeot. It didn't have a vineyard name attached to it, as its most famous vineyard was the walled vineyard called simply 'Vougeot's walled vineyard', which dated back to the Cistercian monastery there. Despite the various political upheavals over the eight hundred years that followed its construction, the building and the walls survived. The *clos* itself was originally farmed and vinified by the monks themselves. During the Revolution in 1789, a colonel in the army called Napoleon Bonaparte – by repute a great fan of the wines of Burgundy, despite being a Corsican by birth – persuaded the monks to pass their ownership of the vineyards on to the State in his name. In exchange, it was said that Napoleon secretly defrocked the monks and arranged for their heads to be shaved in a different way, so that it didn't look like a tonsure, and employed them to continue making the wine. In 1818, after Napoleon found himself alone and unloved on the most obscure British colony of all, an island in the middle of the South Atlantic Ocean, the French government had sold the whole estate over to a single man, Jules Ouvrard. Over the subsequent 250 years more than 50 different people, by dint of sale and the arcane French inheritance laws, had become owners of the 50 plus hectares of the Clos de Vougeot. The Truchaud family now owned one of those plots.

The Échezeaux vineyard was not that much smaller than the Clos de Vougeot, but there was no long swathe of history to explain this state of affairs. The Laforges had a plot of this. They were both Grand Cru vineyards, which to some explained the meaning of 'Grand Cru' as the potential of the land to make great wine. Maréchale had tasted some distinctly ordinary bottles of wine bearing the Échezeaux and the Clos de Vougeot labels in the couple of years he had been in Bourgogne, though they weren't anything he had had anything to do with. When they were younger and in their prime, both Old Mr Laforge and Truchaud Père had made very fine wine from their respective flagship plots.

They turned off the Seventy-Four just before the wall of the clos actually started, and drove down a narrow lane uphill to the west, with the wall on their right shoulder. Truchaud wondered when they had laid the original Tarmac, and how they would go about replacing it when its time was finally due. At the bend in the wall they stopped and parked the little car, and got out. First, they turned left, and walked up an unmetalled track, with the vineyard called Grand Échezeaux on their right. The Grand vineyard was a separate appellation, and Maréchale saw its wine as a target to aspire to. Its history also was thought to date back to those same winey Cistercian monks in the twelfth century who, when they outgrew the confines of the walled clos, started planting vines outside it.

Maréchale wandered through the vineyard, looking under leaves at individual vines, muttering quietly to himself. Neither Truchaud nor Bruno knew these vines, as they were nothing to do with the Truchauds, but they did know some of the other people working in that vineyard. Nobody objected to their being there.

'Come,' said the winemaker. 'Sylvain appears to have this all under control too. Let's have a quick look at your *clos*, just to be sure.' They walked back down the track to the little road, past the car, and through a gap in the wall. This gap was certainly large enough and flat enough to drive a tractor through should one be so minded.

They walked up through the vineyard, keeping the fine old chateau on their left. 'One day, Uncle Shammang, I'm going to be invited to dinner in there,' said Bruno. 'The Chevaliers du Tastevin held their regular dinners in celebration of all things Burgundian in the chateau.'

'I would hope that one day you'll be a knight in your own right, then you'll be able to invite your old uncle to dinner there, when he's in his dotage,' Truchaud returned with a grin. They both looked at the winemaker, 'Simon?' they both asked.

'Who knows?' he replied. 'I'm only an employee at the moment. It would be fun to look into the future, wouldn't it?' He was looking at the vines of the Truchaud plot and nodding at them. He seemed happy with them too. Most of the flowers had pollinated on the clos, and the lemony scent was certainly everywhere. 'To Nuits-Saint-Georges?' he asked them.

Just then, Truchaud's phone went off in his pocket. He looked at it for a moment and answered it. 'Yes, give me five minutes or so. I'll be there.' He paused and shut the phone off. 'Can you drop me off at the town hall on your way past?' he said, 'Apparently my new job calls, and I would hate to create a blob on my first day. Don't worry about me. I'll walk home from there.'

Chapter 5

Chemnitz, Germany, Saturday morning

Renate loaded the last of her luggage into the boot of the Škoda. *Where the hell is that girl?* she thought. There was movement from the front door of the block of flats and there she was, pulling her bag on its wheels with one hand. In the other hand, she carried a paper bag. On her head was a sunhat and shades. Her mouth was just visible underneath the headgear. Below that she wore a tee-shirt with a slogan in a Cyrillic script that Renate didn't understand, her favourite battle shorts and ankle boots. Otherwise, all that was visible was flawless golden skin. Renate raised an eyebrow so that it disappeared under her fringe. How did her friend manage to bronze so naturally and quickly, without the painful pink and peeling phase that accompanied Renate's attempts to get the look she supposed to be gorgeous and Californian?

'I just thought we ought to be forearmed in case anything goes wrong with the car,' Dagmar grinned. Her bag went into the boot too. 'Anything else we can think of? The water bottles are in the front, and I've got lunch,' she added, tossing a paper bag onto the back seat. 'Do you want to drive first?'

Renate shrugged and slid behind the wheel, muttering, 'Why might you think anything would go wrong with Gretel? I checked her all over yesterday, and she's fine: oil, water, fuel, air, all absolutely spot on.' It had been Renate's responsibility to make sure that the car that they had bought together was in full running order, and as she generally drove it on a day-to-day basis, this was a responsibility she was happy to take on.

Dagmar settled slightly uncomfortably into the passenger seat. The leatherette had become somewhat warm in the sun, as the backs of her slender legs reminded her uncomfortably for a moment.

The block of flats had been built as part of the Marshall Plan reconstruction after the War. It had been carpet-bombed by the Allies, probably mistaken for Dresden a little way further east due, either to inaccuracy or under the thought, *There's a German city. Let's get rid of these bombs and get out of here.* Renate's grandmother, who had grown up on a farm outside Chemnitz, used to tell a story about one of those raids. When they were going on, everyone would dive into the cellar and wait till all the noise stopped. One night, when it appeared to be stopping, they all crept out again, and there, coming down on a parachute was an airman right into their back yard. Her grandmother had never seen a black man before, and her first thought was that he had been terribly burned. *Opa*, who had fought in the Great War in the trenches, and had seen Americans and Tommies of every hue, grabbed his shotgun and met the man as he landed. They captured him and took him, and his parachute, down into the cellar. *Opa*, whose Great War experience made him feel honour-bound, as one old soldier to another not so old, kept the airman hidden in the cellar until a detachment of the Regular Army came by. There was no way he was going to hand him over to the SS: there was no knowing what that lot might have done to this unfortunate man, who no doubt had been drafted by his country to fight on their side, as so many young Germans had been drafted to fight for the Führer, with scant regard to their individual feelings on the matter.

Anyway, the block of flats had been built in the form of a square round a courtyard. In the middle of the courtyard was a patch of grass with what was now a large mature tree. The girls could remember when they were young, sitting on the grass surrounding the tree, and surrounded by the Trabant cars that each family had earned from the State for their work. Renate's family had been very proud of their funny little plastic-bodied Trabant. Theirs had been fairly reliable, she seemed to remember, but not everyone had been so lucky. She remembered the fury of one of the neighbours who told of their first car, which had lasted precisely three days before it had caught fire simply because it had wanted to. That was on the Autobahn to

Dresden, and it had burnt to a cinder while they had stood by and watched. They had all managed to get out all right, obviously, but they had had to wait another eight years to be allocated a replacement. She had been born too late to ever remember first-hand the German Democratic Republic, but she did remember sitting in the front room listening to the old people talking about it, and being really relieved when her best friend, who lived in the flat upstairs, came down and asked if she could come out and play.

Renate and Dagmar had been fated to be best friends forever. Born only a few weeks apart, they had passed all their milestones together: they had gone to their first day at school together; taken and passed their exams together; supported each other through their various rites of passage; and when Dagmar's brother had moved west, and her mother caught that terrible illness and died, it was only to be expected that Renate would move out of her own overcrowded flat, with her drunken father and boisterous army of brothers, into the flat upstairs. The housing authority was happy about that too, as it meant that there wasn't a multi-occupancy flat occupied by one single girl only. Not that there was a housing shortage in Chemnitz, but every bureaucracy needed its boxes ticked.

Renate engaged the gear and drove towards the archway out of the square. 'Pair of dykes!' shouted a male voice from nearby, 'Bloody waste.'

Dagmar wound down her window, gave the voice her finger, and shouted back, 'Just because we aren't interested in your prick, you prick, it doesn't mean we aren't amenable to quality prick if some crops up.'

'Who was that?' asked Renate from the driving seat.

'Stupid Gregor,' she replied with a shudder, and they both laughed as they pulled out onto the street into the traffic, not that it was particularly busy at that time in the middle of a Saturday morning. They worked their way down to the main road called Leipziger Strasse, and from there, up onto the motorway pointing west.

West! Now there was a word. They were going west. They were actually going to see the Rhine with their own eyes. They had seen pictures of it from time to time. Dagmar's brother had sent them occasional texts with photos to her phone, and had even sent them a real postcard once. 'We're actually going to see it in the flesh … well, you know what I mean.' Dagmar had been unable to hide the excitement from her voice. They were going to see her brother, Horst, who had moved west and had ended up in the small tourist town of Boppard, just upstream from Koblenz. He had a job in a drinks shop, and as both wine and beer were part of the local industry, as well as tourism, he had settled in nicely. Usually, Horst came home for Christmas, but that hadn't happened last year, somewhat to the relief of Renate.

For the past couple of years he and Renate had slept together when he stayed, but last Christmas, Renate had been quite seriously involved with a real boyfriend for once, and sleeping with Dagmar's brother would have been a little difficult. That boyfriend was now a thing of the past, so she was quite looking forward to the next few days, and hoped that Horst hadn't got a current girlfriend.

Now they had both got jobs, they had a bit of money, but this was their first real holiday that they had spent together, which didn't also involve work for diplomas or degrees or anything, or a holiday job to stoke up the bank balance to cover the next term of study. They were taking a road trip to see Dagmar's brother and the Rhine. They hadn't heard from him recently, but that was typical Horst. She heard nothing for six months, and then suddenly he wouldn't shut up for a fortnight, texting and phoning at the most inconvenient times. Just because he could make a call in the middle of the working day at his job, it wasn't so easy to be on the receiving end, when you were a primary school teacher and surrounded by a classroom full of kids.

The Autobahn was a fairly new construction and the surface was smooth. The day was bright and sunny, and neither girl had any dreams of becoming racing drivers, despite the certain pride they both felt that Sebastian Vettel was German. They cruised along the road at roughly the same speed as the lorries. Renate was aware of the occasional Mercedes howling along at who knew what speed, and kept well out of their way. They pulled into the services area just west of Eisenach and had their lunch. Dagmar had made a *bierwurst* sandwich each, and had put a bottle of water into the bag.

'Do you think this is where the Iron Curtain actually was?' Renate asked as they got out.

'Somewhere round here, I guess,' her friend replied. 'You'd never know it to look at it.' They munched quietly on the *bierwurst* sandwiches. 'As it's my stint next to drive,' Dagmar continued, 'and we know how the road is, have we decided which way we're going, to do the final bit?'

'Remind me what the choices are.'

'Well, the Internet says that down to Frankfurt, then along the Rhine and straight through the hills on a road that isn't an Autobahn, through Braunfels and Limburg, is much of a muchness as far as time is concerned. But looking at the map, there are also roads on both sides of the Rhine that follow every squiggle it takes if we do the Frankfurt route.'

'And you want to drive that one?'

Dagmar grinned at her friend. 'I do.'

'South and lots of Rhine it is. Decision taken.' They finished their sandwiches, and like all good German girls, put the paper bag in the bin provided, then they swapped seats and Dagmar drove off west again. Near Giessen, the road wound south towards Frankfurt on the Main. 'Do you happen to know which Frankfurt gave its name to the sausage?' asked Dagmar as they drove past. 'Theirs or ours?' She was referring to the East-German Frankfurt on the Oder up by the Polish border.

'Probably this one. After all, which nation is the real fan of the hot dog but the Americans, and they say that this Frankfurt is still full of Americans who forgot to go home. The Americans are really good at re-importing German ideas back into Germany. Think of the Hamburger, for example, and the Berliner as well.'

The road guided them through built-up areas round Frankfurt and they headed towards Wiesbaden, through various other built-up areas. They didn't leave the Autobahn until they were on the west side of Mainz, and pulled off onto a road signed to Erbach and Rüdesheim. The road and the Rhine came together near Eltville and they drove along it. At Rüdesheim they were amused to see that an old-fashioned car ferry across to Bingen on the other side was how they would get across; there was no bridge.

Up through the villages, with names like Lorch and Sankt Goarhausen, they drove, and on the other side of the river, Bacharach climbed the river gorge, and around its borders were vineyards too. As they approached Sankt Goarhausen they both saw rocks in the river, which looked quite treacherous, and a big sign announcing the Lorelei. Now everyone knew the story of the Lorelei who sat on a rock and distracted the sailors by singing so sweetly, naked and beautiful as well, that they didn't look where they were going and crashed their boats, whereupon wreckers would plunder the sinking vessels. They drove into a tunnel.

'I think we're going right underneath the Lorelei Rock,' said Dagmar. 'We must get Horst to bring us back here later on, so we can be proper tourists.' They both remembered learning Heine's poem in school and its wonderful, powerful rhythm.

It was only when they reached Kamp Bornhofen that they realized that they were on the east side of the river, and they hadn't seen any form of bridge whatever since the far side of Rüdesheim. There, however, was Boppard on the west side of the river, again climbing up the side of the Rhine Gorge. And there was another ferry. 'Well, there's bound to be an Autobahn bridge near Koblenz, another ten miles or so upstream, or there's the ferry. Offset the cost of the ferry against the cost of the diesel. I want to use the ferry,' said Dagmar as she drove down the feeder road to the ferry, which was just loading so she drove straight on. It took about ten minutes to cross the river on the ferry, and she set the satnav to Horst's address.

The satnav wiggled them up from the expensive looking riverfront hotels and the tourist boats, up through one or two streets that certainly looked so narrow that they would wipe off the wing mirrors of any car much larger than Gretel. They drove under a railway bridge and then up into the newer part of the village beyond, and there was the address. They parked outside the door, and went up the steps and pressed the bell.

The door opened, and a rather bewildered middle-aged face that certainly wasn't Horst looked out.

'Hello?' he said, 'Can I help you?'

'Hello,' said Dagmar. 'We're looking for my brother, Horst. Is he here?'

'Horst?' said the man. 'There's no Horst here. I'm Werner.'

'But my brother Horst lives here,' she said, pulling out a rather crumpled piece of paper with an address on it. 'Look.'

The man looked at the piece of the paper, and then shouted indoors, 'Darling, what was the name of that chap who lived here before us? I think we've got his sister at the door.'

A disembodied voice came out from inside the house somewhere. 'Wasn't it Horst Witter?'

'Oh, that's right, so your brother used to live here, but I'm afraid he doesn't anymore; we do.'

'Do you know where he lives now?' asked Dagmar decidedly bewildered.

'No, I'm afraid I don't. But hang on. When we took over the flat, there was all sorts of clutter lying around which we boxed up, in case he should come back. You know … letters and stuff. You're very welcome to have a look at those if you want.'

'How long have you been here?' asked Dagmar increasingly dismayed.

'We've been here three months now. We were allocated the place by the local housing office. I gather he had gone off, and not paid the rent or anything for three months, so he was evicted and we got the place,' he replied. 'Look, if you hang on, I'll go and get the box for you.'

The man went back into the flat. He left the door open, but as he hadn't invited them in, they stayed on the doorstep.

Dagmar looked in dismay at her friend. 'Where the hell is he? What are we going to do? We've come 500 kilometres to see him, and he's not here.'

'Let's wait and see what the box tells us,' replied Renate in a sensible tone of voice, but inside she felt as dismayed as her friend.

'Here it is!' said the man as he came to the door with a large cardboard box, which claimed to contain a dozen large bottles of curry ketchup. 'Um ...' he continued uncertainly, 'do you have any form of identity? I would hate to hand over his stuff to total strangers without at least checking that out.'

Dagmar passed over her identity card. The only thing that might have proved that she was Horst's sister was the surname 'Witter'. She wondered what would have happened if she had already got married. That wasn't unheard of for young women in their early twenties for one reason or another. However, her card seemed to be adequate for the man called Werner.

'One other thing,' added Renate from behind Dagmar, who was carrying the box down to the waiting Škoda, 'Do you know where we might find a cheap but comfortable bed and breakfast nearby? You see we were expecting to stay with her brother, and we haven't made any other arrangements.'

The man's wife appeared behind him. At least Renate assumed she was his wife as she looked very pregnant. 'Mrs Gruber down the road,' she suggested to her husband. So there definitely wasn't going to be an offer from them to put them up for the night.

'Yes,' he said thoughtfully, 'that might be a good idea.' He explained to Renate how to get there, and wished both girls good luck, and then, quite firmly, shut the door.

'I'll drive,' said Renate. 'If it's where he says it is, it'll be just round the corner.'

Silently Dagmar got into the passenger seat, her eyes glistening slightly. She blurted, 'I'm so sorry, Renate. This was supposed to be an exciting road trip, and now look what's happened.'

Renate patted her friend gently on her brown slender leg, before pulling out. 'Don't worry. We'll get to the bottom of it. Let's hope this Mrs Gruber has a room.'

The house that the man had directed them to certainly had a sign saying '*Zimmerfrei*' – empty rooms – in the window and Renate rang the bell. A large grey-haired woman, who would probably never see sixty again, answered the door. 'Yes?' she asked.

'Your sign says you have a room available for the night,' she said, and explained the missing brother story.

'Yes, I have a twin room, if you don't mind sharing,' she replied.

'My friend and I share a flat at home, so that won't be a problem. We've got a box of stuff we've got to go through, if that's okay.'

'No problem,' said the old lady. 'Follow me.'

She led them, Renate carrying a bag and Dagmar carrying the box, up the stairs and into the room. It was very feminine, pink being its predominant colour, with matching curtains and duvets with flowers. There was a washbasin, and an added walk-in shower and loo. It looked as if the en-suite had been a recent addition as it appeared to have been built into the room itself.

The girls dropped their bags and boxes onto the beds, 'One other thing,' said Renate, 'where would you recommend we had supper tonight?'

'There's a nice little bar just round the corner,' said Mrs Gruber, 'called *Zum Wilden Hirsch*. They serve an excellent schnitzel.'

'Thank you,' said Renate, and the old lady, having given them a key to the room, and explaining that it also opened the front door, left the room. 'Right,' she continued, 'here's a plan: we have a quick rummage in that box, then we go out and get some food and beer inside us. I'm famished.'

Dagmar sat on the bed and looked at her friend with big moist puppy dog eyes. 'What are we going to do?' she asked.

'Stop trying to be pretty,' Renate replied, 'you know it doesn't work on me, and pass me some of those papers. Let's see what Horst has been getting up to in the last few months.'

They both thumbed through papers on the beds, and both had an 'aha!' moment at the same time. For Dagmar it was an envelope with her mother's death certificate in it. The envelope also contained Horst's birth certificate, and even more interestingly, their mother's parents' death certificates. Dagmar had never consciously known that her grandfather's name had been Armand Laforge. That wasn't a German name by anybody's count. The death certificate was dated in the early fifties, so Mum had only been a baby when her father had died, but that was very interesting.

Renate, meanwhile, had slit an as-yet-unopened envelope addressed to Horst. The postmark was smudged, but in it was a letter, dated at the end of last year, most of which was written in a language she didn't understand, but right at the bottom of it was a little bit in pig-German. 'We have your Kombi in our pound, so please come and collect it from the Gendarmerie in Nuits-Saint-Georges.'

They shared the information with each other. 'Well, if we are going further, the next place we have to visit is this Nuits-Saint-Georges place, which from the letterhead appears to be in France.'

At that point they decided to go and fill themselves full of supper, and make plans and a decision. They would have a look at the satnav and see where exactly Nuits-Saint-Georges was. Decisions would come from there.

Zum Wilden Hirsch had a large painted sign outside of a stag looking out imperiously over Lorelei Rock and the river below. It did indeed look welcoming. They walked in and sat down. Immediately a middle-aged woman with a long white apron on was at the table.

'Ladies?'

They asked for a menu and a couple of beers. The menu was collected from another table and brought directly to them. The woman also made a gesture at the bar.

In five minutes she returned with two plates of salad and knives and forks. They had heard from Mrs Gruber that the schnitzel was good, so both decided on a *Jägerschnitzel*, a pork steak in a cream sauce with wild mushrooms. 'What potatoes would you like with that? Chips or pan-fried?' They both chose the pan-fried variety.

Another five minutes after that the beer arrived in a stemmed glass which appeared to be very cold, with a doily around the stem. The woman took a mat off the holder on the table and put the glasses on it. She took out a biro, and made two marks on the edge of one of the beer mats. The beer had a head on top, which gave Dagmar a frothy moustache when she took a pull at it. 'Oh that's good,' she said. Both girls realized that it had been a very long day.

They had looked at the satnav in the car before they walked round to the bar. It appeared that Nuits-Saint-Georges was roughly the same distance further on as they had already driven that day.

'The decision is basically do we go on another 500 kilometres south-west, or do we go back to Chemnitz, and perhaps spend the rest of our holiday going somewhere like Prague?'

'Where we've been before! And we still don't know what's happened to Horst, or who Armand Laforge was. I bet that's why Horst's Kombi is there … because he went to find out.'

'Quite.' More beer was swallowed. The beer stoked up the spirit of adventure, so they had already made their decision by the time two huge plates, piled high with slices of pork cooked in breadcrumbs, doused in a white sauce and covered in button mushrooms, were placed in front of them. 'Can we have another beer each?' Renate asked. When the beers arrived the woman made two further nicks on the beer mat with her biro.

At the end of the meal they settled up, and the woman counted the nicks on the beer mat as well as the meals. They were feeling quite worn-out as they wended their way back to Mrs Gruber's.

'I'm going to take a quick shower,' said Dagmar, 'and then I think I'm going to bed.'

'I think I'm going to miss out on the shower till tomorrow morning,' replied her friend.

When Dagmar climbed out of the shower and was rubbing herself down with the towel provided, spotlessly clean, but slightly starchy perhaps, Renate looked at her friend and realized that she had absolutely no tan lines at all. She was golden brown all over. 'Is that a synthetic tan?' she asked, somewhat disappointed.

Dagmar grinned for a moment. 'No,' she replied. 'Pure sunlight.'

'May I ask where?'

'On the roof on top of the flats, just behind the lift tower, there's a perfect spot to catch the morning sun.'

'With nothing on? Supposing someone were to come along?'

Dagmar waved a hand at herself, 'Then they would have got to see all this. But,' she added wistfully, 'nobody ever did; not even Stupid Gregor.'

'But you'll make your boobs all leathery.'

Dagmar pinched at her breasts thoughtfully for a moment. 'Not at the moment. I won't.'

'I never knew you were doing that.'

'You never know anything at that time in the morning. You are a strictly one-syllable girl until you are deep into your second cup of coffee in the morning.' Dagmar's voice caught and changed. 'I'm so worried about Horst. I have a horrible feeling that something unpleasant has happened to him.'

Renate had no idea whether that was true, but didn't say anything.

Within a couple of minutes she had dried off and had climbed into bed. She turned over and within minutes she was asleep. When it became obvious that Dagmar was out for the count, Renate wondered how it was possible for that to happen. She flipped off the light and closed her eyes hopefully. If they were going to drive another 500 kilometres tomorrow, then she was going to need a good night's sleep too.

Chapter 6

Nuits-Saint-Georges, Saturday morning

Truchaud smiled at the girl on the reception desk as he walked past her, but she gave him the usual response. Or, putting it another way, she didn't. He followed the sign to the Municipal Police and walked through the door. A middle-aged man in uniform looked up wearing a question mark on his face.

'I'm Commander Truchaud,' he said.

The middle-aged man brightened up considerably. 'Ah,' he said, putting a face to the name. 'I'm Officer Fauquet,' he replied. 'You have a visitor waiting in your inner office,' he added, pointing to a closed door off to the right. Truchaud shot a questioning look at Fauquet, but didn't receive any sort of response, so he walked through the door.

'Charlie!' came an exuberant male voice as soon as he got through the door. 'How do I put it? How the mighty are fallen?' It was Jean Parnault. Jean had been a contemporary and good friend of Truchaud's elder brother Bertin at school. He also had a sister who was a direct contemporary of Truchaud's and who, at the time, the detective had considered to be capable of walking on water. 'I just had to see if it was true that you're now our local Municipal Police Chief.'

'Only temporarily, while we sort my father out.'

'Well, it's good to see you, and pleasant to know someone that our taxes are paying for, for a change.'

'If you think you can get away with driving away from a posh dinner with your eyeballs swimming in wine, just because you know who I am, please think again. The prevention of drink-driving is part of my brief, and in general, the prevention of all sorts of crime.'

'Of course, of course. Do you have any mugs here?' Parnault asked, producing a thermos from the bag that hung off his shoulder.

'I don't know, I'll ask,' he said and put his head out of his door. A moment later he came back into the room with two slightly chipped mugs that in no way matched. 'That's something that I need to get for this place: a set of half-decent mugs.'

Parnault poured a slug of strong milky coffee into each mug, and they sat down on either side of the desk. 'I don't quite get it though. Why are you sitting in that chair?' he continued.

'The Divisional Commander made me an offer I couldn't refuse,' Truchaud replied. 'The locals need someone to sit in this chair from time to time, and the Old Man told them he knew just the chap: me. I suppose that means he's not expecting me back any time soon, and it also guarantees my income at the same time. I don't know how Nuits-Saint-Georges can afford a police commander on their budget, but that's their problem not mine. How has your flowering season gone?' he asked, changing the subject.

'At this point, I can't complain,' replied Parnault. 'Moderately encouraging, I suppose.'

'I went round all the big plots with Bruno and Maréchale this morning before I came in, and Bruno seemed especially excited about it all, but you would expect that from the boy. At his age, he hasn't got many years to provide a comparison.'

'Tell you the damnedest thing though,' Parnault continued, 'You know we have that nursery plot up at the top of Nuits-Saint-Georges, on the way to the Hautes-Côtes?'

'You mean you have your own vine nursery?' asked Truchaud.

'Sure. Don't you?'

'No,' replied Truchaud genuinely surprised.

'What do you do when a vine dies then?'

'We dig it up at the end of the season and go and get some new vines from the professional nursery near Dole, and plant them in the hole in the spring.'

'So you've got the occasional very young plant among your old vines?' It was Parnault's turn to sound surprised.

'Yes, but only the occasional one. They don't die off very often, and we don't put the grapes from the new vine into the vat until the plant is adult enough for that to be appropriate. So what is it you do?'

'Well, we have an extra step in the system. We buy our replacement vines from Dole, like you, but we plant them at the top of the village until such time that they are needed, and then we dig them up, and replant them in the appropriate place, so that they're ready to go. We know which vines they are, of course, and we give them a good year or so, to learn which vineyard they are part of. If they've been up at the top for a few years and are producing grapes, those grapes may well end up in our basic Bourgogne.'

'Or even a Grand Ordinaire?' Truchaud asked innocently.

The reply was terse in the extreme, 'We don't make a Grande Ordinaire! Wherever did you see one of those with our label on?'

'I didn't,' replied Truchaud backtracking fast. He continued, changing the subject, 'So as you were saying, what has actually happened?'

'Well, right up by the edge of the wood, there's a strip of very new vines that we planted this year, perhaps a couple of metres long that has just started dying off. I think that someone must have sprayed just that strip with some sort of chemical vine-killer. Why someone would want to do a thing like that, I really don't know. Have we got vandals in Nuits-Saint-Georges?'

'Yes, it sounds like the excuse that kids make in Paris when they've failed a drug test. 'It wasn't me, *ossifer*. Someone must have spiked my drink. I mean why would anyone want to put expensive drugs into someone else's drink?'

'Date rape?' replied Parnault, suggesting an explanation.

'Oh yes, I get that. But no, I wasn't talking about Benzodi-azepines or other sedatives which will make people somnolent and pliant, I was thinking about stimulants and narcotics.'

'But who would want to date-rape my vines?'

'Are the others nearby flowering at the moment?' Truchaud asked.

'Not so as you'd notice; just growing fast with lots of leaves.'

'Hell of a thing,' agreed the detective. 'Do you want me to ask Simon for an explanation of what it's all about?'

'Why would Simon want to kill my vines?'

'I'm not saying he would,' replied Truchaud backtracking, 'I'm just saying he might know why somebody else might. He's got that sort of exploratory mind. In another life he would have made a half-decent detective. Do you think someone could be trying out a new chemical on the vines, to see whether it stimulates growth, or, as indeed appears to have happened, inhibits it, but they didn't want to try it out on their own patch in case it turned the grapes into grapefruit?'

Parnault chuckled at the joke and sucked at his coffee for a moment, and smiled. 'I see what you mean,' he replied, and changed the subject. 'So, what are you planning to do with this new job, now you've got it?'

'Work out a way of giving it back as soon as I can,' replied Truchaud drily, glancing at the door to make sure that nobody was coming through who might repeat that remark to somebody else. 'I have to get my dad sorted out and then get myself back to Paris. I'm a serious crime detective, not a car park attendant. Right now I feel like a duck out of water.'

Parnault was suddenly very aware that the detective was not particularly happy with how things had panned out. 'Did you think of taking over the family firm?' he asked.

'I'm not a winemaker,' Truchaud replied. 'How could I do that?'

'But you employ a winemaker to do that stuff for you.'

'But he isn't going to be there forever. Looking into the future, assuming his relationship with Suzette stands the test of time and they get married, he'll be your nephew-in-law, and as such he'll be a part of your family.'

'Just remember that I have put in a bid to buy your domaine, should you ever want to sell it, and then you could be running

Société Parnault et Truchaud SARL. Yes, our very own petro-chemical wine industry.'

'I do hope you're joking,' said Truchaud, sounding almost desperate.

'Of course! Do you really think I would put any of my precious Chambertin into a communal vat? I could no more do that than you could allow your Clos de Vougeot to get into one of those. Even those fake Richebourgs of yours weren't industrial wine: they were beautifully made and very well blended to make a really good imitation of what they claimed to be.'

'But if you remember correctly, I had nothing whatever to do with the making of that stuff.'

'Maybe not. Once you knew about it and what it contained, you were absolutely damned sure it wasn't going to end up in some vat labelled "Bourgogne Grande Ordinaire", which, as you've just said is the lowest of the low, and probably the only labelling it would have been legally allowed to wear on the market place.'

'Hmm,' Truchaud grunted.

'Tell you something else: it wouldn't have stayed on the shelves very long; it would have been the best damned Grande Ordinaire I have ever tasted, so I'd have bought a few cases for my personal cellar.'

'But that's only because it would have been cheap,' Truchaud replied drily.

'Being a Grand Ordinaire, it would have to have been; that's what the name is all about. It's not a compliment, it's a judgement. I suppose you could use ordinary Grand Ordinaire as a cooking Burgundy.'

'Only if you were doing a mass-produced meal, for a staff canteen or something,' added Parnault with a grin.

'But your Grand Ordinaire would never have got into a staff canteen meal; it would have been nicked and replaced by the chef, long before it got into his coq au vin for the troops. Anyway, that's not the point, what we're talking about is what you could be doing with your own life, and the options that lie in front of you. Being the director of your own domaine would not stand in the way of your also being the local Chief of Municipal Police. You could even stand for Mayor in an election. What do you think of that?'

Truchaud shuddered. 'God forbid!' he replied.

'Don't you want to be a politico?' replied Parnault grinning. Truchaud could tell that the man was having the time of his life. Whether he was being amiable, however, Truchaud was less than sure, though if he weren't, why would that be? Was it something to do with his sister? For heaven's sake, that was a quarter of a century ago and absolutely nothing happened: nothing at all; *rien; nada*. Maybe that was the problem.

'Okay, let's leave that for the moment, and see where we could go from here.' Parnault swallowed the dregs of his coffee.

'Well,' said Truchaud, 'accept that I will let you have Maréchale, when you let him make an honest woman out of Suzette.'

'Do you think she's currently a dishonest woman?'

'No, but you know what I mean.'

'She's my niece, my sister's daughter, and the girl that my sister made with the local doctor. I really don't think I have a lot of say in the matter.' Parnault shrugged.

'But you're the titular head of the family.'

'You don't think we're one of those feudal families that arrange the marriages of their children, do you? We left that sort of claptrap behind before the Revolution.'

And there it was. There wouldn't have been barriers put up to prevent any relationship between Truchaud and Geneviève at any time in the past. Whatever Truchaud wanted to say, now was not the time to say it. He was the local Chief of Municipal Police, and also someone who would soon have the power of attorney over his father's affairs. He would not want to be thinking about 'what ifs' or 'unlesses'.

Chapter 7

Boppard, Sunday morning; Nuits-Saint-Georges, Sunday afternoon

Breakfast at Mrs Gruber's was waiting when they got downstairs. 'Coffee or tea?' she asked. Both girls asked for coffee.

The table had a selection of rolls, pumpernickel, cold and smoked sliced meats, slices of Tilsit cheese, and a couple of hot boiled eggs, sitting in egg cups. Renate wondered how on earth Mrs Gruber had timed the eggs so perfectly. 'It's not just the trains that run on time,' said Mrs Gruber, 'in *Haus Gruber*, breakfast works that way too.'

After breakfast they paid the bill and loaded the car. They set off back through the small town, under the railway bridge and down towards the river. It was as they were leaving the built-up area that Dagmar suddenly pulled off the road into a small car park. It looked like an old garage-cum-filling station, except that it no longer had any petrol pumps.

She went through the double door with Renate following her, trying to get an explanation for why she had stopped. The question was quickly answered as she heard the conversation with the man inside. 'Yes, this is where Horst Witter works. Why?'

'Well, I'm his sister, and I'm looking for him, do you know where he is?'

'Er, no, I haven't seen him for a while.'

'His campervan was impounded in Nuits-Saint-Georges in France, and we're off there to see. Mind you, if his camper has been impounded, then he probably wasn't in it.'

'Well, he told me he had found some relations in France and he thought he might go and look them up. He seemed quite excited about it.'

59

Dagmar looked surprised. 'Oh? I thought I was the only relation he had left.'

'Apparently not.' Acknowledging the huge question mark written over her face, he continued: 'I've no idea, he didn't say. He didn't mention any names or anything, but he said he'd tell me all about it when he got back, if it had amounted to anything.' He rummaged around behind the till, and produced three bottles in a small carry-box.

'Tell you what … give him these from Hans; that's me. He likes this stuff. And while you're about it, tell him that I've got his wages here for him when he comes back. He might even still have a job if he gets back soon, and the story's entertaining.'

Dagmar looked at the bottles of dark red wine, which had, on the label, 'Cabernet Dorsa', made by a man called Michael Schneider. She looked at Renate, 'Any relation?' she asked her friend.

Hans chipped in. 'I doubt it. It's just down the road he makes that. He grows the grapes up on the vineyard they call "The Hook", which you'll drive past if you drive north from here, which you will if you're looking for the motorway to Trier, which is the way to France from here.'

Dagmar asked him for more detailed directions, but it really was very simple: go north with the river on your right shoulder, all the way into Koblenz, then follow the signs to Trier via the motorway.

They were both looking to their right at the river bank as they travelled due south. It stood proud, perhaps several hundred metres tall and half a kilometre from the Autobahn. If they had any doubts on the matter the signs by the side of the road pointing to 'La Côte', illustrated with bunches of grapes and bottles, told them that they were in wine country. The next road sign told them the next pull off was to Nuits-Saint-Georges. They were nearly there.

They turned down the pull off and there was a little cabin with a barrier blocking the road; the other half of the tollbooth system. There was nothing in German written on the cabin, but there was a slot, with a picture which suggested they might stick their ticket in it. Renate took the ticket and did so. Lights flashed and the machine appeared to wake up. It demanded twenty-two euros. Bloody hell ... that was five bottles of wine where they came from! There was an array of slots in the machine, which appeared to accept coins, credit cards, and did that one take bank notes? She gently teased the bank note slot with a ten-euro note, which was pulled greedily from her fingers into the machine, and the count on the machine dropped by ten euros. She expected the machine to belch, but was disappointed. 'Got another ten?' she asked Dagmar.

'Pennies?' asked Dagmar.

'No,' said Renate drily. 'Euros.'

Dagmar fished one out of her pocket, and Renate fed the ravenous machine again, before taking a two-euro coin from her pocket. She fed that into the coin hole, and the count fed back to zero. There was a chime from within the machine and the bar in front of them shot up. She re-engaged the gears and drove under the bar before the beastly thing could change its mind and bring the bar crashing down again, demanding even more money from them.

On their left was a huge white cube, on which was written the slogan 'J.C. Boisset' in enormous letters. It wasn't any architecture they recognised, simply a large white cube, with slightly rounded corners. They were somewhat relieved when passing round the roundabout in front of them that the buildings they passed were more recognisably houses. They were not tall, two storeys or bungalows, but were in good condition, and there were tall green trees in front of many of them.

Suddenly a car shot out of a side turning. Renate managed to slam her foot on the brake to avoid a collision, just, and stalled the engine. 'What the ...?' She got the engine going again but was very cautious when she came up to the next junction, which signed her to turn left to the centre, and right to Dijon and Vosne-Romanée. She cautiously turned left, but didn't see any more junctions until she reached the traffic lights.

'Look!' shouted Dagmar. 'There, on the left, on the other side of the road, it says *Gendarmerie*.' There appeared to be a car park outside it. She turned across the traffic lines, not that there was much traffic still and pulled into the park. 'Now,' said Dagmar, 'Where's Horst's letter from the Gendarmerie?'

Having found the letter, they pushed through the large wrought-iron gates and went up the step to the door. There was a button on the wall by the door, so assuming that they were meant to push it, Dagmar did so. There was a slightly drowsy sounding bark from within, so they turned the handle and walked through the door. That was, of course when they realized their next problem. They didn't understand a single word that the man in the uniform on the other side of the desk said to them.

'German?' asked Renate, and the policeman shook his head. 'Czech?' she asked, and the policeman looked bewildered and again shook his head. 'English?' Dagmar added. The policeman scowled before shaking his head again. Dagmar passed him Horst's letter, and he looked at it for a moment. If it had been a cartoon, a light would have gone on, on the top of his head. He looked at them, almost smiled and pointed to the floor, and then went into the back room.

'I think he wants us to stay here,' Dagmar observed.

A couple of minutes later, the man came back with two more people in uniform: one a stocky slightly red-headed woman with freckles; the other, a middle-aged man with a lot more silver braid on his uniform than the others. They tried the same language game that they'd tried with the first man on the desk. 'Captain Duquesne, and I'm Constable Montbard,' said the woman in German, firstly pointing at the man in all the braid, and then to herself. 'And you are?'

Dagmar, very relieved to find someone who spoke German, explained that she was Horst's sister and they had come about the campervan as it said in the letter, but the woman didn't seem to understand what was being said, and looked puzzled.

'Campervan belongs to man. Horst Witter is a man,' Montbard said. She obviously didn't understand a word Dagmar had said. The two policemen looked at each other and shrugged. 'English?' Renate asked again. The two policemen looked at each other and said 'English' to each other in French.

The woman looked at the girls and said, 'Coffee?' which was fortunate, because it sounds the same in French as in German, even if it is spelled completely differently. They smiled and nodded, and were invited through into a room with a table with plastic chairs round it. The woman said in her best German that they were going to get someone who spoke English.

Three cups of strong black coffee appeared each with a wrap of two sugar lumps and another wrap with a small biscuit. The red-haired policewoman sat down smiling and helped herself to the third cup. By her behaviour she was trying to tell the girls that in no way they were in trouble, and the gendarmes were all very friendly, and were just trying to find someone who would be able to communicate with them. The girls smiled very politely back at the woman, whose name they gathered was 'Mo'bar', but didn't say anything to each other, as that would have been potentially very rude as 'Mo'bar' obviously wouldn't have understood what they were saying. The coffee was good though.

About ten minutes later a small man in a trench coat, looking every inch like a detective they had seen in 1940s' imported black-and-white films was shown in. 'Good afternoon,' he said in English. 'I'm Commander Truchaud of the National Police. Can I help?'

'I'm Dagmar Witter,' said Dagmar. 'I look for my brother.'

Truchaud's face lit up, 'Aha!' he said in English. 'You're the sister.' He turned to Mo'bar and reeled off a bit of French, who replied also in French.

The detective turned to the girls, 'Do you know where he is?'

'No,' replied Dagmar. 'We went to his flat in Boppard last night to discover he moved out three months ago.'

'He left his Kombi here over six months ago,' replied the detective. He nodded to Mo'bar and she confirmed six. 'The gendarmes here put his Kombi in their car park, where it has been ever since.'

Dagmar's eyes were getting wider by the moment, 'Six months?' The only thing you could tell with Renate was that her eyebrows had disappeared under her fringe. 'That's why he didn't come and see us at Christmas,' she said in German to her friend. She then said it in English to the detective, and continued. 'He also didn't go back to his flat in Boppard, because they rented it out to someone else.'

Truchaud looked at Montbard. 'I think we've got a real missing person case here, gendarme. He wasn't only missing here, but he was missing in Germany as well. He turned back to the girls, 'Whereabouts in Germany are you from?' he asked, and they told him.

He wandered over to the phone and dialled. He was calling a number in Paris. 'Hello, *chef*,' he said. 'Have you got Natalie working on something at the moment?'

The voice on the phone came back, 'Well, we've just promoted her to sergeant, and she's bored to the back teeth filling in the forms. Why do you ask?'

'Well, I could use her help to sort out a little problem I've run into down here, since you pushed me into taking over the Municipal Police Force,' he replied distinctly pointedly.

'Good lord, man! You've only been down there a couple of days; they haven't got you working on a job already!'

'I'm afraid so. We've got a missing German, who apparently went missing six months ago, but the various people from whom he was actually missing only met this afternoon, and realized he was missing from all of them. Now his sister has arrived from Chemnitz in Thuringia, deep in Eastern Germany, and our German-speaking gendarme here doesn't understand a word they're saying. At the moment we're getting by on my schoolboy English and theirs, but Natalie speaks good German, though whether she will understand their version of it I don't know. Can we borrow her to find out?'

'She knows where to find you?'

'Either at the Gendarmerie or the domaine. Tell her we'll have a room for her at the domaine.'

'She'll see you later tonight,' replied the Divisional Commander.

Truchaud explained to the girls that he was arranging for a member of his team, who spoke good German to come and see them, and she'd be down this evening. They both looked relieved.

Truchaud then phoned Michelle and told her he'd invited another guest to stay, but when she heard who it was, and what it was all about, she was quite positive about the whole thing. She had obviously liked Natalie last time she had been down. She then went on to suggest that the German girls could park their camper in the courtyard as well. 'It's not their camper; it's their brother's.'

'Well, they've got to sleep somewhere. If the whole thing is now too tatty for words, then we'll have to work something else out.'

Truchaud went back to Montbard. 'Is the Kombi still in the pound?' he asked.

'As far as I know.'

Once again Truchaud reverted to English. 'We're going to try to get the Kombi started. Have either of you ever driven it?'

The girls looked at each other and shook their heads. 'Okay,' he continued, 'we'll get Lenoir to drive it round to where I live. The interpreter will be joining us this evening, and we'll see where we go from there. Okay?'

The battery was flat and the Kombi needed jump-starting from a police Mégane, but once it had got going and stopped belching out rather foul black smoke from the exhaust, Lenoir set off for the domaine. However, for once, Lenoir didn't make the tyres squeal. Perhaps he thought that as they hadn't turned over at all for six months they might well explode if they were strained in any way. Truchaud got into the passenger front seat of the Škoda, and Renate got into the back. Within five minutes they were all back at the domaine. Lenoir asked if Truchaud had a battery charger. Truchaud found one in the garage, rather

65

covered in spiders webs, but it was a good powerful device that they used to reactivate the tractors each spring. Lenoir set the battery on charge, and meanwhile the girls explored the camper. The mould was confined to the outside, and it was quite dry within.

'Can you sleep in it?' he asked them.

'We can try,' replied the girl, who answered to 'Dagmar'.

'Come and meet my sister-in-law,' said Truchaud. 'It's she who invited you to park your camper in the yard.'

'How do I say, "thank you" in French?' asked Dagmar.

'*Merci beaucoup*,' said Truchaud.

'Mercy bo-coo,' she tried out.

'Not bad,' said Truchaud in English again.

'I have a favour to ask you,' she said. 'We were given a couple of bottles of wine by a friend of Horst's in Boppard, to give to him when we next saw him, and the weather's far too hot to leave them in the car. Do you have somewhere we can put them out of the sun?'

Truchaud smiled. 'We have a cellar. Follow me.' He led them down the steps to the cellar door, and took out his keys. *Funny*, he thought, *that I have a key to the family cellar even when I'm on a case in Paris.* He inserted the key into the lock, and turned it. The door swung open and the stone steps continued downwards into blackness. He was aware of a drawn breath behind him. He felt along the wall to the right and twisted the light switch, which lit the area near the bottom of the steps. The far depth of the cellar remained dark, and the girls couldn't see the far wall. 'Have you got the bottles?' he asked.

'Here,' said Dagmar, and passed the box to him. He put them in a rack alongside the back of the steps. He then went to a large barrel standing on one end and picking up a magic marker, wrote 'Dagmar' on the end of the box. 'There. Now everyone will know they're yours and won't try to sell them.'

'You sell wine from here?' she asked.

'A little. Most of it goes to the local shops or big merchants.'

'How big is that cellar?' she asked, waving a hand into the darkness. He flicked a switch bathing the depth of the cellar in light for a few seconds, before turning it off again. Both girls gasped at the size of it, both the racks on the walls and the barrels lying down.

'We don't leave the light on longer than we have to,' he said. 'Young wine doesn't like being exposed to light.'

'I thought you said you were a policeman,' she said after a while.

'I am,' he replied.

'But this is a wine farm,' she continued.

'This is my family's business, but I am a policeman. There are a couple of other things I have to tell you: the first is that my father isn't very well, so forgive him anything he might come out with. He doesn't mean anything by it; it's just how he is at the moment. Oh, and my nephew is twelve, and may well fall in love with one of you, maybe both of you. He's that age, you know.'

Dagmar smiled. 'I don't think anyone has ever fallen in love with both of us at the same time. That would be a first for all of us.' She then translated into German for Renate's benefit, who chuckled too.

'Michelle, these are Dagmar and Renate,' he said in French, to Michelle, and to Dagmar and Renate, he said in English, 'This is my sister-in-law, Michelle.'

'Mercy bo-coo!' said Dagmar and everybody smiled.

They settled down to supper, with Bruno explaining to the girls in the English he had learned that day in school, the technique of tasting fine wine, firstly by nosing it, then by swirling the glass and sniffing again. Finally, he showed them how to suck up a little in their mouth and to suck and blow, his cheeks moving the wine round their tongues. At last, he swallowed. The girls followed suit, and looked at it in amazement. 'Is good?' asked Bruno.

The girls looked at him wide-eyed. 'Is very good,' they agreed.

'My father and grandfather made that ten years ago,' he said, waving at the old man, who was completely ignoring all the new company they had round the table. 'It's from the next village to the north called Vosne.'

'Vone,' pronounced Dagmar, savouring the word. 'Very good. Your father is where?' she asked.

'He's dead,' the boy replied.

'Oh!' she said uncertain what she would have said even if they had a real language in common.

'I've made a coq au vin, so that Natalie can have some when she gets here, if she wants,' said Michelle. 'She may have stopped off on the way down.'

'Why should she have done that if she knew she was going to have some of your home cooking on arrival?' Truchaud grinned at his sister-in-law.

'What do you think of them?' she asked, well aware they wouldn't understand what she was saying.

'I think they're like lost sheep,' said Truchaud in reply. 'They went to Boppard to see the dark one's brother. He wasn't there, but he left them some clues as to where to go next, and the paper chase has led them here. They're totally out of their depth, and I'm so glad you offered to help them out. I don't suppose they've got much money, and they're going to have a fit when they realize how much more expensive everything is here than in Germany. Hopefully, Natalie will understand their accent. Nobody else seems to understand them when they speak their own language. They seemed to understand Montbard when she spoke in school German to them, but when they came back at her in their accent, she couldn't fathom a word of it.'

'And if Natalie doesn't?'

He grinned. 'In that case we send her back and ask the Divisional Commander for another one who speaks proper Thuringian.'

'You wouldn't do that,' she said, 'that would be too unkind. You know she adores you.'

'Don't be silly, woman. You know she's nearly young enough to be my daughter.'

Michelle raised an eyebrow and said nothing more. 'Does anyone want any more food?' she asked in French, which

Bruno helpfully translated as 'More?' into English for their guests, with hand gestures at their plates.

Truchaud waved the wine bottle round as a suggestion as well.

'Dunno why you're wasting good wine on English tourists,' muttered the old man from his end of the table.

'But they're not ...' Bruno started to say.

'Because they're our guests,' interrupted Truchaud, very uncertain how the old man would react to the information that the girls were German. His father had been too young to remember the occupation himself, but he was sure his grandfather would have talked about it often enough round the dining table.

'Coffee?' suggested Michelle. 'A digestif?'

Bruno translated into English. *Café* and *Kaffee* sounded much the same in French and German, and he had no idea how to say 'digestif' in English.'

'Brandy?' said Truchaud in English.

'Now he's offering my best cognac around to bloody tourists,' muttered the old man.

'Would you like a cognac or a marc?' he asked the old man pointedly.

'No,' he came back. 'I'm going off to bed.' And true to his word for once, he got up and stomped out. Truchaud poured a small brandy for himself and Michelle, and offered the bottle to the girls, who nodded enthusiastically at him. He produced a couple of small brandy balloons and poured some into each, and placed them in front of them. 'No driving tonight,' he said. 'You sleep here.'

It was a warm night, with stars out as they sat out in the courtyard nursing their glasses of cognac and little cups of sweet black coffee. Their lives had moved in a completely different direction than they had thought possible when, less than thirty-six hours before, they had been telling Stupid Gregor where to get off. The ambient sound was mainly insects, and there was a faint citrusy aroma to the air.

A Renault Mégane pulled into the courtyard, and a woman got out. 'Hello,' she said to the girls in German. 'Is the chief in?'

'They're all in there,' replied Dagmar, also in German. The woman walked into the house with her case.

'She must be the policewoman they were talking about,' said Renate. 'Looks classy.'

'Looks expensive,' replied Dagmar drily.

A few moments later, she put her nose out of the door again, and continuing in German she said, 'I'm just going to have something to eat, and then I'll come and join you, if that's all right. You're not planning to go to bed immediately, are you?'

Chapter 8

Nuits-Saint-Georges, Sunday evening

'That's better,' said the smart Frenchwoman, delicately dabbing the corners of her mouth with a napkin as she came out of the house again. 'I'm Natalie Dutoit,' she said. 'Commander Truchaud asked me to come down as I speak German. Do you understand what I'm saying?'

Both girls told her that they did, and then went on to say that they had also understood what Constable Montbard had said to them. The problem had been that Constable Montbard hadn't understood a word of what they had said in return. Raising an eyebrow Natalie replied, 'Oh, you do have fairly strong regional accents, don't you,' she said. 'I can understand Constable Montbard having difficulties.' She took a pull at her coffee. 'Now, I understand you're looking for your brother?' she continued, looking at each girl in turn.

'Mine,' said Dagmar, and told Natalie the whole story of the past couple of days. She left little out, and even included Hans's bottles of wine, at which Natalie smiled. 'I think you'll find you didn't need to do that. You've ended up in an area where they make quite a lot of wine, and some of the people who make it are of the opinion that the stuff they make is the greatest wine in the world. My boss, who you've just met, is cut from that jib. Even if Horst is completely illiterate he couldn't have failed to have spotted the vines on the hill, and the bottles outside people's houses with signs to come in, try some and spend.' She rolled her eyes as she said the last word.

'He isn't illiterate,' continued Dagmar.

'So, do you know why he's in Nuits-Saint-Georges?' asked Natalie, getting down to the business at hand.

'I didn't even know he wasn't in Germany till last night,' she

71

said. 'And I don't think either of us were aware of the existence of Nuits-Saint-Georges till then either.'

'So how did you get here?'

'Satnav,' replied Renate drily. 'We were offered a free satnav when we bought the car, and not knowing anything about it, and as they used the "free" word, we said yes. First time we've really used it in earnest was yesterday to get to Boppard; wonderful thing.'

'Yes, up until then we had always known where it was we were going, but Gretel's satnav took us up to Horst's flat without missing a beat,' continued Dagmar.

'Except of course, it didn't tell us we were on the wrong side of the Rhine, and that there wasn't a bridge for seventy kilometres.'

'But it did guide us to the car ferry at Boppard.'

Natalie coughed. She could tell that these two girls would need regular guidance to keep them on topic. She did sympathize with them somewhat, as they were far away from their known territory. She hadn't come from as far as them, but she was also off the patch she knew. 'Tell you what. Shall we go and see that woman at the campsite tomorrow?' she said. 'From what I understand, she's the only person we know who got to know Horst well. Did you know that last autumn wasn't the first time he had been down here?'

'No. Really?'

'You had no idea?'

'Not at all,' said Renate.

'Do you think he had found a girlfriend?' asked Dagmar.

'Instead of me?' said Renate cutely.

'Instead of you, hun,' replied Dagmar.

'Him finding a girlfriend 500 kilometres away, not telling us and emoting down the phone twice a day, at least to you? I don't think that's very likely, do you?' replied Renate acidly.

'I don't think that anything about Horst is very likely without his contacting me and telling me all about it.'

'So you were close then?' asked Natalie.

'Well, I thought so, though right now, I'm suddenly not so

sure. Do you know what I mean? I mean, it must have been two years since he moved west, but until he didn't show up for Christmas last year, he was always in close contact.'

'Did you hear from him after Christmas?'

'You mean texts and things?'

'Yes, anything like that.'

'I'm sure I did. Hang on, I'll have a look.' Dagmar suddenly looked very worried and started fiddling with the incoming call record on her phone. Her eyes got slowly wider at the truth that she hadn't received a text from her brother for over six months. She had sent him a few, and had always assumed he'd replied. But her texts had always been gossipy things that hadn't required an immediate reply. She looked at Renate, who was looking at her phone with a worried expression too.

'I was going out with Willi for a while this spring, so Horst wouldn't have called me.'

'Only if he had known how possessive Willi was.'

'Actually, if he had known how possessive Willi was, I suspect that Horst would have been phoning me all the time I was out on a date with Willi, just to piss him off. That's your Horst to a tee.'

'So,' continued Natalie, 'the bottom line is that neither of you have actually heard from Horst Witter since last year?'

Dagmar looked downcast. 'I think that has to be right.' She paused, and then flung out an expletive, 'Fuck! What have we missed?' By the uncomfortable way the word came out, Natalie realized the girl didn't swear that often.

'Absolutely nothing,' Natalie said. 'Horst came to Nuits-Saint-Georges on some sort of adventure, we don't know what, and he didn't tell you about it. Now whatever he did next, he obviously didn't need his camper, because he left it at the campsite, and never came back to collect it. Right so far?'

'Yes?' Both Germans looked at the Frenchwoman expectantly.

'So that's where we have to go tomorrow, to see if we can find a trail. Follow the trail and find Horst.' She looked carefully at Renate and the worried eyes that peered out from beneath her straight blonde fringe. 'Were you very involved with him?' she asked gently.

'No, we grew up together, because he was my best friend's brother, you know.'

'And you slept together,' nudged Dagmar teasing.

'Only because it would have been icky if you had shared a bed with your brother, and we haven't got a third bed in the flat,' replied Renate in a similar tone of voice, though Natalie didn't need to be a genius to detect a rather more serious undertone to their banter.

'How about another brandy as a nightcap?' she suggested. There wasn't a lot further she could take the hunt for Horst that evening, unless she teased another fragment out of the girls that they didn't know was there. That was a detective skill that Natalie had in abundance. And one of the best ways of doing that, she thought, was to loosen a pair of dainty brains with a little more alcohol. It wasn't as if they were driving anywhere that evening. She stood up and went back into the house with their glasses without waiting for them to refuse.

'Tell me,' said Renate, when Natalie returned with three new glasses and the bottle of brandy, 'how you get to be a detective, when you look like that? I thought you had to be invisible to be a detective.'

'Well, that's one possibility,' she replied smiling. 'On the other hand, if all the criminals had the same view as you, then I suppose they would think that, of all the people in the room, there's no way that I could be the one who's the detective; it would have to be someone else. Mind you, it often is, in fact. Quite often I end up with playing the decoy when a lot of officers are involved in a takedown.'

'But how come you got to be a detective?'

'Because that was the one thing our career guidance counsellor said I would never be. And you know something? I really hated that man.'

'What? Your career guidance counsellor?'

'He was the creepiest of the creepy. He spent the whole time telling me how pretty I was, and how I should maximize my gifts, by being an actress, or even better, a model. Where he really saw me fitting in was as a photographic model. And I was a kid of just fourteen at the time. You must have had that sort of experience, you two.'

'But not on our own,' replied Dagmar. 'They kept trying to pair us up. You know, the blonde one and the dark one: the Tiger Stripes. But Horst, love him, wouldn't have it, and would get really angry with people trying to hit on us. But we never got singled out.'

'That's probably because you were always together, am I right?'

'Yes, that's right.'

'So you two were your own contrast. Me, I was on my own, with just this,' she said pointing to her face. 'And I did absolutely nothing positive to encourage the intense male emotions that surrounded me. When people come up to you and declare undying love all the time, the value of love itself tends to be rather diminished.'

'So you've never been in love?' asked Renate surprised.

'The only time I thought I might have been was with someone who never reacted to my physical attributes, but was interested in my thoughts and opinions. Once I realized why I was feeling that, I stopped being all emotional and gooey about it, and realized that what I was actually feeling was respect, and that it went both ways.'

'You mean you've never had sex?'

'I can't remember ever denying that,' she said. 'Hang on,' and she went back through their conversation so far out loud. 'Boppard; Christmas; Willi; nightcap; fourteen … no, I can't ever remember my sexual experiences coming up in our conversation.'

Renate's eyebrows had vanished again up under her fringe. 'Can you really do that? You know, physically remember everything we've just said and then play it back like a video recorder?'

'Not like that, no. I'm just monkeying about; something to do with the brandy perhaps.' It was now time to soften the conversation again. 'So there's nothing else you can remember about Horst or why he came here?'

Renate's hand shot up, like she was still in class or something. Her fingers felt embarrassed when they realized what they had done.

'Yes, Renate?' said Natalie, sounding suddenly very like a middle-aged schoolmarm. When she didn't get an immediate response, she continued, 'Do you want to be excused?'

'What?' The hand had now come down and she was looking confused. 'No, I was just thinking, in Boppard we found a box with all sorts of papers in it. We haven't been through it very deeply yet, but I wondered if that contains the secrets we are looking for.'

'Oh yes, I expect that could be very interesting indeed. Do you want to wait till after breakfast tomorrow morning to rummage through that? Where is it? We need to be sure it's safe.'

'It's locked in Gretel's boot.'

'Gretel?'

'The name we gave our car,' replied Dagmar. 'A car's got to have a name. Everything else does. Tell you what we did find in Horst's papers: my mother's death certificate. There was one thing I learned from that which I didn't know before: my mum didn't have a German sounding name when she was born.'

'Oh yes?' said Natalie sounding interested. 'What was it?'

'Laforge. Sounds fairly French to me.'

At this point Natalie's interest became genuine. 'There's only one family round here that I know called Laforge, and if it was them that attracted Horst down here to Nuits-Saint-Georges, I'm fairly sure our Commander might be interested too. I think we might involve him in the morning.'

'Why? Who are they?'

'They are Commander Truchaud's family's partners in wine.'

'Huh?'

'They all make wine together, and I think you may find you're in for a treat, as they do make very good wine. I think we'll invite ourselves to meet with them tomorrow.'

Chapter 9

Nuits-Saint-Georges, Tuesday morning

The first awake face at breakfast was Bruno, who had rushed round to the bakery and got twice as many croissants and baguettes as they usually had on order. 'We've got unexpected guests,' he explained.

'You mean your uncle who's the new Police Chief?' replied the baker with an amiable smile. Even Bruno, who was part of it, was impressed with the effectiveness of the local grapevine

'And we've got a couple of German girls in a camper, and my uncle's sidekick from Paris, and they're all gorgeous.'

'But the sidekick from Paris is the most gorgeous because she's French,' replied the baker, in a tone that suggested he would have ruffled Bruno's hair if his hands hadn't been covered in flour.

'Yes, how did you know?'

'Intuition,' said the baker, grinning.

'Bakers' intuition?' asked the boy. 'I didn't know there was such a thing.'

'Which goes to show how much you still have to learn about life. Now run along home. One other thing you'll have to learn about running a harem is that you don't want any of the pretty ladies to starve. They make life very difficult for a lad if they go hungry.'

Bruno carried his bread back home, quietly wondering if the baker believed anything he had said. Then he thought more about it and wondered whether he was bothered anyway.

He dumped all the bread on the table in the dining room, where his mother and uncle both were looking slightly cloudy, stirring cups of as yet untasted coffee. He knew their faces would clear as the coffee got into their systems. Bruno was the

77

only Truchaud who didn't need a cup of coffee to switch him on in the morning. As for poor old Granddad, no amount of coffee was capable of completely turning on all the lights any more. He knew that too. However, as a twelve year old, Bruno was developing a taste for coffee, suitably milked and sugared, and helped himself to a mug from the pot.

'What's news?' Truchaud asked his nephew, who knew the boy and the baker would have touched base when he picked up the bread.

'The main news is that you're back in town, and you're the new Chief of the Municipal Police.'

'So, nothing much then.' Truchaud grinned at his nephew, who glanced down at his uncle's mug and saw that it was already half-empty. He should have been able to tell that from the way his uncle had woken up.

Down the stairs from inside the house, Natalie appeared, looking, in jeans, far less expensively elegant than she had the evening before, but a lot more up and ready for action. 'Morning,' she said to everyone. Michelle offered her coffee, and explained that the bread, jam, croissants, cheese and ham were all on the breakfast table. 'I think there's a salami in the fridge and I can find you a very sharp knife if you want to cut yourself a hunk.'

'No, thank you,' replied the younger woman. 'There's everything I could possibly need on the table right here.' Changing the subject, she asked, 'Are the girls up yet?'

'They haven't been in here yet,' replied Truchaud. Then catching the way that Bruno was gazing raptly at Natalie, he added, 'You need to close your mouth when you gawp. You'll look less gormless, and won't end up swallowing flies.'

Bruno looked slightly offended at his uncle, and continued demolishing his croissant.

Dad appeared. 'There's a van with a German number plate in the yard,' he said.

'I'm impressed, Dad,' said Truchaud airily. 'How did you know it was German?'

'Cos it's got a big letter D on the back, and everyone knows that that's short for Boche.' Truchaud shuddered. He hoped his dad wasn't going to be overly difficult with the girls, or at the very least that they weren't bright enough to understand when he was. *We'll soon find out*, he thought, *because here they are.*

They were both in slacks and blouses, without a great deal of skin on show, much to Bruno's disappointment. 'Goo-oo-ood Mooornink,' they both said in very pidgin French, while Natalie explained that they were to help themselves to coffee, and a chair, and anything they wanted from the table.

Truchaud asked them in English if they had slept well, and they were momentarily taken aback at a different language being launched at them.

'See,' explained Granddad in French. 'Told you they were German.'

Michelle piled in and said that it was English that her brother-in-law was talking to the girls, but that yes they were German, and Bruno, wasn't it about time he was off or he'd miss his bus to school? Truchaud and Natalie were suitably impressed how many conversations she could have simultaneously.

Bruno made his disappointed exit from the breakfast room, but waved and said in his best German, '*Auf wiedersehen*', which threw the German girls even more.

'Don't mind him,' said Truchaud in English. 'He's always showing off to women.' He switched to French. 'So what's the plan for today?' he asked Natalie. 'Anything come out of last night?' he added, almost as an afterthought.

'Answering the second question first,' she replied, 'yes. And in answer to your first question second, I think Dagmar wants to meet some Laforges.'

'Oh yes?'

'She produced her mother's death certificate last night, and it appears that she was born a Laforge, and so far that is the only reason we have found to explain why Horst kept coming down here. There weren't any jobs, or girls, or boys that we've found so far.'

'Where was she born?' he asked still in French, not thinking. He hadn't fully pre-loaded with coffee.

Natalie translated into German, and when Dagmar replied 'Chemnitz', she translated back: 'Karl Marx Stadt, as it was known at the time.'

Truchaud apologized in English, and suggested that they delayed further conversation until breakfast was over.

'See,' said his father, 'I told you they were German. You're German, aren't you?' he said, waggling a bony finger at them.

'Please don't worry about Dad,' he said in English. 'He really isn't very well.'

'No problem,' said Renate, also in English, probably the first thing anyone had heard her say that morning round the breakfast table.

'So how did a Laforge get to Chemnitz?' asked Truchaud. 'That is, of course, if she was related to one of our Laforges.' He had a sudden idea, which looking at Dagmar for a moment already began to sputter and die. 'When was she born?' he asked, without waiting for an answer to his first question.

'1960,' she replied. That killed that idea! The late Young Mr Laforge hadn't started his seed-sowing walkabout round Germany at that point. In fact, he would still have been at school in the Côte-d'Or, so she wasn't the result of one of his peccadilloes. Why had Horst come here then? Laforge was a common enough name in France, implying something to do with a blacksmith's shop, and they would have been everywhere there was civilization, looking after horses' hooves, and they may also have repaired and rebuilt wheels for carts. Round there, smiths may even have made the metal bands for the coopers to make barrels. However, he was aware that there was only one family in Nuits-Saint-Georges called Laforge. Why, therefore, did Horst continue to come back? He also felt slightly guilty about the general content of that thought. He knew that Jérome had gone to university in Paris in the late sixties, and had got involved with the left-wing counterculture of the time.

80

Following that, he had migrated to West Germany and had become involved with the Baader-Meinhof movement. He also knew that much more recently, he had developed a taste for very young girls, but that didn't mean that the two features of his personality had happened at the same time. It was just that, for most people, their quirks were all ingrained by the onset of adulthood. 'And she was born in Chemnitz?'

'Nearby,' came the reply.

Truchaud looked at Natalie and shrugged, 'Don't know. I suppose the next step is to go round to the family and introduce everyone to each other. I think, constable …'

'Sergeant,' replied Natalie.

'Oh, he actually told you about the promotion then?'

'Oh yes, that's why I am here.'

'Tell you something: the system's efficient when it wants to be. Anyway, sergeant, I think the next step is for us all to go round to the shop and see whether we can get any information out of Old Mr Laforge, or from his granddaughter Marie-Claire. If Horst was hovering around the family last year, then presumably someone will remember him.' He paused for a moment. 'I wonder if he got a job during last year's harvest. He may even have been one of the pickers they used to harvest our grapes from the east side of the Seventy-Four.'

'If he was, then he should be on their records.'

'I wouldn't count on it,' Truchaud replied drily, remembering how even a big fish like Maréchale could get lost in the Laforge paperwork if they put their minds to it. 'First thing we do is the washing up. By that time the Laforges will have tidied up their breakfast stuff, but hopefully, following that, they won't have left for whatever they will be getting up to for the rest of the day. Fifteen minutes and we'll be outside the shop.'

The tidying machine got under way, leaving a most impressed Michelle sitting at the breakfast table with her mouth agape.

'Do you want us to follow you in Gretel?' asked Dagmar.

'No, I think we'll all go round in Natalie's car. What would be handy would be a copy of your mum's death certificate, and your grandfather's too. Don't produce them till I say, but it may be interesting to produce them at the right time.'

'You don't think they've done Horst any harm, do you?' asked Renate.

'I sincerely hope not,' he replied. 'Horst was young, fit and healthy, wasn't he?'

'Oh, yes,' said Renate. 'There was nothing wrong with Horst.'

'Well, Old Mr Laforge lives up to his name: he's very old and physically quite infirm, and Marie-Claire, his granddaughter, is Michelle's age, give or take, so I don't think she could have done Horst any harm. They may, however, know where he has gone.'

'And why he doesn't need his Kombi anymore,' Dagmar added.

'Exactly. Go and dig up the documents, and bring them back here. We'll run off photocopies on the machine out the back, so we don't actually take the originals.'

'I think they're photocopies themselves,' she said.

'Do you know where the originals are?'

'No.'

'So they're the nearest to the originals we have to hand, so we copy them, and use the photocopies for the moment.'

'Back in a moment,' said Dagmar and went out, leaving Renate with the tea cloth in her hands. Truchaud looked through the window at her. She had the boot of the car open rather than the door of the campervan where the two girls had slept last night.

'Got them!' she shouted, waving the pieces of paper, and slammed down the boot. He was pleased to note that after that the lights of the car flashed on and off a couple of times, indicating that she had locked it again. She came back into the kitchen again, and he took her into the front room, where a desktop photocopier sat on a small table in the corner. He put the papers through it, and it printed out two copies of each.

'Right,' he said, looking at them and comparing them with the originals. No, there was nothing missing from the front, and there was nothing on the flipside that they needed. 'That's done. Now take these originals and lock them back up in your car, so we'll know where they are when we need access to them.'

She nodded, took the papers and locked them back in the boot of her car. She didn't take any longer than she would have needed just to drop it on the top of a pile, before she was back in the front room again.

'Right,' he said. 'Are we fit? Shall we go?' They trooped out and assembled themselves in Natalie's 'plain-clothes' Mégane. The girls were interested to note that the dashboard was non-standard, and had a radio transmitter in it with a hand-held microphone.

'Does it have blue flashing lights in the radiator grille?' asked Renate in German to Natalie.

'You bet it does,' she replied, 'and a siren. It's a fully equipped, unmarked police car, unlike Commander Truchaud's car, which is his own car with a few add-ons. But we're not going to use the whistles and bells at the moment.'

'The engine?' Renate continued from behind her fringe, showing tomboyish interest in things mechanical.

'Very souped-up.'

'Do you carry a gun?' she asked, changing the subject suddenly.

'Sometimes,' Natalie replied cautiously.

Renate didn't notice the change in Natalie's tone and continued, 'Are you armed at the moment?'

'Pass,' she said softly. 'That's the kind of question you never ask a detective if you're on the right side of the law.' And with that, she pulled out of the gates of Domaine Truchaud and into the street beyond.

Chapter 10

Nuits-Saint-Georges, Tuesday morning, a few minutes later

Even with Natalie doing the driving and the tyres not even thinking about complaining, it only took five minutes from the Truchaud domaine to the Laforge's shopfront. They climbed out of the little car and pushed at the door. As it didn't give under pressure, Truchaud rang the bell. A face he vaguely recognised appeared from over the counter. 'Coming,' said the girl. She walked round with a huge bunch of keys in her hand. 'We're not really open yet,' she said, 'but seeing as it's you, Mr Truchaud …'

He scratched around in the back of his brain for the girl's name. Somehow he thought of music, which considering she was quite a plain girl, was odd. Hmm, a tune perhaps? Aha! 'Good morning, Mélodie,' he said. 'How are you?' The girl looked flattered that he had remembered her name, and replied that she was fine, and asked what she could do for him.

He replied that they were looking for Marie-Claire, and was she out the back? Mélodie responded that she had been five minutes previously, and would he like to have a look for himself? He beckoned to the others to follow him round the end of the counter, past the till and through the door behind the shelves. Mélodie followed them, apologizing to Marie-Claire, and anyone else in earshot, for letting them all through and that she hadn't meant to, only Mr Truchaud – you know … like because he is the Police, and Michelle's brother-in-law – and that she had no idea who these other women were, but they had followed Mr Truchaud through.

Truchaud glared balefully at her and she stopped talking. Marie-Claire Laforge also recognised Natalie from the dinner,

85

which they had shared at the Café du Centre a few weeks ago. They all kissed the air beside each other's ears, much to the amusement of the German girls, who Truchaud then went on to introduce by name, but didn't yet explain why they were there.

'Is your grandfather here?' he asked.

'I'm sure he's about, though, personally, I haven't seen him up this morning yet. Jacquot said he'd seen him, before he went off to catch the bus for school. Would you like a coffee, or a cup of tea or something?'

'We've only just finished breakfast, so may we take a rain check on that one, but you might be able to help us with something. Do you remember a German lad from the end of last year, to the beginning of this year? Young lad called Horst Witter?'

She thought for a moment. 'Tallish lad, quite dark, didn't look in the slightest bit German?' she asked.

He translated the question into English, and Dagmar nodded.

'Sounds like him,' he said, and waved vaguely in Dagmar's direction. 'This is his sister. When did you last see him?'

'During the harvest. He was one of the many students we employed as pickers and sorters at harvest time. No! Hang on, he came back in late November sometime, to see my uncle. I can't remember exactly when or why, but I remember seeing them in the office talking, sometime late November.'

'Do you remember what they were talking about, madame?' he asked slotting into detective questioning mode.

'No, not at all. I wasn't close and I was very busy. I really didn't take any notice. It didn't seem important. Why? Was it?'

'It may well have been,' Truchaud replied. 'We can't find anyone who's seen him since.'

'You mean he's vanished?'

'Whether that's quite the right word, I don't know, but missing without trace is certainly one way of describing it, yes.'

'And his sister doesn't know where he is?'

'That's why she's here,' he said, taking Marie-Claire's question as a statement. 'Did your grandfather meet him while he was here?'

'Granddad's always on display during the harvest. He may not get out much, but he's always entertaining, and very good value at dinner. We always feed the labourers at the end of the day, and fill them full of wine. It's always our wine, and usually a clean skin … you know, without a label on it.'

'So, how do you know what it is, madame?' asked Natalie from behind her *chef*.

'I know what bottles are racked where … in the outer cellar anyway.' She added the last with a smile, as she was aware that until a couple of months ago she'd had no idea how deep their cellars went, and that Truchaud knew that.

'What sort of wine would you have served?' Truchaud asked.

'Oh, it would have been a red table wine, possibly from your grapes from the east side of the Seventy-Four. Granddad has always liked that stuff, and that way we would have been able to give him the same wine as the workers. He would probably have told them that they were drinking the fruits of the labours of previous pickers, and that the fruits of their labours would be enjoyed by another generation further down the line.'

'It's a shame that your uncle isn't here to answer any questions about him.' Marie-Claire's uncle had been killed the previous spring, and Truchaud had been involved in the investigation of that crime.

Marie-Claire didn't reply to that comment, and Truchaud didn't push it. He was also aware that this uncle had abused Marie-Claire in her early teens, and her son Jacquot was the result. Her grandfather had kept the story within the family, blaming an itinerant worker for the pregnancy, but making absolutely sure that his son left his granddaughter alone thereafter. Truchaud was quite happy to leave that story buried. Marie-Claire and Michelle were now the business heads behind the two domaines, working as closely as they could together, without the two firms formally joining together and becoming just a single unit. They also both employed Maréchale as their chief winemaker.

He had explained to Truchaud only yesterday that he didn't feel he had two separate jobs; he felt that the two women were partners, and he did the same things for both women's domaines. He kept the juice from the separate vineyards separate, in exactly the same way that the winemakers from the greatest of domaines did. There was no way that any drops from La Tâche ever got into a barrel of Romanée-Conti, even though they were both monopoly vineyards belonging to the same fabulous domaine. Truchaud thought for a moment about the walk that he and Bruno had taken with Maréchale the previous day, when they had visited vineyards belonging to both families.

There was a bark at the door, and an elderly face, ravaged by time, looked past it. 'Is there any coffee on?' he asked, and then apologized for disturbing them. Truchaud noticed that he got his request in before acknowledging that he might be interrupting a meeting. The old boy was still as slippery as he claimed to have been in his youth.

'May I make him a coffee?' asked the detective.

'Feel free,' she replied with amusement as Truchaud, followed by his entourage of pretty young women, made his way deeper into her house. She couldn't quite picture the rather plain and stubby Commander Truchaud with a harem, but there he was and there *it* was behind him, right in front of her nose.

'Oh it's you, Truchaud,' said the old man, with a wave of recognition.

'How do you like it?' he asked.

'Taste buds got shot off in the War, so as it comes. I won't know the difference.'

'Really?' said Truchaud in amazement. 'How did you taste the wine all those years when you were the main force behind the domaine?'

'Figure of speech, old boy,' the old man replied. 'Blame everything on the War including the ageing process; a tip your dad should consider too.'

'I don't think my father would remember there was such a thing as the War by now,' said Truchaud sadly, looking at the old warrior perched unsteadily on the stool.

'I think I prefer to be in my condition than his,' he replied grimly. 'Anyway, tell me about these girlies you're showing off to make an old boy very happy. Who are they all?'

'Well, going in rank of hair colour,' Truchaud grinned, 'the ash blonde lass is called Renate; the honey blonde is a sergeant in the National Police in Paris called Natalie Dutoit; and the dark-haired girl here is called Dagmar Witter.' He introduced Dagmar last, and her surname last of all, to see if it produced any recognition in the old boy.

The only response he got was with regard to the names themselves. 'Apart from your sergeant, they don't sound very French.'

'They're not; they're from Germany.' Truchaud was ready to be very cautious with the old man, from both sides of the fence. The end of his childhood had been spent as a cellar-rat here in Nuits-Saint-Georges, keeping the cellars free of the occupying Germans during the War. His role had been to feign innocence, and throughout the occupation they had believed him.

The old boy turned to Renate and Dagmar, and said, '*Guten Tag.*' The girls were once again stunned that someone was speaking to them in German. He continued in French that he was afraid he had forgotten most of his German over the years, and could someone explain that to them.

Natalie chipped in quickly translating into German, and Dagmar replied equally quickly. 'Think nothing of it. She feels most honoured that anyone speaks to her at all.'

The old man raised an eyebrow at Truchaud. 'Okay,' he said, stirring the coffee the policeman had just made for him, 'I'm suitably impressed. Who are these German girls that you consider important enough to bring a police sergeant from Paris as an interpreter?'

'Do you remember a boy last autumn called Horst Witter?'

'German boy, who worked the vintage for us. Dark lean lad?'

'That's the one. Well, Dagmar's his sister.'

'Can't be. Horst spoke pretty good French.'

'I'm told that Dagmar speaks pretty good Czech, but that doesn't make any difference. They're both German, and that's what they both speak as their first language.'

'Go on,' said the old man sipping his coffee. 'Nice coffee,' he said and added. 'You'll make a good wife for someone once you can master one or two other domestic activities.'

Natalie giggled and the men ignored her, Truchaud out of embarrassment.

'Well, we're looking for Horst, and the last place anyone saw him appears to be here. Any bright ideas where he might have gone next?'

The room went quiet and although they didn't understand the conversation, it was fairly obvious that Truchaud had asked a fairly portentous question that the old man was taking his time over answering.

'The last time I saw him,' said the old man slowly, 'was in early December. He was talking to my son, Jérome, in the office. That was way after the harvest. We laid off all the students early in October, in time for them to go back to university or knitting school, or however they normally wasted their time, and he was just one of the many students we shook hands with and sent on their way. I think he turned up about four or five weeks later to talk to Jérome, and they went off together.'

'Did he say what it was all about?' asked Truchaud.

'Jérome said he had come back to ask about a job.'

'How do you mean?'

'Well, he wanted a job at the domaine apparently. Jérome said we weren't employing at the moment, but told him that if we ever were looking for someone, we'd make sure he heard about it.'

'That was good of him. Did he send him anywhere else?'

'If he did, he didn't tell me where.'

Natalie was busy translating the conversation to Dagmar as it went along. Finally, she chipped in with a question. 'Where Horst lived in Germany there is also a flourishing wine trade. Did he say why he wanted to work here rather than in Boppard?'

The old man shook his head and said, 'Not to me, he didn't anyway.'

'His main job was selling beer and wine in the local take-away. If he was looking for a job here, it might have been in your shop where he was looking to work.'

The old man looked at her. 'Wrong gender,' he remarked. 'Now if *you* had made that offer to Jérome, he might have been more interested.' Natalie looked slightly uncomfortable translating that, and it was her embarrassment that carried the intended innuendo, rather than anything in the words themselves.

Dagmar looked at the old man and then at his granddaughter. Following that, she did some mental arithmetic, wrinkled her nose and said, 'Ew!' which didn't need translating.

'I entirely agree,' the old man came back rapidly. 'But my son was how he was.'

Truchaud coughed to regain control of the conversation. 'So you have no idea where he went?'

'None whatever,' replied the old man.

'And you saw him once in December?'

'Just the once, and he and Jérome went off out.'

'So your nephew went out with him just to discuss a job that didn't exist anyway?'

'Well, if you put it like that, yes that does sound a little odd, but you have to remember that I didn't discuss the episode with Jérome till much later in the day, after he had come home again.'

'So you remember a conversation that you consider trivial now, but still perfectly six months later.'

'You have to understand that it is the physical part of my body that's worn-out; my mind is in perfect working order, and so is my memory, particularly in matters concerning my son. Surely, under the circumstances, you would understand that, even though you're not a father yourself.'

Truchaud shrugged. 'I think it's about time we went to see the lady at the campsite, but we'll be back.'

'Why don't *you* go and see the lady at the campsite,' said the old man with a smile, 'and leave these young things with me and see if we can't find out some more.' None of them were sure whether the old man was actually trying to be helpful, or was just being leery. 'Oh, for heaven's sake!' he said. 'I couldn't do anything even if I wanted to. I'm old and infirm, and I really think that the sergeant here, at least, could put me over her knee, and I wouldn't be able to do a thing about it.' He grinned, showing rather fewer teeth than he had been blessed with in the past, and added, 'Even if I wanted to.'

Truchaud looked at them all, and softened slightly. 'Tell you what, we will go and see the lady at the campsite now, and then we'll come back and we'll all have lunch in the café over the road. How does that sound?' Truchaud felt that at the very least he would like Dagmar to be with him when he went to the campsite, in case any questions came up.

Chapter 11

Nuits-Saint-Georges and Prémeaux, the rest of Tuesday morning

The visit to the campsite turned out to be a big disappointment. It was certainly luxurious as far as campsites went, or at least as far as he could judge, but, apart from Truchaud – during the National Service phase of his life – none of them had actually been camping. Even in Truchaud's case, the main point of it had been to toughen him up. Things like hot showers and nice warm loos had not been on the agenda in those days. Now they were part of the advertising for campsites. Somehow the concept of roughing it in comfort bewildered him slightly.

The main problem was that the woman who had been running the campsite last winter, Madame Blanchard, was away on holiday at present, and unlikely to be back much before the harvest, when, the young man who was there explained, the place was likely to be packed with itinerant students. They would all be hoping for jobs in the vineyards to stoke up with experience and knowledge, with which to impress their tutors during their next term's studies. No, he explained, he hadn't been there last winter or during the last harvest, as he'd been somewhere else. He had no idea where the woman was on holiday.

Truchaud asked to see the register, which was slightly more informative. In late November of the previous year, there was an entry for Horst Witter, which had a comment asterisked at the bottom of the page: 'Camper abandoned; passed on to the Gendarmerie at Nuits-Saint-Georges', and the date of the alteration. There was also a 'fee-owed comment'. Truchaud then flicked back to September and there was Horst Witter again. That time he'd stayed a fortnight.

93

There was a '3' and the word 'more' by his name this time. Truchaud flicked back to the December entry: yes, there was a small '4' by his name. This led the inspector to flick back in the records again. It wasn't so difficult as it was the guest who filled in the book and not the site manager, so every entry was in a different distinctive hand, and only the comments, few that they were, were written in the manager's hand. Therefore it was not difficult to find the entry for his stay in June, a year before, again for a fortnight.

There was a little comment beside the '2', written in the same ballpoint ink as the numeral: 'he's learned some French'. The final entry that year was a long weekend over Easter. There were no annotations to it at all. This did suggest that the site manager had been the same the second time as the first, as the comment about his having learned some French implied he had known none the first time the person who made the comment had met him.

The bottom line was that Horst Witter had been to that campsite four times in the last year. Now, if someone was going to visit that small part of France in a camper then that would have been the site where they would have parked it. There were one or two others about the Côte-d'Or, including one in Dijon itself, and another on the far side of Beaune, but if travelling locally on a bicycle, it would be quite hard work, and distinctly risky along the Seventy-Four. It was a maximum ten minutes by bicycle to Nuits town centre from Prémeaux.

But why did Horst keep coming back? The third visit was the easiest: he had got a job during the harvest. Looking at the June visit, perhaps he had arranged the harvest job while he was staying then. And if his first visit had been in Easter, and he had fallen in love with the place and decided that that was what he wanted to do, fine, but he might have realized that he needed to learn a bit of French in order to land the job. So, he could have gone back to Boppard and taken some French lessons after Easter. That probably explained the first three visits, but what was the mysterious fourth one about? And where did he go at the end of it?

He voiced these thoughts to Dagmar in English to see if she had any ideas. She shrugged and said that she didn't. However, she did then volunteer the thought that she had a box of Horst's papers that they still had to go through in Gretel's boot back at Truchaud's domaine.

Truchaud looked at her and at Natalie, and in a combination of English and French suggested that that was where they should go now. He would leave them there for an hour and wander into the town hall, just to surprise the Municipal Police and to show everyone that he was taking his new job seriously. They would meet again at the domaine around midday, with a view to lunch in the café across the road from Laforge's shop with Old Mr Laforge, and Marie-Claire if she felt so inclined, as they had originally agreed.

Officer Fauquet looked up as Truchaud walked into his new office, with a smile on his face. '*Bonjour, commandant,*' he said. 'What can we do for you today?'

'Nothing really,' he said. 'I just thought I'd pop in and see if you needed anything: papers signing; me to arrest someone perhaps; or anything else that crossed your mind.'

'No, sir. As far as I can tell Nuits-Saint-Georges is behaving itself perfectly this morning. Mind you, it's still a little early for the drunks to venture out in their cars,' he said with a chuckle at his own joke.

Truchaud joined him quietly in polite laughter. Those were the sort of things he was expected to police now: drink-driving. 'Anybody doing any building alterations we should be looking out for?' he asked, just letting Fauquet know that he was aware of the other jobs he would be expected to keep an eye on too.

'Not that I know of, sir; none at all. We could just go out and listen for people drilling in walls. That would find the little tricksters.'

'I don't think so. Sooner or later it's going to annoy someone and we'll get a complaint. That's the thing about policing: if you stay alert, it'll do the work for you.' He wondered whether the Municipal Police were aware about the demolition of the underground walls Lenoir had done a couple of months ago.

Well, he thought for a moment, Molleau did; he had been there at the time, and Molleau had been his predecessor in this job. Though there was no doubt in his mind that he was going to perform this role in a different way from how Molleau had done.

After a further moment of foot shuffling he decided that he would go back to the domaine. After all, there was a job to be done; a missing person to be found. It may, technically, not have been part of his role as Municipal Police Chief, but if somebody was going to get uppity about it, he could build up a case for it being his job. 'Crime Prevention' would cover a multitude of sins. 'Have you got my mobile phone number?' he asked.

The policeman picked up the phone from the desk and tapped the dial a couple of times, and after a moment Truchaud's pocket rang. Fauquet put the phone down, and Truchaud's pocket stopped. 'Yes, sir, I think we have.'

'Well, don't in any way worry about calling me, if you need to,' he said in his most benevolent-sounding voice.

'Believe me, sir, none of us will. Just as a matter of form, is there a time that you would like to meet all of us? There are six of us in total. I could call a parade.'

'Don't you think that would be a lot of work for everyone? If I haven't met everyone over the next few days, during the course of a normal working day, we'll have a rethink about that. Rest assured I will be in on a regular basis.'

'Very good, sir.' Fauquet came calmly to attention and saluted despite the fact Truchaud was not in uniform, and he commented on it.

'I am saluting the man, not the uniform, sir. Anyone who has attained the rank of commander deserves respect, however he achieved it, and so, sir, I salute you.'

Truchaud smiled and said, 'Thank you for that, officer, and if I were in uniform, I would salute you right back.' The two policemen smiled and Truchaud left the office with a spring in his step. He liked Fauquet, and, for the first time, he liked his new job.

When he got back to the domaine, all three young women were sitting in the camper with a box on the table and all had pieces of paper in their hands. The side doors were open, but they still looked distinctly warm. The camper certainly pre-dated the time after which all motor vehicles had air-conditioning built in. He looked round the door. 'Anything interesting?' he asked, inducing a catch of breath from both the German girls, and a sideways look from Natalie, who he hadn't surprised since forever. 'Tea? Coffee perhaps?' he offered.

'If you're making coffee that would be nice,' said Natalie, 'and we'll tell you what we've found when you get back.'

Truchaud wandered into the kitchen and having filled the kettle, switched it on. Michelle was sitting at the dining room table, surrounded by papers too. *That's what life has come down to today*, he thought, *just paper*. She accepted a coffee too. *So life was about paper* and *coffee, was it?*

Having passed a steaming mug to Michelle, he took a tray out to the campervan. Renate took the box off the table and put it on the floor, so Truchaud could put the tray down. Natalie then squeezed up the bench seat so he could sit down. 'Well,' he said, stirring his mug, 'what have you got?'

'You'll never guess the family dynamics we've uncovered,' said Natalie in French.

'Don't tell me, Horst was a Laforge?' he replied.

'How the hell did you work that one out?' she asked amazed.

'Well, that would explain the visit to see Jérome before Christmas. Do you have any proof of that guess?'

'Oh, yes,' she replied and asked the girls a question in German. Dagmar replied and produced a buff piece of paper. It was all written in German, but typed on the form was the name 'Armand Laforge' and a date over fifty years ago.

'What's this?' he asked.

'It's an East-German death certificate,' Natalie replied. 'It's Dagmar's grandfather.' It didn't have any other information on it that Truchaud understood. He was fairly sure he wouldn't have understood the diagnosis of the cause of death, even if it had been written in French.

'So,' he said in English, 'your grandfather was called Laforge?' and Dagmar nodded. 'So this was why Horst kept coming back: he had found some new relations.'

'Yes, I think so,' she replied. 'Scary, huh?'

He turned to Natalie and said in French, 'What does this say to you?'

'That he either didn't go away, or that Jérome found a different strain of Laforges that he was more closely related to, and who were so excited to see him that they came steaming down from Wherever-with-two-Churches in their luxury limo, and whisked him off to their mediaeval chateau. No, I don't believe that either! If that had happened, then presumably they would have wanted to meet the sister too.'

'Quite,' said Truchaud, and switched to English. 'May I run this through the copier another couple of times? I also think we ought to hide this particular document somewhere particularly safe. I am concerned that once it is out there, someone may make all sorts of efforts to lay their hands on it.'

'Why?' asked Dagmar. 'Who was he? Apart from being my grandfather, of course.'

'I don't know yet, but I suspect we will know at lunchtime. And by that time, it will be known that we know all about it. Back in a moment.'

He took the piece of paper with him to the photocopier back in the house, and ran off half-a-dozen copies. He then pulled out his phone and dialled. Lenoir answered. 'Gendarmerie?' he replied.

'Constable, Truchaud here.'

'No,' came back the reply, quick as a flash. 'I know a few Truchauds, and none of them are constables. One of them's a commander in the National Police.'

Truchaud chuckled, 'Twit!' he said. 'I'm Commander Truchaud, and you're Constable Lenoir. What I want to know is, do you have a secure location in your station?'

'We've got a safe, yes.' He replied. 'But so have you in the town hall.'

'Yes, but I'm not sure I feel comfortable using that yet. I don't know who's got access to it, whereas I trust you lot,' he paused. 'Implicitly.'

'Thank you, sir. I take that as a compliment.'

'Any chance anyone could come over and pick up a box of papers from the domaine office to put in your safe?'

'I'll be with you in five minutes.'

'No chance it could be ten, could it? As I'm now the Municipal Chief, it's my responsibility to prevent accidents, and I would rather you didn't hurtle about the streets of Nuits-Saint-Georges when it isn't an emergency.'

'Ten minutes it is, sir.'

Truchaud walked out to the campervan clutching the papers in his hands. He dropped the original back in the box, and passed the copies over to Dagmar. 'I've called the Gendarmerie, and they're going to send someone over to collect all this stuff and lock it away. Somehow I don't want it to disappear while we aren't looking.'

'You're taking this very seriously, aren't you?' she said.

'You've got me and Natalie involved,' he said, 'and we are among the best puzzle-solvers in all France. You must let us do what we do best.'

Truchaud had forgotten to time Lenoir, but it wasn't long before he arrived at the domaine. And just to show off, of course, after he passed through the gates into the courtyard, he did a hand-brake turn, spraying gravel everywhere. How he avoided hitting any of the parked vehicles already in the courtyard, Truchaud could have only put down to divine intervention. Renate looked horrified as the Renault missed her beloved Gretel by a fraction.

Lenoir leapt from the driving seat and sprang to attention. 'I suppose I deserved that,' said Truchaud drily, 'but I'm not sure any of the others did. These girls have scrimped and saved to pay for that car themselves, and watching it become a near-miss incident was not funny. Are you ready to take the box?'

A suitably chastised Lenoir stuck out his hands, and Natalie passed him the box and avoided catching his eye. She too was annoyed by his showing off, and was determined to show him. As soon as he took the weight, she looked back at the girls and spoke to them in German, with her back to him. Lenoir put the box in the boot and climbed back into his car. 'Tell the *capitaine* I'll see him soon,' said Truchaud to Lenoir as he left the premises very sedately.

'Laforge?' Truchaud said to the three young women who were back and seated in the campervan.

They climbed out again and climbed back into Natalie's car. 'So could you make this car do hand-brake turns and stuff?' asked Renate.

'If I needed to in a particular set of circumstances, yes,' she replied. 'This is a standard police car; it just doesn't have the standard paint job that the Gendarmerie cars do. Under the skin they're the same; just a different idiot behind the wheel.'

Dagmar put a couple of copies of the death certificate back in the camper, and folded a couple more and put them in one of the pockets of her jeans. 'If the camper does get burgled looking for the master copy of the death certificate, then they'll find those, and assume I had a copy made of the copies already in the camper. The master could be back in Germany or anywhere.'

'You're becoming quite a tricky little fox, aren't you?' Natalie told her. 'We'll find a job for you at the Quai des Orfèvres in no time.'

Dagmar looked at her and asked, 'Where?'

Well, at least she had worked out it was a place, Natalie thought. 'It's the police headquarters in Paris where Commander Truchaud and I work,' she explained.

'If anyone wants to walk, to work up an appetite,' said Truchaud, 'that's fine, but I do feel we ought to have one car nearby, in case someone needs me in a hurry. I do have another job. I don't mind driving your car in an emergency, sergeant, as long as you don't mind my doing so.'

Natalie shook her head, 'No problem,' she replied, faintly amused by the sudden formality of his term of address.

She parked the car opposite Laforge's shop, just next to a little café, which was beginning to bustle. 'You go in and grab a table,' said Truchaud. 'I'll go and collect Old Mr Laforge, and see if Marie-Claire wants to come.'

Mélodie was beginning to think about closing up the shop for lunch, so Truchaud got in just in time. 'Just going to grab the old man for lunch,' he said, conjuring up a rather unwelcome picture in her mind, and he ran through the back door of the shop into the office. The only person in there was Celestine, who was filing her nails. *Was she creating a weapon?* he wondered. He threw the same line at her as he went through the office into the house. The Old Man was in the parlour, and was momentarily surprised when Truchaud walked in. 'Lunch?' Truchaud asked.

'Yes, please,' came the reply. 'I didn't think you were serious when you said that.'

'When a Truchaud says something, always assume that it's genuine.'

'Including your father?'

'Er, perhaps not now,' Truchaud acquiesced, 'but me, certainly.' The Old Man followed him out slowly, much to the amusement of the employees in the office and shop.

When they reached the café, they found the girls sipping a cold-looking red liquid in a wine glass. 'I remembered you said that a Kir was a local speciality,' said Natalie, 'so I'm continuing the girls' education.'

'I'm impressed,' said Old Mr Laforge. 'They teach you all sorts of unexpected things at Police College.'

'Ah, that was nothing to do with Police College,' Natalie came back. 'That was far more to do with having dinner here with the commandant and the rest of the squad, at the conclusion of a case. A great deal of good learning can go on over dinner.' Remembering her manners, Natalie translated the gist of the conversation into German for the benefit of Renate and Dagmar, as a prelude to bringing them into the conversation. Truchaud ordered himself a Kir, and the old man had a *p'tit pastis*. Truchaud asked him if he knew the wines on the wine list.

'Hope so,' he replied drily, 'they get most of it across the road. Do you want me to pick one, or do you want to order the food first and pick a wine to fit?' Truchaud was aware the old man was making an in-joke at the expense of the non-Burgundian ladies. As if you would pick the food first, indeed! A Burgundian perused the wine list first, and picked the wine he wanted to drink, and then looked at the menu for dishes to complement his choice of wine. He looked at the wine list, and harrumphed. 'They've been round to young Parnault's, I see.'

Truchaud explained in English what the discussion was about and asked Dagmar and Renate whether they would like him to translate the menu for them. They were a little thrown when they realized that the line at the top of the starters said 'snails cooked Burgundy style'. The two girls looked at each other in alarm. 'Snails?' said Renate, her voice rising in tone with increasing concern. 'I thought eating snails was just a slightly racist joke we used to make about the French when we were kids. I didn't realize it was genuine. What are they like?'

'A bit chewy, and served in a rich garlic butter sauce,' he replied. 'Tell you what, if one of you orders them, I will too, and I'll show you the technique of how to eat them. You see, they're served in their shells, and you have to winkle them out and then pop them into your mouth while you dribble butter down your front.'

'Ew!' said Dagmar, and Truchaud realized he hadn't done a particularly good job selling *Escargots à la Bourguignonne* to the girls.

'And what're the other starters?' enquired Renate.

'Ham with parsley, which is a local speciality too. It's served cold and is lumps of ham with parsley and jelly.' The girls looked more interested in that. Much as he thought he might like to have a plate of ham, he felt duty bound to his beloved Burgundy to order half-a-dozen snails as his starter.

The rest of the menu was less complicated, being either chicken or beef stewed in wine. It was only in the really expensive upmarket restaurants, which this place certainly wasn't, that the chicken or beef were actually cooked in the quality of wine that was served at the table. Truchaud hoped that Michelle had never cooked food in his favourite Village Vosne, which his father had always made so wonderfully well.

'Well?' said the Old Man. 'This is nice, but somehow I can't help thinking you wouldn't be feeding me like this if you hadn't either got something to ask me or tell me, and you wanted to soften the pain first.'

Truchaud and Natalie exchanged glances, then the Commander continued. 'You're absolutely right. Satisfy my curiosity. Do you know anyone called Armand Laforge?'

Even Dagmar and Renate understood what Truchaud had just asked.

'I used to know an Armand Laforge,' the old man replied slowly. 'Whether it is the same one that you have in mind, I wouldn't like to say.'

'And who was your Armand Laforge?' asked Truchaud.

'My brother was called Armand, and he died in the War.'

'Are you sure he died in the War?' asked Truchaud gently.

'As far as anyone ever could be during that bloody thing,' he replied angrily. 'Why? Have you any reason to believe that he didn't die in the War?'

Truchaud looked at Dagmar and flicked his fingers at her. Natalie explained that he wanted a copy of the piece of paper she had in her pocket. She fished in her pocket and pulled it out. Truchaud passed it to the old man.

'What's this?' he asked. 'It's all in German. I don't understand a word of it.'

'It's a death certificate,' said Truchaud, 'but if you look at the date of it, it's considerably later than the War.'

'And you think this might be my brother's death certificate?'

'I think it's possible, yes. Tell us about your brother, Mr Laforge.'

'I want to explain to these young ladies here that what I am going to say does not in any way reflect on them. During the War, the Bourguignons and the Boches were not friends. It is now sixty years later, and those mad times are long past. We are all friends in the European Union now; even the perfidious Albion can, for the most part, be trusted.' Natalie was translating as fast as she could, and managed to get a laugh out of the girls with the joke.

Dagmar told Natalie to tell him that she understood, and that he had nothing to worry about.

'My brother was abducted in 1943, as part of the *Service du Travail Obligatoire*. The STO took able-bodied Frenchmen, living under German Occupation, between the ages of sixteen and sixty, to Germany, to work in the factories. I think this was probably to free up young German men to go and be slaughtered on the front line. My father and I saw that as the positive side of what happened to him. We never saw him again, nor even heard from him again, but we always saw him as being responsible for killing a few Boches. Do you know what actually happened?'

'Is this him, Monsieur?' asked Truchaud, still very gently.

'It's certainly his birthday,' he replied dully. He swallowed the rest of his *pastis*, and shouted at the waitress for a scotch.

'Do you have anything to add?' Truchaud asked Dagmar. 'Were there any stories about Armand that you were told when you were little?' He turned back to Old Mr Laforge. 'We think that Dagmar here is Armand's granddaughter, and Horst, wherever he is, is his grandson.'

'Where the hell's that whisky?' the old man bellowed and then softened. He looked at Dagmar for a moment, and said to Truchaud, 'Pretty girl, which would certainly suggest my brother's genes might be involved.'

Natalie looked at him slightly askance. 'Dagmar was born long after Armand died. Why would he have anything to do with her prettiness or otherwise?' Truchaud was pleased to note that, interpreter or not, she was still on the ball.

'Well,' said the old man, 'my brother was always a good-looking beast, and could pull all the girls. I supposed that was why he got dragged off by the STO. I was always a little squirt, which was how I got away with pretending I was younger than

I was. Armand couldn't get away with that. If he survived the War and managed to pull a girl in Germany, it stands to reason that she would have been a splendid looking girl too. Am I right?' Natalie translated that to Dagmar. She had known her grandmother for a while.

'*Oma*?' she thought out loud. She had carried herself with a certain panache even when she was old. She didn't remember her colouring. In her memory *Oma* was silver-grey and lined, and they had never had a camera or photographs of anyone from those days. But yes, she could have imagined *Oma* being young and eye-catching, especially as she could certainly remember her mother, who she always considered to have been the most beautiful woman she had ever known, with her raven hair, soulful eyes, and tragically later on, the diaphanous pallor of the cancer that killed her.

'Do you know how they met?' he asked her gently.

'From what I heard, *Oma* was a nurse when she was young. *Opa* was a patient in the nursing home where she worked. The Russians liberated a number of concentration camps when they raced west to be the first in Berlin. She supposed that *Opa* had been in one of them. He was far too ill to be repatriated and wasn't expected to live. But *Oma* says that he had seen her, and from that day on, he refused to die, until he and *Oma* had created my mum.'

'Did they get married?' he asked.

'*Oma* always said they did. She certainly described herself as a young widow.'

'Did she ever get married again?'

'No. She looked after my mum, and helped her grow up. She got the sort of help from the State that she wanted, being a war widow with a child. I didn't follow that myself as Mum was born years after the War had ended.'

'Your *Oma* was a Cold-War widow,' Old Mr Laforge chuckled. 'Well, well, well! Isn't today a remarkable day? I think it calls for a rather bigger wine to celebrate.' When the girl produced his whisky, he whispered in her ear. She looked at him, smiled and nodded.

Chapter 12

Nuits-Saint-Georges, Tuesday afternoon

Old Mr Laforge became increasingly genial over lunch, and Truchaud was very impressed with the cleanskin bottle that had emerged from the cellar to accompany it. He had a feeling that it was a Grand Cru; it had that sort of pedigree about it. And if it was a Grand Cru, grown and made by the Laforges, it would have been an Échezeaux, because that was the only Grand Cru they had in their Portfolio. It certainly wasn't a Truchaud Clos de Vougeot: he would have recognised that immediately, and known what year it was too. He was thoughtful as to how an unlabelled bottle might have got out of the winery across the road. Truchaud had no idea, and wondered whether the old man was already testing him, and showing off to his new great-niece. As the new Chief of Municipal Police, unlabelled and untaxed bottles fell under his purview as 'crime prevention'. The old man wasn't letting on what it was, but looked very happy when Dagmar said that it was really nice, and she looked increasingly contented when he told her that it was 'hers'.

Following the coffee, he insisted that they all went back over the road for a digestif. Truchaud could see the afternoon vanishing into a haze of celebratory alcohol, and thought that sooner or later, he would have to take his leave of the newly enlarged Laforge family and do a little proper work. He had a father to look after as well. He had a little word in Natalie's ear, while they walked back to Laforge's.

'Feel free to stay with them, to act as their interpreter and to keep a general eye on them. I'll take your car back to the domaine, so that you can walk home. I've got to go and sort out one or two things, but if you need me urgently, give me a

107

call and I'll be with you immediately. I'll have my car with me, and I'll certainly be within the town limits.'

'Okay, chief,' she replied. 'They'll be safe with me. Of course, they may well be a little drunk when you get them back, if the old man has anything to do with it.'

'In which case, I'll make sure that their car and the camper are both disabled,' he added, wondering exactly how he would go about disabling the vehicles without actually totally wrecking them. The Volkswagen Kombi pre-dated any training he ever had, and a Škoda …? When he was a trainee, who would ever have been seen dead in one of those?

She smiled and Truchaud let himself out of the shop, past a very confused Mélodie, who looked acutely aware that there had been a sea change in the family dynamics at lunchtime, and seemed vaguely concerned that it might adversely affect her status within the business.

He parked Natalie's car at the domaine and drove out in his own, down to the Gendarmerie, and pressed the button. There was a stentorian call of 'Enter' from within. Lenoir was behind the reception desk, and he sprang to attention, saluted and announced to all within earshot that the Municipal Police Chief was in the house.

Truchaud touched his forelock and enquired whether Captain Duquesne was at home. He was led through into the captain's office, and Lenoir dusted his seat with a pocket handkerchief that looked moderately clean. Lenoir announced that he would get both of them a coffee immediately and left the office.

Duquesne chuckled at the back of the departing constable. 'I think you've frightened him,' he said. 'Do tell me how you did it, in case I need to do it too, at some time in the future.'

'I think you have to be the Municipal Chief of Police, and threaten his driving licence,' replied Truchaud, returning the smile.

'So what's happened? I see you sent Lenoir back here with a box of papers.'

'Well, since then we've introduced Old Mr Laforge to his long-lost great-niece.'

'What?' exclaimed Duquesne, and Truchaud told him the story. By the end of the narrative they both realized that they had uncovered more problems than solutions.

'I certainly think we have to consider that Horst Witter is now officially a "missing person",' said Truchaud. 'The questions are: when should we formally announce it? And which of us should actually be running any investigation?'

'This is even more confusing. Last time we worked together there were really only the two of us: I was the local man; and you were the national policeman. Now you're a local policeman too. When should we involve the Investigating Magistrate?'

'The reply to that is relatively simple: when any conversation between the two of us becomes *official* I think one of us should consider calling him in; when one of us thinks we're ready, or when either of us thinks there is a case that needs to be answered, send for Monsieur Lemaître.' Truchaud looked at the gendarme slightly upwards and to the left. Duquesne nodded slowly.

'You don't think that there will be a problem between us, do you?' asked the gendarme slowly.

'I think the only way we'll find an answer to that is if one of us wants to call in the magistrate and the other has a reason not to.'

'Do you have a picture of Horst, so we can put together a poster?' asked Duquesne. 'I think that's the first thing we do.'

'Can you take a picture off a phone to make a poster?' asked Truchaud, 'because if anyone has a photo of him, surely it'll be one of the girls, on their phones. If not, I'm sure there will be an official photo of him in the German National database. I'm sure Natalie can get hold of a copy of that from Karl-Heinz in Bonn.'

'Karl-Heinz?'

'A friend of hers in the *Bundespolizei*. He seems to be the guy to go to in Germany for information, or at least that's who she went to last time we needed to contact their internal force.'

'Now I come to think about it, if we're going to start putting posters up, we ought to let Mr Lemaître know what it's all about. Then he can decide when he gets involved. He may even ask the Municipal Police Chief what he thinks,' Duquesne added with a chuckle.

'I like your thinking,' Truchaud replied. 'Now I have to potter back home and see what Michelle is getting up to with my father. After all, he is supposed to be the main reason I'm down here. Every time I get down here for family reasons, I get involved in police work. In this case, it may even be international police work.'

'You haven't changed your phone number, have you?' Truchaud reassured him he hadn't, and with that, they bade each other farewell, just as Lenoir was walking in with cuppas. He didn't stop, but did thank him on his way out.

He drove back to the domaine and pulled up in the courtyard. There were more vehicles parked in there than normal, so they needed to be parked quite militarily, and at the same time leave space for the tractor to get in and out should Maréchale need access to it. He, therefore, parked just in front of the camper: firstly so he could get out easily; and secondly, so that there was no way the camper could get out without moving the BX first.

He walked into the house, which was unlocked, so presumably someone was home. Michelle was not in the back of the room, which she used as her office; nor was she in the kitchen. Kitchen. The word reminded him of the cup of coffee he had just walked out on in the Gendarmerie, so he set up the filter machine.

While the machine was doing its thing, he shouted upstairs, but there was no reply. He wondered whether he should wander up to the flat his father called home, just to see if there was any problem there that she was busy solving. He walked back across the courtyard and tried the door, but that was locked, so he returned to the kitchen where the machine had just about finished doing its business. The coffee made, he sat down at the table to read the paper, in the hope of finding information about what was going on in Paris.

In the end he phoned the office and ended up talking to Lieutenant Leclerc, wondering why he felt like he was missing the urbane young Parisian. He felt so much more in control in Paris than he did down here. 'How's it going up there?' he asked.

'Is it true,' came the reply, 'what the *commissaire* said?'

'I imagine that rather depends on what the *commissaire* actually said,' replied Truchaud rather drily, 'and which *commissaire* it was who said it. Go on.'

'Commissaire De Chagny said that you aren't coming back, and that therefore I've been promoted to commander.'

'Well, I spoke to the Divisional Commander before I left, and he said he was minded to promote you, and I agreed that you deserved it, but we didn't discuss it with De Chagny; at least, he wasn't there when we were talking about it.' The *commissaire* was Truchaud's immediate superior in Paris. He was an aloof individual who, on promotion, seemed to have settled down into the bureaucratic role very comfortably. While the squads went out, solved crimes and caught criminals, he made sure that quotas were kept and budgets were up to date. It was, no doubt, essential work, but as far as Truchaud was concerned, it didn't appear much of an incentive to aim at for promotion. Maybe one day he would get tired of fieldwork, and yearn for a seat behind a desk. Maybe; maybe not. Most of the discussions Truchaud had had with a superior had bypassed De Chagny completely and had been directly with the Divisional Commander himself, an amiable old cove, with whom Truchaud had assumed he had got on fine. With this news that apparently he wasn't coming back, he was suddenly less sure.

'And how's Sergeant Dutoit?' Leclerc asked. 'Any idea when she's coming back?'

'She's got rather embroiled in the same missing person's case that I've got caught up in at the moment,' Truchaud started.

111

'A missing person's case?' said Leclerc. 'I thought you were down there looking after a sick relative.'

'Well, that was how it started, but then this person went missing, and someone from up in Paris set me up as the temporary Municipal Police Chief down here. At least I bloody well hope it's a temporary post.'

'So, how is Sergeant Dutoit involved?'

'She's the only person that the relation of the missing person we've got to hand can communicate with. She's East German.'

'Who, Natalie?'

'No, fool; the relation. However, she speaks German with a very thick accent, and Natalie's the only person here who can understand it.' He found himself suddenly wriggling to make sure his erstwhile sidekick did not demand his sergeant back. He felt that once she had gone he might never see her again, and that was a situation he wasn't prepared for yet, though he wasn't sure why it worried him so.

'I thought you spoke German, sir?'

'No, English. My German is fairly rudimentary, you know … I can read a menu on the Swiss side of the border perhaps, but when this girl speaks, it's like listening to someone gargling musically, like a foreign opera in its own language; very strange. I would be grateful though, if you would find out exactly the source of this rumour that I'm not coming back, and if it is genuine and true, it would be nice for somebody to put it to me formally, so I can work out where that leaves me and the town of Nuits-Saint-Georges. As now, speaking as its Police Chief, I think I'm responsible for its budget, like De Chagny is up in Paris. I can't see him leasing me to this nice little town indefinitely, paid out of his budget.'

'I'll have some quiet words in discrete ears,' Leclerc replied. 'You know you can count on me.'

'Yes, I do know that.'

'Meanwhile, sir, how's the wine down there? Any indiscreet hints on any good investments?'

Truchaud laughed. Leclerc's knowledge of wine was, like any urban Parisian's, to be found on the taste pages in the colour supplements. Yes, he could quote *Le Monde* and *Paris Match* like the best of them, but he couldn't tell a Burgundy from a Bordeaux without reading the label. Mind you, it was the label rather than the wine in the bottle that the wine investor bought.

'It would be extremely indiscreet for me to recommend a Clos de Vougeot by Domaine Truchaud,' he said, 'and at this moment in time the only person that would benefit would be me. It's our flagship wine and the last bottle I tasted from it was very fine, but it was made by my dad, who was then very well, assisted by my brother, who was then still alive.'

'I'm sorry. That was a tasteless question. May I take it back?'

'Oh, don't worry about that, it's not a problem. It's just that, at this moment in the year, we have absolutely no idea what the new wine that's growing now is going to be like.'

'Last year?'

'Oh yes, I have some idea what last year's is going to be like, but still very little idea what it's going to say on the label. Tell you what, it won't be an investment, but I will let you in on a little secret for your own cellar, once I know what it's called and how you'll be able to lay your hands on it.'

'As you know, sir, just like you, I live in a flat and don't have a cellar.'

Truchaud had no idea that Leclerc didn't have wine storage facilities in his block of flats. The landlady at his block had ample storage space for wine, which she made available to all her tenants, as well as forwarding their mail and cancelling their papers. 'Don't worry,' he said. 'We'll work something out when the time comes, and you can certainly rest assured it'll be worth the wait.'

'I think I'll say thank you for that, in anticipation.'

'Meanwhile, I'll say nothing to Sergeant Dutoit about our conversation at this moment. I know she won't object to being in your team. Do the rest of the team think I'm not coming back, like George, for example?' Truchaud thought about the young policeman involved in the road accident on the way back from Nuits-Saint-Georges a couple of months ago.

'I haven't talked about it to anyone, and they haven't talked about it to me, but that doesn't mean that Commissaire De Chagny hasn't had individual conversations with everyone else without telling me yet.'

'I appreciate this conversation, my friend, and please be assured that if you ever need support from anyone, you can count on me.' They bade each other farewell, and Truchaud sank back in the chair. He glared at the coffee and realized, to his annoyance, it had gone cold in the cup.

Chapter 13

Nuits-Saint-Georges, Tuesday afternoon

Truchaud poured the cold coffee down the drain, and started to make another pot. He was stunned and felt betrayed. He knew he shouldn't be shooting the messenger for the contents of that conversation. Leclerc wasn't to blame, but was it the *commissaire*, or even the Divisional Commander himself, who hadn't the stones to tell him the bad news, and had, therefore, left it to his own deputy to tell him? He was also sure that Leclerc was a loyal enough friend not to want to receive his own promotion at Truchaud's expense, however much he wanted promotion to a commander's post.

The filter machine started making noises as if it were dying of pneumonia, and Truchaud put a splash of milk into his cup and then poured the coffee on top. He tasted it. Yes, that would do, so he sat down at the table and thought. He paused awhile, trying to prioritize his activities. He was waiting for the magistrate in Dijon to come back to him about his father. His role in the Horst Witter missing person's case was as the local Municipal Police, but when Horst was found, his continued involvement in the case would depend on the condition Horst was in when he did appear. However, if Horst's condition made the 'Horst case' a case for the Gendarmerie and the National Police, it would be the branch based in Dijon, and not that from the Quai d'Orsay that would be dealing with it.

He assumed, at that point that his sole responsibility would be the protection of Dagmar as a crime-prevention issue; that was, if a crime had even been committed. That would constitute a problem, as neither he nor Dagmar spoke an enormous amount of English, and that was the sole language in which they could communicate. Moreover, there would be no place

115

for Natalie in Nuits-Saint-Georges, so she would be expected to return to Leclerc and Paris. He wondered whether he could arrange for them both to be assigned, at least temporarily, to the Dijon Branch of the National Police. However, if he was assigned to Dijon, however temporarily, he would then be expected to take responsibility for whatever they might care to pass his way as well. In fact, he might not even be involved in any case in Nuits-Saint-Georges. And working on a case of cattle rustling somewhere beyond Is-sur-Tille, in the north-east of the *département*, wouldn't make life any easier in terms of his looking after his father, which was, after all, the main reason he was down there in the first place.

He took a slurp of coffee and nearly scalded the inside of his mouth. That was better. He had to stop feeling sorry for himself and start thinking constructively. He had to stop feeling that he was being persecuted and get on with the case in hand. There was a young man who was missing, and a young woman who needed his help to solve the problem. Was the young man away on a wild adventure in another quadrant of the world? Or had he met with a tragic end? If the latter was the case, was that end here in the Côte? If the latter was what had happened, then the case needed to be solved, and he and Natalie constituted two components of the best crime-solving team he knew. Therefore, the case needed to be solved, before his colleague was summoned back to Paris to get on with whatever they thought they were paying her to do.

So the question came down to this: if Horst had been killed, then was it by accident or by design? If it was accidental, then the body might still have been disposed of to prevent uncomfortable questions being asked. Where might it have been disposed of, or hidden? Truchaud's mind immediately went to the tunnels under Nuits-Saint-Georges. If the Maquis had successfully hidden weapons, men and fine wine in there from the Germans during the War, then surely a corpse could be hidden down there now?

He thought about that for a while. Would it have been possible to hide a corpse down there from December to April? He and the gendarmes had been all over those cellars like a rash in the spring. He would certainly have recognised the smell of decaying meat, and he felt the gendarmes would have recognised that odour too. The cellars, after all, never got cold enough, even in the middle of winter, to deep-freeze a corpse; a constant temperature of around eleven degrees centigrade was what they were all about. The fine wine from the twenties had been bricked up at least two years before the Germans marched into Burgundy. Even if a corpse had been bricked in that winter, the brickwork would hardly have had time to dry in the intervening time. Truchaud was already unconvinced that a body had been hidden in any part of the cellars that they had explored the previous spring. There was a tunnel upstream of the underground wharf that they hadn't explored when he had been down there, but somehow he expected Lenoir to have done so since, simply because it was there. He would obviously check it up with him.

One question he wondered about was what was behind those locked doors that he had never got past? Was that possibly access to the family crypt in the churchyard? That would be ironic: Horst being buried surreptitiously in his family's crypt via a secret entrance. However, Old Mr Laforge, on being asked about it a couple of months ago, had said that door was between different cellars that had belonged to the same owner back in the mists of time. However, he would have said that, wouldn't he, if he had known that there was a fresh body down there that had no business being there? That was, of course, assuming that that door did lead to the crypt in the first place, and not into someone else's wine cellar. Truchaud continued to mull all this over in his mind. The bottom line, as far as the cellars were concerned, was that there was no evidence of any recently hidden corpse down there. He would need to ask the funeral directors whether they had performed a funeral at Saint Symphorien's Church in December or January. If they had then they might need to re-open the particular crypt involved, to check that they had not, in fact, buried two bodies at the same time.

117

The more hopeful story, on the other hand, was supposing he had vanished off to a recently discovered gold mine in, say, Ecuador? Was he likely to go off without telling anybody? Well, yes, that was well within his character. He had been visiting Nuits-Saint-Georges all last year without dropping even the slightest hint of what he was doing to his sister. He might say, when they finally found him, that he had been waiting to tell her that he had found a whole new swathe of family until he was totally sure of it. Fair enough, and therefore there was a case for saying he might wait until he could send her a nugget before he told her about his gold mine in Ecuador. And he would have had no idea that she was already on his trail looking for him. Okay that worked, but he didn't feel comfortable about it.

The other possibility, which kept dragging him back, would be an accidental or intentional killing, whereby the body had been buried, either sneakily into a re-opened crypt around the time of a funeral, with the body being put down there under, or even in an old casket during the night before the formal interment ceremony. *See above*, he thought. A second solution might be that he had been buried in the woods above the vineyards. There was a lot of wild ground up there where nobody went. But he did feel that if a body had been buried there up in the woods, it would have attracted a lot of attention from the local insect and feral wildlife population, and surely that, in its turn, would have attracted the attention of some of the farmers or other folk up there. The question that needed asking was if a wild boar had died up in the woods, and surely from time to time a boar or a stag died of reasons not to do with hunting and the table? That would still have attracted bluebottles and carrion scavengers. Would the locals know?

What other solutions might there be? He could have found a girl in Gevrey-Chambertin, ten kilometres up the road, and be shacked up with her at present, while working in her village shop, or perhaps bar. He knew about bars and drinks; after all, he had worked in an off-licence in Boppard, and it was in the German blood to know how to pour a beer with just the right amount of head on it. But wouldn't he have told Dagmar that he had met the love of his life, and was presently shacked up with her? Even if he thought Renate was madly in love with him – itself a moot point – surely he would have told his sister that news? The answer to those questions would come out with Duquesne's 'missing person' poster.

He slurped some more coffee, which was managing to remain hot a lot longer on this occasion as he was being positive. It had gone cold very quickly when he was talking to Leclerc. What other possible solutions could he come up with that would have ended up with Horst disappearing, but leaving his campervan behind for six months, and never making any attempt to retrieve it, or at the very least to make sure it was all right?

Had he been involved in a robbery and was currently on the run? Or had he been locked up perhaps, and was tucked away in a Swiss jail, currently serving twenty years? The Swiss authorities might not have considered notifying the Nuits-Saint-Georges Gendarmerie, though they would surely have informed Boppard authorities that they'd got one of their citizens banged up, and that they wouldn't be getting him back any time soon. That question might involve Natalie asking Karl-Heinz if there was anything that had come down the line into his mail box.

Accidents? he wondered. Could he be a John Doe picked up on the roadside near any of the other towns, and be languishing in a fridge awaiting identification? Would an unidentified corpse be kept in a fridge for six months? He couldn't remember if Dagmar had said whether he'd left his identity card in the camper, but that was a question that he needed to ask her.

He sat and thought, and the more he thought, the more he came up with alternative scenarios that would fit with the information he had to hand … which came down to not a lot.

To each scenario he appended one question, which would either rule out that scenario from requiring further investigation, or alternatively, point to the possibility of that scenario being the solution, or at the very least requiring further investigation. Interestingly enough, each question would require an answer from a different member of the team.

He decided he needed to clear his head, and putting his mobile phone in his pocket he wandered out.

Chapter 14

Nuits-Saint-Georges, Tuesday afternoon continued ...

He walked down through the town centre, past the Place de la Résistance, where he was pleased to see that the tables and chairs were out in front of the bars, and people were sitting in them under the parasols drinking coffee or beer. He walked past the post office and the tourist office to the Seventy-Four. To his right stood the Gendarmerie. He thought about walking in to see Duquesne, and then thought about it again. *Not yet*, he thought.

Once he spoke to Duquesne he would have to tell him that he no longer had a job at the *'Sûreté'*. He had no idea how important that was to Duquesne, but right now, he didn't even know how important it was to himself. He walked on, passing the block containing the Gendarmerie, past the Hotel de Ville with the banner over the main entrance advertising a blood donor session the following week, and into the eastern residential part of the town. His feet knew where they were taking him, even if he wasn't aware of it himself.

Even when he knocked on the door he wasn't really sure where he was. When a familiar pair of green eyes looked out from behind the front door, he became fully aware of where he was, and why he was there.

'Charlie!' she said, 'come on in.' Geneviève, Parnault's sister, with whom, back in the day Truchaud had always felt he had an understanding, although, despite that, nothing had ever come of it, asked him if he was alone, whether it was a social call and whether he would like a coffee or a snifter, all in the same breath. He accepted the coffee and was led into the kitchen.

'Is this work or pleasure?' she asked.

'Oh pleasure,' he replied. 'Work's a four-letter word, and I really felt I needed my hand held.' He told her his story, about how he had been dumped on the local Municipal Police by his bosses in Paris.

'Well, that seems strange,' she said. 'You were born and brought up here. I didn't think anybody was allocated to the towns of their nurture.'

'I think I was posted here simply because there was a vacancy, and I was already on the spot. Possibly my having some responsibility for there being a vacancy in the first place might have had something to do with it too!'

'How do you mean?'

'Well, you do know it was me who shot Molleau in the first place?'

'Yes, but that was in self-defence.'

'I don't think they're punishing me for shooting the man by giving me his job; it's not that tedious. I'm just sad that my little bit of compassionate *temporary* leave looks like it's been made awfully permanent.'

'Well, cheer up. You're on a case here currently, the grapes are in flower, and in your favourite part of the world at the best part of the year, even though you are still dressed in your warm coat. Why do you do that?'

'What? The coat?'

'Yes, that old thing.'

'Lots of pockets, and because of them, it saved my life in the Molleau affair.'

'You mean you've got a pistol stashed in one of its pockets now?' Her blazing green eyes opening distinctly wider, Geneviève looked alarmed.

'No, but I do have my phone in there.'

'And a desk with a fax machine on top would fit in there too!'

'Now you're just having a laugh at my expense.'

'No, I'm not, but I am trying to make you smile; you look as if you're in desperate need of one.' She smiled at him, which had a very beneficial effect.

'I must take a picture of that smile on my phone,' he said, 'so that any time I feel miserable I can look at it and it will make me feel better.'

'Do you know how to do that?' she asked.

'Haven't the faintest idea. I've only just got the hang of sending a text, and the point of doing it, too,' he added drily. The great advantage of the sending and receiving of texts was that the sender and recipient did not have to be online at the same time.

'You're not very up to date with technology, are you?' she said sadly.

'Depends which technology you mean,' he replied. 'With the latest police technology to catch criminals, I'm right up there with the best of them. Facebook and Twitter, I agree, not so much. I live in fear of people I've never met phoning me to tell me they've just got into the bath, or have just down-loaded the latest record by a group I've never heard of. I'm still very content with my LPs and my turntable. I have got into CDs, enough to be able to play them in the car when I'm on the move. I have even worked out how to make a copy of my favourite LP onto a CD, so that I can play it in the car, without jiggling it silly. You see, I can see a point to *that* technology, and if a piece of tech wants me to get into using it, then it has to justify its existence first. No doubt the kids of today really want to know all about the bathing habits of total strangers; me, I can do without it.'

Geneviève chuckled. This was the Charlie Truchaud she remembered of old; warm and silly. She wondered whether her daughter discussed her bathing habits on Facebook. She shuddered at the thought, and prayed that she didn't text the pictures. 'What are you listening to at the moment?' she asked.

'Still the Grateful Dead, Claude Nougaro and Beethoven,' he replied.

'In other words, tunes by dead people.'

'Most of the Grateful Dead are still alive,' he replied, 'though I have to admit they aren't very young anymore.'

'So why are they called the Grateful Dead when they're still alive?'

'They were all alive when they started using the name; it was just a name that one of the guitarists dug up in a book about Tibetan mysticism somewhere, I understand, because the name they were currently performing under was already being used by somebody else.'

'I can't imagine you listening to heavy metal music,' she said.

'It's not; it's soft and jazzy, and at times, quite out of its tree. It's one of those things where you just go into your own space, and let it say to you what it wants at the time. Every one of their concerts was different, and I understand that they recorded most of them, so they will be continuing to release a new concert from time to time for people like me to go and listen to in the confines of my living room.'

'And it goes with the Pinot Noir?'

'It has been tried from time to time, and it generally worked out fine. Mind you, that was in Paris. I haven't plugged into the Dead in Nuits-Saint-Georges, so I have no idea whether its magic will work here.'

'Do you want to bring some round and you can introduce me to it?'

'All my LPs are in my flat in Paris.'

'Do you have any CDs in your car? We've got a CD player here.' She pointed at a boom box at the far end of the kitchen with two small speakers at either end of the device. Truchaud shuddered inwardly. He could just tell that it would sound tinny, and would never produce that fat, warming sound, and the feeling that went with it that a really good Grateful Dead recording could produce. It was one of those devices that people used to put music on in the background while they were doing the dishes, or perhaps the ironing. He couldn't imagine having music on as a background to anything; it took concentration to listen to music.

Sometimes he did listen to music when driving, but it wasn't on in the background, it was the other thing he concentrated on, and kept him calm while he waited for that idiot, so close behind him that he couldn't see the number plate, to crash into his tail gate. He would have to think of an excuse to not expose the Dead to that boom box, however much he would like an excuse to enjoy this company.

It was Geneviève who changed the subject by asking how the current case was going.

Truchaud thought for a while and then came up with a non-committal, 'We haven't found him yet.' Then he thought about it and asked how she knew he was working on another case down there in Nuits-Saint-Georges.

'Well, Simon came round last night looking for Suzette, and of course she wasn't here because it was Monday, and she's still putting the finishing touches to this semester's project. He said he had just popped into your domaine to have a word with Michelle, and the place was full of German cars and girls, and Michelle told him all about it. Apparently, a German boy, who was in Nuits last harvest, has gone missing, and you and your constable from Paris are looking for him. Why you and her?'

'We appear to be the only two people in this town who can communicate with the relatives. They speak highly accented German. Natalie can speak to them in German, the Germans and I get by in English, and that's about it. The Germans can understand what Mac Montbard says to them in German, but that isn't a lot of help when she can't understand their replies in their mist of patois.'

'Any idea what happened to him?'

'I have an uncomfortable feeling of exactly that: something happened to him.'

'No, no, no. I didn't mean it that way. I was simply saying do you know anything?'

'Know? No. But I am very concerned that he has been killed, either accidentally or on purpose, and his remains have been hidden. As to the five questions, I have no idea.'

'Five questions?'

'Who? How? When? Where? and Why? They're the five questions that a homicide officer needs to know about a case. Plug a fatal road accident into that formula and you get Mr Everyman, last Friday at ten twenty-three, on the A6, skidded at high speed avoiding say a stray cow, rolled over, caught fire, and curtains. There are your five questions about that case in a nutshell.'

'I didn't hear that anyone had been killed on the A6 last Friday. It wasn't in the local paper.'

'No, it didn't actually happen, I was just giving you an example of the five questions of investigation, and how that questionnaire might be used.'

'Oh, I see,' she said, but he wasn't sure she actually did. She wore a distinctly muddy expression. 'So why are you working on the case now, if he was killed on the A6 last Friday?' she asked. Yes, he knew she had missed it.

'No,' he said, trying not to sound annoyed. 'He wasn't killed on the A6 last Friday. In, as far as I know, nobody was killed on the A6 last Friday.'

'But why did you say he was then? I don't understand.'

'I was just using the A6 as an example of *where*, and "last Friday at ten twenty-three" being an example of *when*. We don't know any of the answers of the five questions about Horst, apart from the objective "who?" The answer to that is Horst. It opens up other questions.'

This time she did look as if he had answered her in a way she could understand. 'I see,' she said. 'I suppose you could use that form of five questions to answer any sort of mystery. Do you remember when you lost something and you asked your dad, and he'd say, "where you put it", and your mum would blame the "international gang". I can remember the lines of frustration on your face as neither of those answers were in the slightest bit helpful.'

'Because neither of them could be bothered to help me answer the five questions. Mind you, "where you put it" was probably the closest to an answer, wasn't it?' He thought for a while.

'So, we could say exactly the same thing to Jean, when he jumps up and down about the strange differences in the growths of the vines in his patch of new vines.' Truchaud remembered her brother talking to him about that when he had come round to his office in the town hall yesterday. Had he actually been trying to ask him something? He hadn't cottoned on to that. Why would a small patch of grapes grow faster or slower than those around them, especially as they were the same clone of the same breed?

'Does he actually want me to think about that?' he asked.

'I think we'd all be quite keen if someone would make an effort to find an explanation as to why it's happening. He's becoming really boring, banging on and on about it.'

'Exactly where is this plot?' he asked. She showed him on the sepia art map of all the vineyards of the Côtes de Nuits that most winemakers had up in the public areas of their domaines. Geneviève used one to decorate her kitchen wall. He looked at it carefully, as she pointed to the exact spot, and he noted it down in the notebook that he always kept in one of the pockets of his trench coat.

'Tell him, I will look into it in the next couple of days. If he has discovered someone doing a spot of sabotage, he has then shared it with Domaine Truchaud already. Perhaps I will need to discuss it with Simon and tell him to look out for it.'

'I don't suppose he will mind you telling Simon about it. After all, when he marries Suzette, he will become one of our family anyway, and then will be working for us, and all Simon's tricks and secrets will come with him.' Truchaud was tempted to suggest that she shouldn't count her chickens before they hatched, but decided not to be so unpleasant. After all, he had seen Simon and Suzette together at her digs in Dijon, probably more together than any of them had really wanted, and that was only a couple of months ago.

'Is that your pocket ringing?' she asked.

He wasn't concentrating and suddenly he realized it was his phone that he was hearing.

'Hello?' he asked, having forgotten to look at the number ringing him before he pressed the answer button.

'It's Michelle. Are you free to talk?'

He looked across to Geneviève for a moment, realizing his manners were distinctly suboptimal. 'Go ahead,' he replied.

'Are you still in Nuits-Saint-Georges, because your car is still here?'

'Yes, I just went out for a walk.'

'Can you pick up some bread on your way back? I'm not sure I want to leave Dad here on his own at the moment.'

'Why? What's he doing?'

'Oh, he's just being difficult.'

'I'll be right back in fifteen minutes, via the baker. See you shortly.' He looked sadly back at his erstwhile girlfriend, 'I'm sorry; Dad's playing up, by the sounds of it, and I've just told Michelle I'm going to help her with him. I'm afraid I have to go.'

'Do you want a lift? I can run you back quicker by car than if you walk.'

'Via the bakers?'

'Of course.'

'That would be very kind. Thank you, I'll accept that offer.'

'What are old friends for, if not for driving people about when they need it?'

'I can think of a lot of other responses to that question, but we'll leave that unanswered at the moment. Shall we go?'

Chapter 15

Nuits-Saint-Georges, later still that afternoon

He let the baguettes tumble out of his arms onto the kitchen table, while Michelle shook hands with Geneviève and kissed the air beside each other's ears. 'Thank you for bringing him back,' she said. 'I didn't disturb you at all, did I?'

Meanwhile, Truchaud was looking at the surly figure of his father sitting at the dining table. 'Now, what have you been getting up to?' he asked putting on his best cross-sounding parent voice.

'Nothing,' replied his father in just the same tone of voice as a child does when on the receiving end. 'I haven't been doing anything.' Was that a little tremor in his lower lip?

Michelle came back into the room. 'I'll put the kettle on,' she said. 'If we were English we'd all have a nice cup of tea to clear the air.'

'But I haven't been doing anything,' his father wailed. 'Honest, Shammin, I haven't.'

'If you say so,' she replied frostily over her shoulder.

Truchaud had already realized that neither of them were going to tell to him what had actually happened to explain the unpleasant atmosphere in the house, or why he had been summoned back from the delights of Geneviève's kitchen. Dammit; he hadn't taken that photograph either. Oh well, there would be time for that later no doubt. He was sure she would smile at him again sometime.

'If you want to go out,' he said, 'I'll stay here with Dad. We'll wait for Bruno to roll up and then I'll get the Tarot cards out and we'll have a game. I'm sure Dad will remember the rules, won't you, Dad?'

'What, Tarot? Why would you think I would forget the rules?'

'Well, that's just it; I don't think you would.'

'Why don't you bring that girl round? She plays very nicely.'

'Suzette, you mean? She's still in Dijon, working on her end-of-term paper, so we'll have to wait for Bruno. He won't be long, will he, Michelle?'

'Bruno?' she asked. 'Who knows how long Bruno's going to be? Who even knows where he is?' Truchaud realized that the tensions in his family home now ran very deep and none of the family members were communicating constructively. For a moment he thought that his father was probably in the best place, not being fully aware of what was really going on.

He got out the pack of cards and shuffled them, and, realizing that it would be a pointless exercise, he nonetheless dealt two hands: one for himself and one for his father. It was a totally unmanageable hand with thirty-nine cards in each hand, despite the extra length of a Tarot card. 'There's no point in bidding as there's only the two of us,' said his father.

'Oh, I agree,' he replied. 'I just thought we would find it fun to play a few hands off the top. That way we'll both be back in practice when Bruno gets here.'

'Very clever,' the old man replied. 'He's a sharp one that Bruno. Now we'll be ready for him.' They both re-organized their cards into suits in their hands. Truchaud had heard of a way that two people could play Tarot, each playing two hands, and playing alternately from one hand and then from the other. It seemed terribly complicated to him, and would have been impossible for his father. The old man suddenly tossed the Knight of Hearts out. 'What's that?' he asked, wondering why the old man had thrown away a pretty good card.

'That's my lead,' he said. 'The Knight of Hearts.'

Truchaud understood, and looked at his own hand.

It wasn't terribly interesting playing just the two of them, they knew exactly where every card was that wasn't in his own hand; and he did feel kind of sorry for Bruno, when the poor lad popped home, ostensibly just for a few minutes, and found himself involved in a three-handed game of Tarot with the old folks. On the other hand, the interest in the game to Truchaud increased instantly.

'What are we playing for?' asked Bruno.

The old man replied with the twinkle he once had of old, 'The loser gets an Alzheimer's Test,' he replied.

'I thought you'd already failed one of those, Granddad,' replied the boy.

'No,' replied the old man with a twinkle. 'I passed mine: I've got it.'

Truchaud was stunned by the little by-play between his father and his nephew, and decided not to break the spell. He dealt the cards to all three of them, in threes, counterclockwise, dropping the odd card into a separate pile. The three of them played together amiably enough for an hour, until Natalie and the girls were brought home by Maréchale in his car. Truchaud could tell that, without a doubt, the German girls had had a fairly alcohol-fuelled time, and were slightly the worse for wear.

'Hello, men,' said Maréchale to the various generations of Truchaud sitting around the table. 'Who's winning?'

Bruno said, 'Me!' which was perfectly true. Truchaud was quietly impressed with the smarts Bruno had shown with his play. 'What's happening with the vineyards today then, Simon?' he enquired.

'Nothing new,' came the reply, 'apart from the new family member.'

Bruno's eyebrows shot up; he obviously hadn't cottoned on to Dagmar's new status.

'So that's definite?' Truchaud said.

'Certainly the old man seems convinced that she's his brother's granddaughter, yes,' replied Maréchale. 'And he appears fairly excited about it.'

'How's Marie-Claire taking it?' the policeman asked.

'As far as I can see, she's okay about it. She's never been particularly money-driven. I think we'll see her final decision when Dagmar decides what it actually means to *her*.'

'And Jacquot?'

'I haven't seen him, but I would imagine he'll be busy working out how he could best manage to get his hands all over his new second cousin. He'll have already worked out that a relationship with a relation that distant is not forbidden, and look at her: she is a bit of a honey, isn't she? I'm sure that's the way his mind will work.'

'Were we all so lecherous as teenagers?' Truchaud asked Maréchale, forgetting Bruno was in earshot. Bruno, however, quickly reminded him.

'What's *letch'rous*, Uncle Shammang?'

'You take that one,' said the winemaker. 'You said it!'

'Er, it's when a boy, or a girl for that matter, can't keep their hands to themselves.'

'You mean like they've got Desert's Disease?' he asked.

Truchaud was stunned that the lad knew that sort of language. But when he came to think about it, Desert's Disease with the wandering palms was something that he had talked about when he was at school. It was obviously a joke that had gone downwards through school from one generation to the next. He remembered Jean Parnault talking about it a couple of months ago.

His mind moved off that train of thought, and moved over to Parnault himself. There was someone he needed to talk to. 'Excuse me,' he said, and pulled his phone out of his pocket. Parnault's name was on speed dial, though he couldn't remember ever having put it there. Perhaps Jean had put it there himself, during Truchaud's last sojourn in the little town.

'Hello?' came the reply.

'You remember that problem you brought to me at my office yesterday morning?'

'What, you mean about the dying off of some of the vines in our nursery?'

'Yes, that's the one. Have you got time to show me the plot this evening?'

'I'm not doing anything right now, if you want me to come round and pick you up.'

132

'That'll be fine. I'll be at my domaine waiting for you.' Click.

'What was that all about?' asked Maréchale sounding interested.

'I'll ask his permission to tell you, as I suppose I should.' Truchaud grinned for a moment. 'His sister thinks you should know anyway. As far as she's concerned you've already been landed.'

'What?' The winemaker looked worried for a moment. 'You mean Suzette?' and Truchaud, still smiling nodded.

'He's not going to marry Suzette; I am,' came from Bruno's corner of the room.

'Shammang,' came from a rather plaintive elderly voice, also from the dining table, 'can you explain to me what everyone's going on about. I don't understand them at all.'

'Don't worry, Dad,' he replied, 'I don't think you're alone in that.'

Ten minutes later, Jean Parnault rolled up at the domaine in his rather loud four-wheel-drive Mercedes *Champs-Elysées* tractor, which was greeted by an immediate, 'Can we get one of those, Uncle Shammang?' from Bruno.

'I think you may have to wait until you marry Suzette, then maybe he'll let you have that one as a wedding present,' he replied.

'Oh, alright,' came back, in a tone of disappointment.

He climbed up into the passenger side of the Merc, and was greeted with, 'Do I want to know what that conversation was all about?' from the occupant of the driver's seat.

'Probably not,' he replied, feeling slightly guilty that he had abandoned his family to the delights of looking after his father again.

It didn't take very long to get up the hill past the church. The culvert that passed through Nuits-Saint-Georges had by now turned into a proper stream known as the Meuzin. Parnault turned off the road to the villages in the Hautes-Côtes, up a pebbly track which forded the stream, and then turned right alongside the border of the woods. He stopped the truck at a point where any further progress would have massacred the young vines in front of them, and they got out. Truchaud looked downhill to the east. Below them lay the little town with its panoply of vines on either side; some of them very fine indeed. As the Charmois wood was in the way, he couldn't see any of Les Saint Georges, further to the south, which, he had heard, was being put forward for upgrading to Grand Cru status. Neither of them had a personal stake in that vineyard, but they would both take great vicarious pleasure and pride if that came off. It would mean that their town had a Grand Cru, all of its own.

'Here,' said Parnault, waving at a line of vines to his right. 'What do you think of that?' He was right. There stood a couple of rows of vines, as you counted them horizontally, with about six vines in each that looked distinctly dead. The next couple of rows downhill from them looked as if they were desperately struggling, but still technically alive. Everything about them looked … less: the stems were thinner and feebler; the leaves were smaller and weaker. Certainly they were not in flower. He looked at the little vines behind him. He couldn't see flowers on them either.

'Have you been spraying vine-killer chemicals up here?' he asked.

Parnault looked very offended. 'We're strictly organic here,' he replied. 'That's how we make the wine that we do.'

'Quite. So, do you think someone else might have had some sort of chemical spillage up here?'

'Why would anyone else be bringing synthetic chemicals up here? This is all Parnault land. Right at the top of this is our nursery, and the next bit down is our Village Nuits. There's barely any topsoil up here, as it has slowly rolled downhill over the years. We do bring some back from time to time, like they do to the upslope Crus in Vosne and Chambolle, and they are still fabulous wines.'

'Have you ever tasted a Romanée-Conti or a Musigny?' asked Truchaud.

'Oh yes.' He raised an eyebrow at Truchaud. 'Have those life-changing experiences still escaped you?' Parnault asked him. 'Leave it to me: I'm sure we can change that, you being the new Municipal Police Chief and all. Anyway what do you think of this?'

'I don't know. It seems to be coming from uphill above the vines, doesn't it? It is, after all, the top vines that are most affected, and as you go downhill they seems to be less and less affected.'

'Yes, I see what you mean.' They both turned round and looked into the thicket beyond the vines. There was untrained woodland beyond with brambles and scrub. And there, about twenty metres or so beyond where the uncontrolled vegetation started, there was a slight, though quite definite depression in the ground. It may have been a metre to a metre and a half long, and ran parallel to the vines. Between the depression and the edge of the vines, the rough vegetation looked particularly dense and aggressive. The brambles seemed to be growling at them, 'Come through here if you've got the guts!'

'Any idea what that is?' he asked Parnault, pointing to it.

'No idea,' came the reply. 'I've never noticed that before. Mind you, I've probably never looked that hard either.'

'Any idea how you would get to it?'

'Rather than trying to fight my way up from here through all the brambles and stuff, I would probably come down on it from above; from further up the road. Shall we take the car and see?'

They climbed back into the Merc and Parnault showed his skill at reversing it back up the track, impressing the Police Chief who was responsible for the driving skills of the little town. Just after they had forded the Meuzin, he turned uphill and then found a track into the woods. He got to within twenty metres or so above the depression, as a tree blocked their way. However, the terrain was passable enough on foot.

They looked at each other. 'Do we know whose land this is?' the policeman asked.

'Dunno,' Parnault replied. 'Certainly my land stops at the edge of the vineyard. I wouldn't be surprised if this was

135

common land belonging to each and every citizen of Nuits-Saint-Georges.'

Truchaud looked around him. The light was beginning to fail now, and he thought that nothing would be lost by waiting till the morning. 'I think, rather than scrabbling around in the dark, we'll come back tomorrow properly equipped. Shall we go, my friend, and see what our nearest and dearest have prepared for our evening meals?'

He climbed back into the passenger side of the Merc, and Parnault drove back into the little town.

Chapter 16

Nuits-Saint-Georges, Wednesday morning

The following morning Truchaud explained to them all at breakfast that he and Natalie had a little police work to do, but to stay around as they wouldn't be very long.

'Mr Maréchale said he would show us round the vineyards this morning,' said Dagmar in English. 'Is that okay?'

'I didn't know Simon spoke German,' he said. But why would he? It wasn't as though they were likely to speak to each other in German, after all.

'He doesn't,' she replied. 'We talk in English. Is it okay?'

'Fine by me,' Truchaud replied. 'But don't get in his way, and remember he works for Truchauds as well.' An amused Truchaud felt like he was talking to a child, giving them instructions how to behave at a maiden aunt's.

Natalie climbed into the passenger side of his BX, and he drove off down the road. 'I think I've found a shallow grave,' he said. 'We're going to collect a couple of gendarmes as witnesses, and we're going to dig it up and see what's in it.'

A ring at the *sonnette* opened the front door of the Gendarmerie, and they were shown into Captain Duquesne's presence. Truchaud explained why they were there.

'Lenoir and Montbard!' called the captain. 'The Commander here has need of your assistance.'

The two gendarmes both rushed in from different directions and leapt simultaneously to attention. Duquesne stood them at ease, and explained the situation. It was only after the explanation that he stood them easy. *The game continues*, thought Truchaud.

'Do you want me to drive?' asked Lenoir.

'No!' replied Truchaud forcefully. 'We're going up in my car. I know where we're going, and you two should fit in the back.' They climbed into the old BX parked in front of the Gendarmerie and set off up through the little town. He drove up the pebbly track and took the turning just before the fords, stopping exactly where he and Parnault had been the evening before.

'Sir! Is that it?' Lenoir pointed at the distinct dip in the earth just in front of them. There were no bluebottles to be seen anywhere, but mixed in with the citrus scent of the vine flowers there was a definite smell of detritus. Was that death they could smell? He would know if they actually found what they were looking for. Truchaud was pleased they hadn't had any 'cadaver dogs' on hand. Personally, he had found them to be irritatingly fallible. Dogs that were trained to find dead bodies, in his experience, usually didn't. They did, however, often delay the process of finding the body that was being looked for, and potentially contaminated a crime scene with their excitability. Past experience also told him that Natalie was totally in agreement with him. What he was glad he had with him was a good crime scene officer.

Natalie knelt down beside the slight but definite depression in the ground. Was that where a body might be buried? If so, it looked like it had been there for some time, and they knew the person they were looking for had been missing a while. Was this his grave? Truchaud explained to the gendarmes, 'When a body is buried, the soil is either heaped up over the body, making it obvious that that is where a body has just been buried, but if the killer thinks he's really clever he flattens the ground off so that the ground looks flat and undisturbed. But there's a problem with that too. During the process of decomposition, the soft tissues slowly collapse, so that the soil above it falls in too, leaving a depression after a while, betraying where the body has been buried.'

'So if you're going to hide a body by burying it,' said Lenoir, 'you've got to keep coming back to fill in the hole.'

138

'Thus increasing your chances of getting caught, yes,' Truchaud assented. 'It also shows the changes in the topsoil, and with that, a change in the vegetation. Different plants grow in the presence of a decaying body, so it will still look very different, and sooner or later you will leave a footprint that will be traceable by the forensics team.'

'So you wouldn't bury a body then, *chef*? Just as a matter of interest, how would you go about disposing of a corpse then?'

'My immediate reply to that is that I wouldn't be going about disposing of corpses in the first place, but that is a bit of a cop-out, isn't it? You would need to find a place where people would expect to find human remains. Where might you find dead bodies, constable?'

'Graveyards, mortuaries, archaeological digs perhaps?' Lenoir was getting quite into the swing of the tutorial.

Natalie, taking on the role of crime scene officer, interrupted proceedings. She instructed Lenoir to tape off the area with yellow tape, and instructed Montbard to start a log of everyone who had moved into and out of the area. It was only valuable up to a point. They had no idea how long this body had been there; if indeed there was a body in that trough. Moreover, if there was a body there, then who or what had been passed since its burial was anybody's guess. Right now there were only the four of them present, but if it did turn out to be a genuine crime scene, then that situation would surely change. If they were lucky, the first new arrivals would be the coroner's team from Dijon. From there on in, any number of rubberneckers would start turning up, including the press. But they had to start somewhere. Truchaud called Captain Duquesne on his phone. 'I think we're onto something quite promising. Constable Lenoir's cordoning off the area as I speak.'

'Call me back as soon as you've got something definite.'

From outside the tape Truchaud and the gendarmes watched Natalie as she got to work with her trowel. She knelt at the edge of the pit, making sure that the other three didn't get too close and contaminate the scene. She pulled on a pair of blue plastic gloves, partly in self-protection, and partly to avoid contaminating the scene further, and then she picked a spot and started to dig. She moved small quantities of earth very gently, casting it aside only when she had made sure that she could see nothing on the trowel. Truchaud watched her at work. He was alarmed to realize he was actually watching her knees, rather than her hands and their contents as she worked. True, her hands and knees weren't that far apart to start with, but it was the pressure of her denim jeans on her knees and her lower thighs that was attracting his attention. Moreover, he realized that his conscious mind was giving him instructions how he could continue to look at what his eyes wanted to look at, and at the same time appear to have his eyes on the job in hand. He was very disconcerted at this self-accusation. This was his officer, for heaven's sake, and she trusted him! How was it possible for him to be looking at her like that? *Was* he looking at her like that? Like what exactly?

To stop interrogating himself like a suspect, he forced his eyes to the blue plastic of her gloves and what she was doing, and away from the pressure of her slender thighs on the inside of the denim that protected her knees from the ground beneath them. Not that he believed in the power of prayer, but he prayed that she wasn't aware of the battle going on between his ears. Was it something that the Divisional Commander had said last week about her legs that was attracting his eyes to them? It wasn't as if he hadn't seen them before, and some-times they had been considerably less well covered than they were at the moment. Dammit! It was her angel face that most people talked about if they were going to discuss Natalie Dutoit behind her back; they didn't discuss the components of her torso, let alone her legs!

Truchaud pulled his mind away from the illicit thoughts to the conviction that it was inevitable sooner or later that she would hit something that stopped her progress. It could be a stone perhaps, or a tree root, or an outside distraction like one of the gendarmes falling over something, or it could be what they were actually looking for. By now, she was lying fully prone, with her arms outstretched into the pit, and if she had to dig any deeper, she was physically going to have to clamber down into it.

She looked up at him when her trowel made a soft metallic *clang*. He nodded at her almost imperceptibly as if to say, 'Go on'. She dug round the obstacle. 'It's bone,' she said. Nothing else quite had that look of matt cream that bone had, apart from dentine or pure ivory. But the source of that bone … that was the question.

'I was afraid it might be,' replied Truchaud drily. 'Any idea what sort of bone?' he asked.

She dug a little bit more, and announced that it looked like a bit of pelvis. Well, that would have figured, considering that she had started digging about halfway down the pit. It would also suggest that the remains were human. Very few animals died with their rear legs stretched out behind them. They were usually collapsed underneath the pelvis. However, it was important to exclude the contents of the grave from being the last mortal remains of a wild boar or a deer, perhaps, which had somehow become buried there. They could have even been formally buried by an amateur hunter who realized that perhaps he shouldn't have done what he had just done, and covered up his *mistake* by burying the unfortunate porker or bambi in a shallow grave. Wild boars were a considerable nuisance round harvest time, as they too had a taste for ripe Pinot Noir grapes. However, the vintners had an agreement among themselves, and some of them even had gun permits, to guard the vineyards from boars. Any boar that was shot during that time would be reported to the Municipal Police, and assuming that due process had been observed, in all probability it would grace a number of dinner tables around the Côte; no doubt including those belonging to certain members of the Municipal Police.

Thinking about it, Truchaud could envisage a particular boar, mortally wounded, escaping into the woods above the vineyards and breathing his last alone, but then why would it have gone to the trouble of burying itself?

Truchaud called Duquesne on his mobile phone again, 'We've found something,' he said. 'Natalie has found a body.'

'Human?' asked the gendarme down the phone.

'I think we have to assume so,' replied Truchaud. 'It seems to have been formally interred. I can cope with the laughter from the coroner's team if it turns out that we've dug up a dead pig. But if it is human, and especially if it's the one we're looking for, then we want it as intact as we can get it.'

'I'll get them on to it, leave it to me,' replied Captain Duquesne. 'Expect a visit from the coroner's officers sometime soon, and I'll also have a word in the right ear to get in touch with an examining magistrate.' He took the directions of the best way to get to the scene with a van, and put the phone down.

Natalie had continued to dig carefully. Aside from the piece of pelvic bone, there were perhaps remnants of skin, and mostly a fatty waxy material called adipocere, whose smell now dominated the proceedings. The gentle citrus scent of the flowering grapes had now been completely vanquished. She stood up. 'You know what I could really use?' she said. 'A stiff brush.'

Truchaud laughed, 'I thought you were about to say that you could use a stiff drink.'

'Well, that too,' she replied, her face dripping with sweat, despite the old adage that only horses sweat, it was definitely sweating that Natalie was doing in the heat and from the work she was doing. There wasn't any glowing involved. 'You know something? This corpse hasn't had any maggots working on it, so if it is the remains of a pig, then it wasn't shot during last year's vintage. It will have been buried in the cold of last winter's frost, and that would have needed one fit man to dig the grave, or a hole that had been pre-dug, before it got really cold. I don't think you could have got a mechanical digger in here without seriously damaging the plant life nearby.'

'What was last winter like?' Truchaud asked Lenoir, knowing that the winter in Paris had been bitter, but then it often was.

'Cold,' said Lenoir drily. 'Oh yes, it was very cold: minus five at least for most of the time, even when the sun could be bothered to show its face.'

'That would have been enough to do this to a corpse,' Natalie said from beside the grave. 'And by the time the thaw came, it would have been too late for the bluebottles to have their way with the juices, and lay their eggs. They wouldn't have been interested.'

'So you're qualified in entomology too?' asked Montbard.

'I keep my ears open at crime scenes,' came the reply. 'And being part of a Serious Crime Squad in Paris, we get to see a fair number of corpses that shouldn't have been dead at a particular place or time.'

Knowing the shape of a pelvis, she knew which direction to keep uncovering earth. When she hit the bottom of the rib cage about a foot north of the pelvis, she remarked that it was the right size to be an adult human, but continued since that still didn't exclude a boar yet. At this point she wasn't trying to dig up the body, merely to uncover it a bit so that the coroner's team could take over when they arrived. At the top end of the thorax was a clavicle, and by now she was fairly convinced it was human. 'Boss, I think when I hit the skull, I shall stop, assuming that that looks human too. I think I shall have disturbed the crime scene enough for someone more official to take over.'

Truchaud acknowledged and watched as the skull appeared. Now he was sure. There was no way that that skull belonged to any other species than *Homo sapiens*. The next question was whose? The body had been stripped before it was buried, or so it appeared from the amount of it that they had uncovered so far. It would be a question for the crime lab to work out when the corpse had been buried. Little by little they would work out the identity of whose remains were lying in that pit.

'How will they work out when the body was buried, *chef*?' asked Montbard from behind his left shoulder.

'You used the word not five minutes ago, constable; entomology,' he replied. 'It's the study of insects, and precisely which

143

insects there are present at the scene. Bluebottles can smell death from over twenty-five kilometres away. They arrive and lay their eggs in every open orifice they can find, be it a mouth or a laceration. The life cycle of a bluebottle larva's egg to the next generation is a fortnight, and the larvae in between, called maggots, devour decaying human tissue. Bodies have been found with a greater mass of maggots than human tissue once they really get going.'

Montbard looked fairly disgusted. 'I wish I hadn't asked,' she said, 'and I wouldn't have, if I had known you were going to get really revolting.'

Natalie had stood up and was brushing her clothes down with her hands to remove as much dust and dirt as possible. 'Of course, in this case, an entomologist would be no use whatever, as there aren't any maggots,' she said. 'The amount of decay may be a guide, but probably the best bet would be to identify the body, and then work out when he or she was last seen alive. We can then assume he or she was buried at some time after that.' She was looking into the narrow trench she had dug and what was visible of the corpse within it. She knew that the corpse's facial features would no longer be recognisable, but if the girls got to see him, they would find it a most unpleasant experience. Renate had appeared to be flippant about her feelings about Horst, but if anything, she was too flippant not to care about him. Natalie had a feeling that she just didn't want her friend to know how much she cared. As far as Dagmar was concerned, Horst had been her only close relative, and until yesterday evening, the only relative that Dagmar knew she had.

'Commander!' called Lenoir. He was pointing down the road, down the hill. Truchaud walked over to where the gendarme was standing. Between a gap in the trees he could see a column of dust rising from one of the tracks they had come up to get to that place. A large dark Renault van was climbing the hill, and there were one or two vehicles behind it that were fairly indistinct because of the dust the lead vehicle threw.

'Let's hope that's the coroner's crew. And equally, let's hope that the car behind contains the Investigating Magistrate and not a horde of press photographers.' Truchaud's response was dry. 'Mac, are you ready with your pad to note down exactly who has close access to the site?'

Montbard said she was ready for them, and grabbed one end of a large piece of wood lying near where she was standing, and smiling also she said, 'They shall not pass.'

'Unless of course they are the coroner.'

'Unless they are the coroner or her sidekick.'

'Her? Is the local coroner a woman?' asked Truchaud.

'You know, sir, I have no idea about the one we're going to get, but you might think that it could be, don't you think?' Truchaud had nothing to say about that. He had certainly known female coroners' crime scene investigators in his time, and they had, without exception, terrified him. They did not take prisoners.

They watched the van climb up and park next to Truchaud's BX. A woman in a dark blue jumpsuit climbed out, and announced herself to be Mrs Clermont, the Coroner's Scene of a Fatality Investigator. Yes, she was big, strong, middle-aged and scary. He had always considered Mac Montbard to be built a bit like a fly-half in Rugby Union, but this woman was built like a lock forward. He doubted that she carried an ounce of flesh that wasn't involved in power or locomotion. And then again, he thought about that for a further moment as she spoke loudly and assertively in a rasping contralto.

'Who's currently in charge here?'

'You are?' replied Truchaud quietly, almost meekly.

'You're right there,' she replied, 'but from whom am I taking over?'

'I'm Commander Truchaud from the serious crimes unit in Paris, and this is Constable Lenoir from the Gendarmerie in Nuits-Saint-Georges.'

'Not having been notified that the SCU in Paris is involved, Constable Lenoir, I shall take over from you. This is Mr de Castaigne, the Examining Magistrate.' She waved a hand at

145

the silver-haired man wearing a suit that seemed to be at least three sizes too big for him, standing just behind and to her left. 'And you are?' she addressed Natalie still holding her trowel.

'Sergeant Dutoit, SCU Paris,' she replied, verbally at attention.

'Another Parisian flic,' she said. 'Have they moved the capital to the south of Dijon while I wasn't looking? Has anyone been taking a record of people present at the crime scene?'

'Me, Constable Montbard, Nuits-Saint-Georges Gendarmerie.'

'Ah yes,' the Coroner's Investigator replied. 'I know you. Now who's going to tell me about this dig?'

Truchaud told her the story, though he felt he was really telling the magistrate. He was slightly disappointed that it wasn't Lemaître who had come out on this case; he had got on well with him, but he could hardly complain about de Castaigne, who hadn't uttered a word yet.

'Do you know that this is Mr Witter?' asked the investigator.

'Not at all,' he replied. 'Until Natalie exposed what little we can currently see of the skeleton, we didn't even know it was human.'

'Nat-al-ee!' The investigator spaced out the syllables as if it were some childish game. 'You two Parisians seem very friendly with each other, but maybe that's how Parisians are: friendly,' she came back drily.

Truchaud coughed. 'I stand corrected. Sergeant Dutoit and I have been members of the same squad for a fair amount of time.'

The coroner peered at Natalie down her nose, 'You don't appear old enough to have been a member of the police force for a *fair amount of time*, dear.'

'Appearances can be deceiving,' Natalie replied drily. 'However, if we are just going to growl at each other, may I suggest that I pass the scene over to your technicians, and my colleagues and I will depart?'

'The gendarmes will remain at the scene, but the friendly civilians from Paris may go,' the investigator barked.

'Can I have a little word in your ear?' said de Castaigne, the magistrate, in a soft voice to Truchaud, as he was making his way to his car.

'Certainly,' replied Truchaud equally.

'Please don't be upset by her manner. Mrs Clermont is a very good Coroner's Investigator.'

'She has to be with a manner like that,' Truchaud replied drily.

'Are you going to be available in the immediate future?' asked the magistrate, and Truchaud reassured him that he and the sergeant were staying in Nuits-Saint-Georges for the time being, and that he was also the acting Municipal Police Chief.

'Don't you think this scene is a little outside the purview of the Municipal Police?' he asked. 'If you see what I mean?'

'Oh, totally,' Truchaud agreed. 'This piece of excavation came out of an interview with a winemaker yesterday evening who was complaining about the under-activity of the vines in his nursery just over there. Spraying someone else's organic vines with a chemical fertilizer, as he was suggesting, might be within my purview as Municipal Police Chief so to speak.'

'And as you've got experience with the SCU in Paris, you will have some experience of crimes like this.'

'Sadly, just a bit; assuming that a crime has been committed.'

'Oh, quite. I think we'll assume that this is a crime scene until it has been proven otherwise, don't you think?'

'I'm inclined to agree with you, sir. If I give you my mobile number, then you can call me if you want to talk to me. Meanwhile, Sergeant Dutoit and I will take our leave of you, and return to the domaine and drink some coffee. You will keep us in the loop, won't you?'

'I'm quite convinced, Commander, that we shall need to stay in close contact with you. You seem to know far more about this case than anyone else.'

'Quite,' said Truchaud and slipped behind the steering wheel of his car.

Chapter 17

Nuits-Saint-Georges, later Wednesday morning

Truchaud and Natalie drove back down the hill. Truchaud felt a little bruised from his encounter with the Coroner's Investigator. 'I think I lost that round,' he remarked.

'I think you probably did,' she replied, 'though why she felt it needed to be a grudge match in the first place was surprising. She'll need to involve us in the investigation, at least to start with.'

'The Examining Magistrate seemed okay, though it was disappointing that it wasn't Lemaître. I got on well with him last time. However, I think we need to touch base with Duquesne before we go home.' With that he headed for the Gendarmerie.

The captain was very amused with life when he greeted them. 'Coffee?' he offered, naturally, and while he was making it himself, not so naturally, he said, 'I've just been on the blower with Constable Montbard, and I gather you've just lost a pissing contest with old Thunder-Guts,' he chuckled. 'Fierce, isn't she?'

'I assume that she's brilliant at her job, which is charitably where I'll leave it. Personally, I think there is little point in an attitude like hers. Not only was she rude to me, but she was also rude to Sergeant Dutoit, suggesting that she wasn't old enough to be a police officer.'

'I hope, mademoiselle, that you were flattered by that. She's probably only a fortnight older than you, and is somewhat piqued that you've aged a little better.'

'The chap Natalie dug up had aged better than she has,' Truchaud snapped, still furious.

'Now, now!' said Duquesne, 'that's not fair. She doesn't smell that bad.' Changing the subject he began, 'But now we're talking about the body, tell me all about it.'

'From the parts we uncovered,' Natalie started, 'he was buried without a stitch of clothing on. Moreover, I reckon he was buried in the deep midwinter.'

'Do you think that's how he died?'

'I've no idea. I didn't uncover any other obvious findings that indicated a cause of death, but then I really didn't uncover a lot of the body. The investigator took over before I had found anything. There was no sign that the soil had been disturbed after the interment had taken place. So, if he was buried alive, he wasn't conscious enough to have put up much of a fight.'

'Do we know even if the body was male?' asked Duquesne.

'Well, it's tall enough to be an adult male, and there was no obvious breast development on the right side, which was where I had got to. I suppose it could have been a girl with Polen's Disease, or perhaps with Turner's Syndrome, in which, among other defects, female breast development does not occur; in the case of Polen's, on the one side only. Both of those syndromes are extremely rare. Generally, people without female breast development are, unless proven otherwise, almost always male. I hadn't got round to uncovering the midline of the pelvis, as I was trying to ascertain the species of creature we were digging up before the coroner's team got there. I can just imagine how that one would have behaved if it turned out that we had dug up a wild boar.'

'If you do ever dig up a wild boar and you happen to be calling Mrs Clermont about it, please can you call me first? I would simply love to be standing there watching the fireworks from the sidelines.' Captain Duquesne, thoroughly enjoying himself, calmed down again. 'Now, how do we set about trying to find out whether this unfortunate young man is, in fact, Horst Witter?'

'There is no way that anyone is going to identify that body just by looking at it, that's for sure,' Natalie assured them.

'If that's the case, then we're going to have to rely on dental records, or perhaps even DNA testing. How were the teeth?'

'I didn't look that closely in the mouth,' she said quietly. The thought of putting her face that close to the corpse did not fill her with excitement. 'Of course, if it is Horst Witter, he would probably have had any dental work done in Germany, rather than in France.'

'We could probably tell if it is dental work done in Germany, as the quality of German dental work is considered to be nonpareil. But just stating that a corpse's bridge was made in Germany does not identify it as a particular German.'

'Quite. So I suspect we're going to have to arrange to take, at the very least, a blood sample from Dagmar to definitely prove or disprove it's her brother that you've just dug up.'

'Well, I'm sure any doctor worth his salt can take a blood sample without creating severe pain. If the worst came to the worst we could always ask Dr Girand down the road.'

'Well, captain, can I count on you to keep us in touch with what's going on?' asked Truchaud, sipping at his coffee, thinking that the constables made better coffee than their boss, but then thought charitably that it wasn't a bad attempt.

'Sure thing,' he replied. 'Even if Madame Investigator threatened to send me to the guillotine were I to keep you in the picture, you can count on me nevertheless. I need the continuing support of the Municipal Police, even if she doesn't.'

'Well, in which case,' Truchaud added, tossing back the last of the coffee, 'we'll see you soon. First stop is the domaine to reconnect Natalie with her fledglings, and then I'll be off to the office to see whether they need me at the town hall.'

'See you soon,' said Duquesne, and Truchaud followed Natalie out to his car. They climbed in, and he drove her back to the domaine.

Michelle was still in the domaine when they got there. 'Has Maréchale already come to pick them up?' Truchaud asked as he sat down.

'What time do you think it is?' Michelle replied. Truchaud looked at his watch, and realized it was lunchtime already. 'They're all down with Bruno and Dad having lunch at the Café du Centre in the town square, and if you had been five minutes later, you would have got that information in the form of a bit of paper pinned to the front door. Coming?'

'Can I just wash the crud off?' asked Natalie. 'I'll be down in a minute.' She leapt up the stairs two at a time.

'What have you two been doing together?' Michelle added slyly.

'You really don't want to know,' said Truchaud, and then when Michelle raised an eyebrow, and rolled her eyes, he struggled for a moment, and said, 'No, perish the thought. She's just been digging up a body.'

'You policemen!' said Michelle. 'It's a nice sunny day in the middle of summer; the birds are on the wing, and the vines are in flower. And all my brother-in-law can think about is digging up bodies. What strange things you consider romantic! Is it anyone we know?'

'I don't know yet. No doubt we'll find out soon enough.'

Natalie had changed extraordinarily rapidly, had put on a different pair of slacks, and obviously given herself a quick wash and brush up too.

'She does scrub up nicely, doesn't she?' smiled Michelle at her brother-in-law.

'I was having a similar thought, only *quickly* was the adverb that sprang into my mind.'

It was a very short walk into the centre and the day was bright. There was no way that Natalie would let the Truchauds get to the town centre by any other form of locomotion than by Shanks's pony. She was the only one who had done any exercise that morning after all.

The menu of the day was much the same as the menu of every day, but none the worse for that. Truchaud didn't have snails that day, although he noticed a finished tray of them in front of Renate. She was doing her tourist bit. Pâté, beef Bourguignon and a crème brulée was to his taste, and a glass of red: just the one, to keep the food company. 'Well, what have you been getting up to today?' he asked the German girls.

'I think I've learned more today about wine than I have learned during the rest of my life. I have also tasted some very interesting wine indeed. We even had a bit of your family's wine too, which Simon was doing stuff with.'

'Oh yes?' replied the policeman cocking an eyebrow at Maréchale.

'Yes,' added Simon. 'I opened a bottle of your Not-a-Richebourg last night, just to see how it had aged after three months since we last opened it. Incidentally, you'll be glad to know, it is making appropriately slow progress. I think it's a keeper. Anyway, as I already had it open, I gave the girls a taste. We also compared that with a bottle of our own Echézeaux, which was fifteen years old, and which is now really quite mellow.'

'Oh yes,' chipped in Dagmar. 'We'd never drunk wine so old.'

'Ah, yes,' Truchaud added. 'And, yet, at the grand dinners you will have in the future, you will no doubt have a wine that makes even that stuff look ridiculously young. All those very old wines though are already in the cellars of the houses where they will eventually be consumed, certainly round here.'

'Including the Truchaud house?'

'Oh, we've all got treasured bottles in our cellars laid up for days of celebration. I think all of those in our cellars are our own, as we're not merchants. The Laforges, being a merchant house as well, may well have bottles that, at one time or another, they bought from somewhere else.'

'It sounds very exciting,' she said. 'So what were you doing while we were doing the tour with Simon?'

Truchaud looked at Natalie, and said in French, 'What were we doing?' And then back into English. 'A bit of routine police work,' which he immediately translated into French, to show Natalie his first response to the German girls' questions about their activities of that morning. They would need to know about what they had found, but halfway through lunch was neither the place nor the time. He hoped Michelle wouldn't blurt out what they had said earlier, but even if she did, then it would be in French, and he would have time to cover for her. Fortunately, she was deep in conversation with Maréchale and Dad about issues in the vineyards, and wasn't even trying to listen to her brother-in-law babbling away in a foreign language.

Bruno was at the beginning of his summer holidays. For the next three months he would spend a lot of his time with the men, working on the vines. He would return to school after the harvest, nut-brown from the summer sun, as did many of the kids who were from Nuits winemaking families. The harvest was the time when every family member mucked in with the creation of the little town's prime industry: wine. But that was three months away. So far the flowering had happened and it all looked distinctly promising. 'All the vines seem to have flowered at the same time,' he said. 'This suggests that the grapes will be roughly the same size and healthy.'

Truchaud picked up on Bruno's statement to the air, and followed up on it, hoping to leave the general conversation away from his and Natalie's activities of the morning. 'No *millerandage* then?' he said.

'Well, it's too early to state that with absolute certainty,' the boy replied trying to sound thirty-five, 'but we can hope so.'

'*Millerandage*?' asked Natalie never having heard the word before.

'It's when the grapes are all different sizes, and therefore it reduces the size of the harvest, and a smaller harvest means less money.'

'Does it make the quality of the wine worse?'

'Not usually,' replied Bruno, still trying to sound far older than his years, 'there's just less of it.'

Natalie popped a little piece of toast with pâté on it into her mouth and chewed gently. Finally, she swallowed. 'You know something, Bruno, your job is totally as technical as ours.'

'Ah yes,' he replied earnestly, 'but isn't the product at the end of it so much more fun?' Truchaud couldn't resist a chuckle at that.

The meal pottered along gently, with the conversation ambling this way and that, but never drifting into dangerous territory. At the end of it Michelle insisted on picking up the bill on the business. 'Put it down to the millerandage,' she said with a smile.

Truchaud went off north from the café to the town hall. The rest of them, well, he wasn't sure where the rest of them went, but they went off in the opposite direction on leaving the café, and he never looked over his shoulder to see which way they went after that.

Fauquet was in the outer office and, as usual, no one else was about. 'Afternoon, *chef*,' he said. 'I understand that you've been having business with the Coroner's Investigator and the Examining Magistrate this morning.'

'News gets around Nuits very quickly,' said Truchaud drily.

'In this case it isn't the gossip machine: it was the magistrate himself who wondered whether you might give him a ring when you got in. He phoned about ten minutes ago.' Fauquet gave him a piece of paper with a Dijon number on it. 'I told him you were at lunch, and he said it could wait, otherwise I would have called you.'

'I was only five minutes' walk away in the Café du Centre.'

'I know, sir. That's why I knew it could wait for a few minutes.' Truchaud was about to ask how he had known where he was, and then thought better of it, and went into the back office with the piece of paper. He picked up the receiver and dialled.

'De Castaigne,' came the reply. *So this was a 'De' who used the 'De' even when he only mentioned the surname*, thought Truchaud. Many 'Des' would only have said 'Castaigne' when they answered the phone. He filed away this information in his memory for future use.

'Truchaud here. I understand you wanted to talk to me.'

'Ah yes,' he said. 'The Commander-Chief without the "in" in the middle. I thought you would like to know that we've completely exhumed the body, and it's now in the forensics lab in Dijon.'

'That was quick,' said Truchaud. 'If it's not tactless, tell the team I'm impressed.'

'Thank you. If it comes up, I'll mention it. I'm sure that someone would be happy to know that Paris is impressed with something done here in Dijon. Anyway, I thought you would like to know our preliminary findings, especially as you were involved in a shooting down here a couple of months ago, I understand.'

That completely bewildered Truchaud. All the people involved in the gunplay during that case were dead, apart from Truchaud himself, of course. 'You've got my attention,' he replied. 'Go on.'

'The victim received one shot to the back of the head. There was an entry wound but no exit wound at the front of the face. An X-ray of the skull shows a foreign body, very distorted, still in the skull.'

'You mean he was executed with a low-velocity round?'

'It looks like that, yes. You caught on to that very quickly, Commander.'

It was not surprising. Truchaud had come within a whisker of being executed himself in the same way, and were it not for a very lucky shot of his own that might have been that. 'Why are you surprised?' he replied.

There was a moment's silence down the phone. Truchaud could picture the magistrate struggling to come up with a witty riposte. After a moment, he said, 'We'll want to check the bullet with the weapon used in your case,' he said. 'I thought you might know where that weapon might be at the moment. We could look it up, of course, but if you were to happen to know that would save a lot of time and palaver.'

'As far as I know, I think it was last seen in the custody of the local Gendarmerie.'

The pistol in question had belonged to his predecessor in the Municipal Police: one Inspector Molleau. He had been a man who had liked playing with his firearm, which he had disassembled and then reassembled with his eyes closed, in front of Truchaud, sitting at the very desk at which he was now seated. Molleau had, when he had been in killer mode, used a low-velocity round to the back of the head as his modus operandi, like a Khmer Rouge style of execution. The round was fired from a short range, and then slowed down still further as it entered the cranium, and, not having enough momentum to force its way out again the other side, it would bounce around within the vault, turning the cranial contents into porridge. It was not a wound from which there was any chance of survival.

'Was this an execution?' he asked.

'It appears so. The second question I have to ask at this moment, have you any idea who the victim might be? Who were you looking for?'

'I'm guessing, but the Gendarmerie and I are looking for a German boy, who apparently went missing at the end of last year, and had his camper impounded by them. It appears that as no one had claimed the camper everyone seemed to have forgotten about him.'

'So why are you all suddenly looking for him now? Has some new evidence turned up?'

'His sister turned up yesterday to claim the camper.'

'Is she still here?'

'Yes, the camper is in my domaine, and the girl was having lunch with us ten minutes ago.'

'Does she know that you may have just dug up her dead brother?'

'She didn't when I left them to come to the town hall.'

'Can you keep it that way for a moment? The body's in no state to be physically identified, and there has been no dental work done, so a dentist's report would be pointless. We're going to need to do a DNA test to identify him.'

'How would you do that?'

'Take a bit of bone marrow from the femur, and compare it with the sister's DNA. They're blood siblings, I assume? Not adopted or anything?'

'As far as I know, they are true blood siblings.'

'I'd like to pop round and take a blood test from her fairly soon, just to make sure at least part of her doesn't disappear back to Germany when we aren't looking.'

'Very good, sir. May I request that you don't hang around too long in that case? Do you have a German speaker who understands German as spoken by someone from the far east of the country?'

'She's an Osti?'

'If by the word Osti, you mean an East German, then yes, she hails from Chemnitz near Dresden. The Gendarmerie's German speaker didn't understand a word she said, although it worked okay in reverse when the gendarme spoke to her.'

'So how did you get through to her then?'

'I speak a bit of schoolboy English, as does she, and fortunately, it's the same subset of English, but my sergeant from Paris speaks very good German, and understands Dagmar even when she's talking in her native language.'

'Dagmar?'

'It's the girl's name.'

'You do sound like you have become unprofessionally close to a suspect, Truchaud,' came down the phone at him.

'Suspect?' said Truchaud stunned. 'I don't think she's a suspect. I think she's a victim already, and what I'm worried about is that she may yet become the same sort of victim as her brother.'

'How is that possible, Truchaud? If what happened is what we think happened, then the killer is already dead, and you would know that, because you killed him yourself.'

'I hope you're correct with all these suppositions, sir, but if indeed it was Molleau who killed the lad, we need to find out why he did so, to rule out anyone else deciding they had to do a similar thing to his sister.'

'Are you suggesting that there's a copycat killer about, Truchaud?'

'Not necessarily. Put yourself in the shoes of an unnamed Mr Big. Now if both Germans *needed* executing, and I had got in his way by killing his *executioner* then Mr Big would need to find a different killer, who may have a completely different way of going about his business.'

'I think we need to come and see your Dagmar immediately.'

'I'll be at the domaine when you get there, and I will have prepared Dagmar as to who you are and why you've come.'

Chapter 18

Nuits-Saint-Georges, then Dijon, Wednesday afternoon

Truchaud pulled out his mobile phone, and dialled Natalie's number. 'Have you got Dagmar still with you?' he asked.

'Yes. Do you want me to pass you over to her?'

'No, but I need you to keep her there. Where are you?'

'We're still at the domaine.'

'Good, stay there. We're going to have to tell her what we may have just found before the Examining Magistrate gets to her. He's on his way from Dijon as we speak, so I'll be with you in about five to ten minutes.'

'You sound like you're moving quite fast.'

'Yes, and I haven't even left the town hall yet. See you very shortly.' He disconnected, and, having pulled on his trench coat, he dropped his phone into a pocket. It was far too hot to do the coat up, so with its tails billowing out behind him, leaving the front door at a gallop, he crossed the main road. There wasn't a pedestrian crossing as such, but there was a very sharp right-hand bend, and a sort of sleeping-policeman hump in the cobbles. Those, combined with the warning of the traffic lights up ahead, meant that nobody drove fast round that corner, not even Lenoir.

Truchaud made his way through the back streets and was slightly out of breath when he trotted through the domaine gates. All three girls were sitting outside under a parasol round the barbecue table, which, as far as Truchaud knew, had never been used for a barbecue. He pulled up another chair, and parked on it.

'Dagmar,' he said in English, 'I think we may have some very bad news for you.' He quickly said the same thing in French for Natalie's benefit. 'It's possible that we've found your brother.'

'Why is that bad news?' asked Dagmar, not understanding the implications of what the policeman had said.

'Because the person we've found is dead.' Truchaud was as gentle as he could be, but it needed to be out there. Dagmar's expression was just as he'd been afraid it would be. Her face crumpled and her eyes got very wide, and filled up with water. 'Dead?' she said in German. 'No, he can't be. No! Please say it's not true.' At this point Natalie took over in German, and with both friends sobbing, Natalie had an arm round each girl's shoulder.

'It may not be him,' Natalie said, 'but they're going through the identification process at the moment. That,' she continued slowly, 'may not be so easy, as the reason we think it may be him is that the body we found was buried at about the same time your brother went missing.'

'What? You mean he's been dead for over six months?'

'This person has.' There was a further flurry of wailing from the two girls. Truchaud stood back and left Natalie to do the comforting. Rather than sitting there and gaping at the tableau, which he found tempting, he stood up, and went into the house. His father was there mumbling about something.

His father looked up and smiled, without any sign of recognition showing in his expression. 'Hello,' he said, 'can I do anything for you? A bottle of wine perhaps? I'll get my son to go down into the cellar to get it for you.'

'Dad, I *am* your son.'

'No, not you. My other son.'

Truchaud thought for a while whether it would be more or less helpful to his father's well-being to remind him that his other son had been dead these last three months or not. He wasn't sure where Michelle was, and she could probably do without being constantly reminded of it. But then, would she ever forget she was a widow? It wasn't the kind of thing you forgot, even after you'd remarried and had a further couple

160

of kids, which of course, she hadn't. He put his arm round his father's shoulder and purred into his ear, 'Dad. Oh, Dad!' which his father may have found all the more disconcerting. 'No, I don't want any wine at the moment, thank you. Perhaps later we'll have a bottle together.'

His father smiled vacantly at him, and said, 'That'll be nice. You're a good boy.' He then changed the subject completely. 'You know something? Those girls out there are German, but we don't blame them for that, do we? They're nice girls, and somebody's still got to be German after all, so why not them?'

Truchaud thought for a while. He wondered how his father had realized that Renate and Dagmar were 'nice girls'. As far as he knew his father didn't speak German. Bruno was learning German at school, of course, and both of the girls had Bruno's seal of approval, being both, in their own rather different ways, fairly easy on the eye.

'Are you German too?' his father asked.

'No, Dad, I'm your son.'

'Can't I have a German son?' Truchaud was beginning to wonder whether his father was rather mischievously playing on his mental state, but, bearing in mind who was about to arrive, this was not the time to start exploring that, especially as there came the sound from outside of a car pulling into the courtyard.

'I have to go,' he said. 'I think these are the people I am expecting.'

By the time he got out into the courtyard, Mr de Castaigne and a young woman were already talking to the three young women sitting under the parasol. The young woman was talking in German.

'Ah, Mr Magistrate,' said Truchaud. 'Good afternoon. Would you care for a cup of coffee or tea, or perhaps a little *apéro*?'

'No thanks,' said the magistrate. 'It's a little early for an *apéro*, don't you think? May I introduce Constable Roussanne from the National Police. She speaks German.'

Truchaud watched with interest, as did Natalie, who sat back and said nothing. Roussanne seemed to be doing even less well than Montbard had done, as the girls appeared to be struggling to understand what she was saying. Naturally, she had no chance in understanding any of Renate and Dagmar's *Ostdeutscher* patois.

'Perhaps you should use Sergeant Dutoit as the interpreter?' suggested Truchaud. 'She appears to have built up a relationship with the witnesses already. Not in any way denigrating your ability, mademoiselle, but from what I understand, their version of the language is a little difficult to get the hang of. There are regional accents like that that are difficult to understand in France too.' He added the last to be as emollient as possible.

'Would you be so good as to interpret for us, sergeant?' asked de Castaigne in a voice as dry as tinder.

'Certainly,' Natalie replied, 'anything to be of assistance to Monsieur the Magistrate.' Her voice dripped with similar irony.

'Can you first ask which of these two girls is Miss Witter.'

Following a quick dialogue between Dagmar and Natalie, Dagmar pointed vaguely at her cleavage, and said that it was she.

'In which case the other girl does not need to take any further part in the current conversation. Can you explain to Miss Witter that we will need her to give us a blood sample to exclude her brother from the identification process of the body we have in our laboratory?'

'Where will you want her to go to have this blood sample taken?' asked Natalie.

'We have a room in our station in Dijon where the sample can be taken under strictly controlled conditions,' said the magistrate. 'The sample will then stand up in court.'

Natalie explained what had just been said to Dagmar, and she just shrugged her shoulders. She didn't appear to be particularly distressed about having a blood sample taken. 'How long will it take to get the results back?' was all that she asked.

Natalie translated that to the magistrate whose reply was that he would be annoyed if it took longer than a couple of weeks to do the required number of tests to prove it definitely was Horst Witter, but it probably wouldn't take anywhere near that long to prove it *wasn't* him.

He turned to Truchaud and asked, 'May I also borrow your sergeant's services?' as if it didn't occur to him to ask Natalie herself. 'As an interpreter, you understand. She seems to be very good at it.'

'It's alright with me, provided she's happy with it, of course.'

'I imagine it would be. You are still on duty, mademoiselle?'

'I am and I am,' Natalie replied.

The two Germans were deep in quiet conversation, and then Renate spoke up in German. 'Can I come too? I think Dagmar is a little more worried than she is admitting.' Natalie translated that to the magistrate.

'Of course,' replied the magistrate.

'Can we count on a lift back, or would you rather we followed you in my own car?' asked Natalie.

'We'll all fit in our car, and I'm sure Constable Roussanne would be willing to run you back here afterwards,' he said assertively, casting an eye in the plain-clothes officer's direction.

'Of course,' the unfortunate Roussanne replied, fully aware that she had absolutely no option in the matter.

Truchaud watched the magistrate park himself assertively in the front passenger seat of the Renault, necessitating the three girls to squeeze, in a somewhat undignified manner, into the back. As none of them carried a great deal of spare flesh perhaps it was less of a squeeze than it might have been than if the chunky frame of Constable Roussanne had been in the back with any two of them. She, however, climbed into the driver's seat and drove carefully out of the gate.

His father wandered out of the house. 'Didn't you want to go with them?' he asked. Truchaud thought about it for a moment before answering that, actually, he didn't think he did. 'Oh, well then,' the old man continued, 'in which case I shall go up and have a zizz. See you later,' and he wandered across the courtyard and into the flat.

Truchaud wondered what his father would have come up with if he had said that actually he did want to go to Dijon with the Examining Magistrate and the girls, but wasn't going to go there.

At this point his mobile phone rang. It was his office in the town hall. 'Fauquet here, sir. We've got a problem. There's an artic broken down outside the town hall and traffic can't move in either direction.'

'I imagine that tempers are becoming quite frayed?'

'Your imagination is not mistaken, sir. No, sir … or do I mean yes, sir? I've sent for a mechanic, but we need some planning to sort the traffic out, or he'll never even get to the scene.'

'I'll be with you in ten minutes,' he replied. 'I imagine I'd be better off on foot.'

'I imagine you would, sir, yes.'

So this was what his new job was all about: sorting out stroppy motorists and broken-down traffic flow. He wandered out of the gate and headed back to the town centre. When he got to the far end of Place de la République, he could see the problem. There was a large articulated lorry halfway round the sharp right-hander with the raised-up cobbles. It would have been fine if it had completed the bend, but it appeared that an off-side front tyre had failed when it was halfway round and the trailer was effectively blocking the other carriageway. The driver seemed most apologetic to Fauquet, the most senior policeman in uniform present, but there were a number of agitated motorists at this end of the lorry, and he imagined that there would be a fair few on the other side beyond the ruptured tyre.

'Do we have any other uniformed police to hand?' Truchaud asked Fauquet.

'I can find a couple.'

'Good, because we need to divert the traffic round the other side of the town hall, while this gets sorted out, and we need to do it from both ends. Bring them round with a number of diversion signs. I suspect that we're going to have to divert any lorries either out via the motorway, or, if they don't like that, just park them while we get this brute's tyre fixed.'

Truchaud understood what he was trying to do, but it must have been half a lifetime since he had actually directed traffic, and somehow he realized that the mood of the average motorist under stress had changed considerably in those intervening years. "Ere, you. Stop babbling at the plod and let 'im get on with 'is job,' came a voice from a van caught up in the melee. Truchaud looked around and was relieved to see that de Castaigne and his car were not caught up in it. He presumed that Roussanne had spotted the problem as it was starting, and had turned sharply towards the motorway. He wondered if she had used her blues and twos. Naughty girl, if so, as she wasn't driving an emergency. The fact that they were not caught up in the traffic jam was encouraging; it suggested it hadn't been in place very long.

Truchaud watched while Fauquet talked to the crew in the town hall on his handset, and simultaneously to the stroppy motorist face to face. He was quietly impressed with how he coped, explaining that Truchaud was the Police Chief, in mufti, and persuaded the motorist to reel his neck in and stay in his car.

The driver of the truck was looking at the tear in his tyre with dismay. 'Just think, if that had gone at speed on the motorway, rather than slowly here ...' He didn't need to complete the sentence.

'What are you carrying?' asked Truchaud.

'Various non-perishable goods, such as canned food, and there are things like refrigerators and washing machines on board as well.' He paused, 'It's for the Super U in Gevrey-Chambertin,' he added, to explain to Truchaud exactly why he came to be there. 'I came off the motorway about five minutes ago at the Nuits-Saint-Georges junction, and here I am.' He rubbed the back of his head, and joked, 'Take a quick look, I haven't got a can of strawberries sticking out of it have I!'

'Have you got triangles out?' Truchaud asked.

'Your policeman has taken them and put them just round the other corner. With the complexity of this junction here, I think I need about five triangles to cover it adequately.' Truchaud could see his point. There were little alleys that made their way through into the nooks and crannies out of the west of the town, as well as the main thoroughfare of the Seventy-Four, and the road out to the motorway. The lights on the front of the cab were flashing amber.

At this point a mechanic rolled up on the far side of the road with a flashing light on the roof of his van. Yet another municipal policeman had guided him through. *They're all coming out from the woodwork now*, thought Truchaud. The mechanic unloaded a large hydraulic trolley down a ramp from the back of his van, and asked brusquely, 'Where's the driver?'

'That would be me,' said the man in question.

'Good. Sometimes, you know, they just wander off to the nearest café to wait for me. It's a bugger when it isn't the nearest café! Are the brakes on?'

'Yes, and the ignition is off.'

'We need to chock the other wheels.'

The two of them got down to the changing of the lorry tyre. Truchaud stood back and let them get on with it. It was the first time he had been close to the changing of a lorry tyre, and it took remarkably little time for them to get the job done. Once the lorry had a fully inflated tyre on board, the driver and the mechanic agreed to get the lorry cleared from the junction, before they got down to the required paperwork. A hundred yards beyond the traffic lights there was a forecourt in front of a wine merchant and the lorry pulled in, and the mechanic with Truchaud aboard pulled in behind him.

'What would have happened if the lorry had just driven off into the distance?' Truchaud asked the mechanic.

'Then you'd have a real problem next time this happened, as you probably wouldn't have been able to find a mechanic available for 100 kilometres who wasn't already too busy to come and help,' said the mechanic drily.

166

The paperwork only took roughly the five minutes it took Fauquet to clear the traffic and, ten minutes later, you wouldn't have known that there had been any trouble at all. Truchaud was quietly impressed with his team and how they had all worked together. It was a very different form of police work than he was used to, but now he realized why it was necessary, and understood just a little bit about how it worked.

Chapter 19

Nuits-Saint-Georges, Wednesday evening

The dining room at the Laforge domaine was considerably larger than that at Truchaud's, but then, during the vintage, it would need to be, as there were a fair number of casual workers at Laforge's, who needed to be fed. Marie-Claire and Celestine would often be found working in the kitchen during the afternoon, frequently being nagged silly by Old Mr Laforge to produce a dish that would suit his choice of wine from the cellar. Often enough he would change his mind after they had started the prep. On the other hand, the old man had invested in a huge pan so that they could poach two dozen eggs at once, and pour the red wine sauce over them, to make an *oeufs en meurette* entrée for everyone. He would, however, send someone else, usually Maréchale, who knew his way around down there, to actually collect the stuff from the cellar.

Truchaud's favourite *meurette* had a firm white but a liquid yolk, though he had never dared to try to make it himself. He was uncertain why this was; perhaps it was that it wasn't something you would only cook for one person.

That evening the old man sat at the head of the table as he would even if just he, Marie-Claire and Jacquot were having supper. Their guests included his shiny new German great-niece and her friend, their employee, Simon Maréchale, and the Truchauds from down the road. Oh yes, and young Mr Truchaud's rather pretty work assistant from Paris, who, like the great-niece and her chum, was all dressed up for the occasion. Old Mr Laforge was comfortably the king of his domaine, seated on his throne at the head of the table. Marie-Claire had tactfully arranged the seating so that everyone could talk to the person they were sitting next to. Thus Simon, who spoke

English, sat next to Dagmar, and across the table from them sat Renate and Natalie, also together despite both being women. The ability to communicate was more important than gender protocol round this table. Jacquot and Bruno also sat together, as surely no one else would be expected to speak 'teenage boy', it being a language all of its own. Simon was teaching Renate and Dagmar French, and Natalie, like any consummate actress, sat on the other side of the table playing teaching assistant.

Simon was explaining about the wine that was to accompany the meal. There was no neck capsule on the top of the bottle, which was not unusual, as people often cut off the complete neck capsule prior to drawing the cork. What they didn't usually do was soak off the label completely as well, so its absence was something to comment on.

In this case, the bottle had never worn a label or a capsule in the first place. The cellar man who had brought it up for the table knew what it was by its place in the cellar: a bottle that had been laid aside for family consumption, and also for the vintner to taste to monitor the progress of that particular wine over time; a policy that was generally allowed by the taxman, provided the small number of bottles set aside for that purpose never left the premises. Old Mr Laforge, who had already pulled the cork to allow the wine breathing time, would have taken note of the date embossed on its top. All the corks used that year had the date of the vintage printed on the top, and printed on the side of the cork it would have 'Domaine Laforge'. Some of them might even have a vineyard name as well. Truchaud's Clos de Vougeot, for example, did just that.

Old Mr Truchaud, seated tactfully between his son and his daughter-in-law, so that he didn't upset anyone, continually informed his son how nice it was in there. Truchaud wondered whether it would be the last time his father would be invited out to dinner. At least most of his food still ended up in his mouth. Michelle wiped his shirtfront from time to time, but otherwise no one seemed to notice much. Truchaud saw down the table the animated conversation between Simon, the German girls and Natalie, but he was just too far away to make any meaningful contribution, or to hear the French or English components.

'Well, I like our new relation. I think I would rather Simon had brought her into the family, than wandered off with that Parnault girl. If she gets him then he'll probably leave this family long before Jacquot's ready to take it on. I'll be long dead before he's ready,' remarked the old man at the head of the table.

'Oh, Granddad, you know you're going to live forever,' said Marie-Claire from her side of the table.

'You know, I'm afraid you might be right.'

'Did you know her brother?' Truchaud joined in the one conversation that was available to him that wasn't just parental repetitiveness.

'Not as a potential relation of Simon's,' said Marie-Claire, 'just as a polite young German student who was learning French, and making a fairly good fist of it,' she added.

'Yes,' said the old man. 'Wish I'd actually talked to him at the time. Have you found him yet? I understand you're looking for him.'

Truchaud looked at him. So, Dagmar hadn't discussed with her new family where she had been that afternoon, or what she'd been doing. There had been a number of moments like this during his career, when he hoped that whoever's remains they were that they had found that morning really didn't belong to the person they were looking for. He shook his head slowly and said nothing. He remembered one incident where a relative had been with him at a crime scene, and had chosen not to mention it to another relative, and as there was no reason to involve the second relative in the line of questioning, Truchaud had really had no reason to bring up the victim's identity. He thought that doctors and their confidentiality agreements had similar problems, but then perhaps doctors didn't often take dinner with their patients. Truchaud didn't often dine with the families of victims either, and he was beginning to understand another reason as to why that was.

Old Mr Laforge didn't give up so easily however. 'I asked if you'd found him yet.' His voice was clearer and more assertive, but fortunately no louder than before. Truchaud decided he needed some sort of answer.

'We found a body this morning,' he replied quietly, 'but we haven't identified it yet.'

'Well, that's a piece of cake, old boy,' the old man replied. 'Just take the girlie at the other end of the table to have a look at him and ask her if it's her brother.'

'Unfortunately it isn't as easy at that,' Truchaud replied, still quietly. 'The body we dug up was probably buried around six months ago, and isn't really identifiable to the naked eye.'

'Sorry, I don't understand. What's it look like then?'

'Oh, Granddad,' said Marie-Claire gently, 'not at dinner. Only retired warriors like you and perhaps the police would be able to hang on to their dinners during a description of a six-month-old corpse. And as I spent a lot of time in the kitchen this afternoon, I request an immediate subject change now.'

The old warrior deflated, 'As you command, my dear,' he said. 'So, what shall we talk about? I'm not in the mood to discuss your skills in the kitchen, and I'm not allowed to discuss forensic matters with our pet policeman here. So, any suggestions? Religion? The sexual antics of our politicians perhaps?'

'It's nice in here,' suggested the old man on the other side of Commander Truchaud again with exquisite timing. Laforge chuckled.

'I can certainly talk about the history of this room,' he said. 'It may even date back to the rebuilding of Nuits-Saint-Georges after it was sacked in the sixteenth century during the Thirty Years' War.'

Marie-Claire looked pleadingly at Truchaud. It appeared that she had listened to that story more times than she could stand, and she really didn't want to hear it again that evening.

He intervened. 'What periods have you not heard so much about?' he asked her.

'I can't really talk about my childhood,' the old man replied over the top. 'There are Germans present and that topic would appear downright rude.' He said the last part of the sentence so softly that Truchaud wasn't sure he had heard it right himself. Those at the other end of the table apparently heard nothing as the hubbub mimicking the Tower of Babel continued unabated.

'So what's the year been like so far?' Truchaud said airily. 'Hopes for the vintage?'

That comment was heard by the two boys in the middle of the table and Bruno chipped in, 'Oh, Uncle Shammang, don't you listen to a word I say?' And he proceeded to give the elders at the end of the table a repeat of his lecture earlier in the day, about the relative absence of *millerandage*. Old Mr Laforge was impressed, and said so.

'The boy will become a good winemaker one day,' he said. 'I hope you will be proud of him, if he continues to learn his stuff.'

'So do I,' said Truchaud, 'so do I. You will continue to do your homework won't you, Bruno?' he asked.

Bruno shuffled his feet and looked down at his plate uncomfortably. 'I expect so, Uncle Shammang.'

'I think it will depend on the summer from here on in,' said the old man gently. 'At this moment in time, the word, "promising" is the one I'd use. If the weather stays this hot and bakes the grapes nicely, then it will get better than that. But you know as well as I do that one badly aimed hailstorm will knock all the grapes off the vines, and that's it for another year. I can remember one hailstorm was all it took back in '75. Well, that and the rot, I suppose.'

'I was a child then,' replied Truchaud, 'but I remember it well. Every afternoon it was really hot and sticky, and then I seem to remember an electric storm hitting at around six o'clock every evening to cool the air down, so that we could go out in the twilight.'

'I don't think it happened *every* evening,' replied the old man.

'Maybe not, but it felt like it, and remember I was only a lad, so I was pleased that the storm cleared the air from being sticky, heavy and close, to being pleasant, and so much cooler.

It was like someone had put the atmosphere through a cool washing machine.'

'So, it is possibly a good thing you went off to be a policeman then,' replied the old man drily. 'You should have been conscious of the well-being of the grapes as soon as you were conscious of anything at all.'

'You may well be right at that.' Truchaud acknowledged, hoping his father wouldn't hear that.

Needless to say, his father was listening at that moment. 'Told you that you would never make a half-decent winemaker,' he chipped in.

Truchaud looked at his father down his nose. 'I suppose you thought I had that one coming,' he replied tersely, perhaps forgetting for a moment about his father's declining intellect. He caught himself from saying anything else he might have regretted, and added to Old Mr Laforge, 'I may not have been naturally gifted, but I can think of a good many others who are plying a more than adequate trade round here by dint of solid hard graft rather than brilliant talent.'

'Ah yes, but can you imagine someone with the combination of the two: a sublimely gifted winemaker, who was also willing to put in the hard yards?' Truchaud thought for a moment about his brother. *Was that a description of him?* he wondered.

'My son Bertin was one of those,' came from his father from his left. He was obviously thinking the same thing.

'And maybe we both were in our younger days,' replied Old Mr Laforge. 'We made some good wine in our youth, eh, Philibert?' he chuckled.

'And drank a fair bit of it too ourselves,' chuckled Père Truchaud. 'That was until the taxman caught us at it.'

'Yes, and then we had to share it three ways instead of just the two. Damn thirsty that taxman too, I seem to remember. Bastard!'

'Wasn't he just! And he wasn't just into it for the alcohol and merriment. Oh no, he wanted a Premier Cru at the very least.'

'And if we hadn't got any?'

'And Truchaud's didn't; we only have our Grand Cru. Can you imagine getting a taxman rat-arsed on a bottle of Clos de Vougeot?'

'Why do you think we bought that Premier Cru Chambolle? It kept the nuisance off our Echézeaux!'

'You know something,' said Old Mr Truchaud, 'I think I prefer your Premier Cru Chambolle to that Echézeaux.'

Truchaud took a sharp intake of breath. Was this the moment where his father put his foot in his mouth and caused an international incident? Not a bit of it. Old Mr Laforge kept the banter up: 'Like I prefer your Village Vosne to your Clos de Vougeot.' That was a sentiment that the policeman himself was inclined to agree with, but wasn't sure he would voice it in public. He also wondered whether the old man on his right had just admitted his complicity in the wine fraud that had nearly blown up that spring.

Truchaud leaned back and let the two old men banter on about the good old days, and continued to listen carefully, in case there was a clue or two dropped by accident, under the influence of the alcohol, which might lead him to find Horst Witter somewhere else entirely. He also noted that his father found it much easier to remember the distant past than what he had done last week or, even worse, what he had said an hour ago.

The rabbit fillet done Dijon style in a sauce with mustard grains *à l'ancienne* was followed by cheese that gave the rich heady wine a close run for its money. The cheese, made up the road in the cheese factory in Brochon, just on the north side of Gevrey-Chambertin, had certainly ripened up well. Why it was called 'Chambertin's Friend' Truchaud had no idea. As far as he could tell, its main objective seemed to be to slaughter any taste that the wine had left.

Following the cheese, a home-made apple tart and liqueurs completed the meal. Bruno and Jacquot made themselves useful clearing the table, while the adults continued to sit comfortably with whatever they were drinking. The boys made coffee for everyone, but the local Municipal Police Chief wasn't going to let anyone think about driving again that evening anyway.

It was that mellow post-prandial moment when everything was digesting nicely and the eyelids began to feel quite heavy that Truchaud's father chose to kick off. The person who spotted his coming to the boil was sitting across the table from him: Bruno his grandson.

'No, Granddad, don't start now, please,' he shouted making his mother and uncle aware of the imminent problem. Truchaud became simultaneously aware of two problems: the growing puddle underneath his father's chair; and the airborne apple tart. The soft bottom of the apple tart hung together quite well in flight, but on impact it disintegrated in various directions. On the assumption it had been aimed at Old Mr Laforge, his aim was true. The old Resistance man didn't appear to know whether to roar in laughter or fury. Truchaud was not sure which roar it was, but it was well and truly a roar.

'See, that's what you get, eh? Eh?' said Old Mr Truchaud, 'You and your nice big room. Is that how you like it?'

'Shammang, I think we'd better take him home now.' Michelle was in control a moment later. 'Come on, old chap, time to go home.' She helped him to his feet, pulling at his shoulder, and Truchaud followed her lead, applying traction to the other one.

'I don't want to go home,' he protested. 'I like it here; it's nice.'

'But if you can't behave, then it's home you go,' Michelle continued. 'I'm terribly sorry about this,' she said to the room as a whole. 'I had so hoped this wouldn't happen. Would you like me to stay to clear up?'

Marie-Claire accepted the apology instantly, though whether she was aware of the puddle on the old parquet floor was uncertain, and told Michelle it was fine if she just took him home. Truchaud was helping to shield the moist front of his trousers from view.

'Do you want me to come home too?' asked Bruno.

'I think your uncle and I can cope with him all right,' she said to her son, adding, 'but don't be too late.'

'I'll bring him back with us when we come, if that's all right. We won't be long,' said Natalie from her end of the table.

'Thank you,' said Michelle. 'Come along, Dad.' And the three of them left the room and the house.

On the way back, Old Mr Truchaud shouted out once or twice, which Michelle followed with a 'Ssh, people are trying to sleep.' Truchaud was relieved that his father didn't attempt to relieve himself in the street; the idea of having to arrest his father for a breach of the peace appalled him. Once they were through the stone gateposts of the domaine, the old man calmed down and, knowing where he was for a change, he headed for his room, and with a 'goodnight' to both of them, went through the doors into his flat.

It was only when Commander Truchaud sat down on his bed that the image of Old Mr Laforge wearing apple tart on his face came back to him. He suddenly found it unbearably funny, and he lay back on his bed with tears of laughter streaming down his face.

Chapter 20

Nuits-Saint-Georges, late Wednesday evening

Truchaud's room was at the opposite end of the house from where the others slept, so he was sitting on the bed making notes, with some music on. He was listening to a fairly late concert by the Grateful Dead. It was while he was being told by the band to, 'Wake up and find out that you are the eyes of the world' that he became aware that someone was knocking on his door.

'Come in,' he said.

'I wasn't sure if you were still up,' said Natalie, walking carefully through the door. 'I heard you had music on, but that wouldn't have told me anything.'

'Evening,' he said, turning the CD down to a level that he would have found irritating had he not known the music. He then turned it off completely, as he imagined that Natalie would find it just as irritating anyway.

'Don't turn it off for me,' she said.

'But you want to talk to me,' he replied. 'That's why you came in.'

'Yes, but I could have talked to you over the top of it. It wasn't loud.'

'Unfortunately, my brain would have tried to listen to the music over the top of what you were trying to say,' he replied, 'and as a result, I wouldn't have made a lot of sense out of either you or the band. I don't do background music, especially the Grateful Dead. About the only thing I can do, when I am listening to them, is drive a car.

'That was the Grateful Dead?' she asked, 'It sounded somewhat different from how I imagined from the name. I must borrow that off you some time and give it a spin.' He wasn't

179

sure that would ever happen, but he didn't voice that thought. The idea of lending out any of his rare concerts bounced momentarily round his head like a low-velocity round, and then came back into his consciousness with a resounding, *No. That's not going to happen.*

'What can I do for you?' he asked politely, deciding not to convert the thought into speech, and changing the subject.

In one corner of the room was a chair, which later on that evening would be covered with his clothes once he had climbed into bed. Natalie pulled it up and parked herself on it. He became aware that the hemline of her skirt rode up over her knees, displaying a length of thigh, when she sat down. Oh good lord, and he was going to have to look at that … out of politeness, of course. Concentrate on her head, man, it's not that unpleasant, and it is the bit where the sound is coming from.

'I wondered what you thought about tonight.'

'How do you mean?'

'About what went on over dinner.'

'I think I must have missed something,' he replied with a quizzical expression. Natalie had obviously spotted something that he had been completely unaware of. 'Go on,' he added.

'Well, Dagmar didn't come home with us this evening. She's still having a *French lesson* over coffee as we speak.' She did the inverted commas sign with her fingers as she said the word 'coffee'.

'What? You mean she's staying over?'

'It appears so. Renate's distinctly d'off about it.'

'D'off?'

'Hacked off, pissed off, fucked off, anything you like d'off; but whatever sort of d'off you want that's where Renate is, seething in the campervan downstairs, on her own.'

'Well, there's a thing,' he said. 'Did you see that coming?'

'Well, I don't speak an inordinate amount of English, but I don't think you needed to understand a word of the language to understand that the ambience was, at the very least, flirtatious.'

'And she's staying the night?'

'Well, she didn't come back with us when we brought Bruno back, did she?'

'Did she say she was coming back?'

'No, and that's what I've been saying these last five minutes,' she replied testily, but then her voice softened again as she continued. 'But I suppose she didn't say she wasn't going to do so either. Mind you, I thought Simon was in a relationship with that student girl that was with him at that dinner at the Café du Centre the last time I was down.' She was referring to the dinner at the end of the previous case in Nuits-Saint-Georges, when Captain Duquesne formally handed Truchaud's open custody to Natalie, so she could escort him back to Paris. He had still been in open custody at that point, having been responsible for the shooting of Inspector Molleau, in self-defence of course; and the girl in question was Suzette Girand, the doctor's daughter, but in another universe, she might have been his own.

'Yes,' he replied. 'I thought that too. She's still in Dijon, I gather, putting the finishing touches to last year's thesis.' *And that*, he thought, *was a very silly decision to have taken when there are two very pretty German girls hovering around in Nuits-Saint-Georges.* 'Do you think I should wander round in the morning, to tip her mother off that while the cat's away, the mice are at play?'

'That would depend on how appropriate you might consider that plan of action to be,' Natalie replied carefully, and then changing the subject, she continued. 'While we're here, I wonder whether we should be asking ourselves whether Dagmar is putting herself in the same jeopardy as her brother.'

'How do you mean?'

'Well, apart from the woman who runs the campsite, the only people we know with whom Horst linked up are the same people with whom Dagmar is now alone.'

'That's true as far as it goes, but we don't know whether the corpse we found does belong to Horst.'

'Oh, I agree, but if that body doesn't belong to Dagmar's brother, then he has made a brilliant success of vanishing off the face of the earth, without, at the same time, leaving behind any reason whatsoever for doing so. Shall we, just for the sake of argument, posit that the corpse that we dug up does indeed belong to Horst Witter?'

'And that Dagmar Witter is currently alone in the house where her brother was last seen alive?' Truchaud continued her argument for her.

'In a nutshell, that's what I'm saying. Now, I must admit that there are one or two fewer people around now than there were at the time of Horst's disappearance: Jérome Laforge, to name but one. But the only motive I can think that Young Mr Laforge had for killing Horst could just as easily apply to the others still at the house.'

'Another person that isn't there anymore, of course, would be Inspector Molleau, and I know from personal experience that he quite liked shooting people in the back of the head. You know something else? I have still got fairly little idea why he came at me with that gun. Presumably, I knew something that he didn't want me talking about, though your guess is as good as mine what that actually was.'

'Well, I'm very relieved that you didn't stop to ask him, *chef*; that would have been a complete waste of a commander.'

'I think that in all probability one of the main reasons I have survived to become a commander is because I don't stop to ask silly questions.'

'My point exactly,' she replied. 'Therefore, the question I have to ask is, how far should we intervene in Dagmar's activities?'

'She's a grown woman, an adult, and therefore we have no right to be interfering in her activities if she's not in danger. However, do we actually know if she is in danger or not?'

Natalie looked at the Commander for a moment, 'That is the question we have to ask ourselves. I could phone her, I suppose, and ask her if she's coming back, because we need to lock the gates, and she hasn't got a key to them.'

'Good try,' said Truchaud bleakly. 'Unfortunately, Maréchale does, being also the overseer for our estate, so he could let her in.'

'Okay, so he has a key. Then he can let her in, if he's remembered to bring it with him. Shall we make sure he hasn't forgotten it? I think I'll give him a bell to remind him to bring it with him, because we're about to lock up. At least it will let him know too that we're also looking out for her, and that he should bring her back safely, without even thinking about doing her in, or even just letting her walk home all on her own. I can't see him being violent, and I can't actually see him wanting Horst dead. What would his motive have been? We need at least to know that she is safe and in someone's company from minute to minute.'

'Yes, I think that's a reasonable thing to do,' said Truchaud, 'and I agree with you about contacting him rather than Dagmar herself.'

Natalie fumbled in her bag, and pulled out her phone and dialled it. 'Oh hi, yes, it's Natalie here. Just letting you know that the Commander and I are making the domaine secure for the night and locking the front gate, so when you bring Dagmar back, can you remember to bring your keys to open the gate? We'd hate for her to be hanging about in the street till one of us unlocked the place tomorrow morning. Bye.' There were of course one or two spaces where she was listening to what he had to say. Truchaud was impressed. She sounded totally perky on the phone, and there was even a touch of 'nudge, nudge' in there, as well. He was smiling when she turned back to him, job done.

'I think that gave just the right message,' he said.

She looked at him quizzically. 'Yes, I thought so too.' She looked down at her knees, and then at him again, 'Sorry, *chef*, I was just wondering, is there anything the matter with my knees? You were watching them very intently while I was on the phone.'

Truchaud looked up, and, continuing to smile said, 'No, not really. You know, I think it's the first time I have seen either of them since the pivotal role they played in the takedown of the Fox in Paris, and that must have been over three months ago. Evening, lads!' he said chirpily saluting her knees, as if they were constables in uniform. Internally, he heaved a huge sigh of relief that he didn't trip over that last sentence, and that he wasn't tempted to babble on, trying to overcompensate after getting caught gawping. His excuse worked, and she smiled again. He even thought he might now be able to give her legs an occasional eye, if she ever put them on show again, provided he saluted them first.

They walked down to the entrance to the domaine together, talking quietly to avoid waking Michelle and Bruno, and quietly closed the big wrought-iron gates, which didn't squeak normally, but did, just enough to bring Renate out of the campervan.

'What are you doing?' she asked in German. 'Dagmar isn't back yet.'

Natalie explained to her, also in German, about the phone call to Simon Maréchale, and that he would therefore be expected to bring his keys with him when he brought Dagmar back. What Natalie didn't explain was their concern about Dagmar being in the same jeopardy as Horst.

Renate looked crossly at the two police, but climbed back into the camper, and turned the lights off again. Natalie and Truchaud walked back into the house, and climbed the stairs, making as little noise as possible. They bade each other a quiet good night, and gave each other a little salute, and then Truchaud offered both her knees a gruff 'g'night, lads' and a salute, but they were now more or less covered by her hemline, and didn't salute back, although their owner seemed amused. Chuckling quietly to themselves, the two detectives made their way to their respective rooms, to await the arrival of sleep.

Chapter 21

Nuits-Saint-Georges, Thursday morning

Truchaud was the second arrival downstairs that morning. He couldn't actually ever remember a time when he had been down before Michelle; she always seemed to wake up at some unspeakable hour in the morning, and that had been a habit long before his father became unwell.

'Coffee?' she offered.

Truchaud accepted, and parked himself at the dining room table. There was a large basket of croissants in the middle of the table and beside it, a plate with sliced cold meats on the one side and sliced hard cheeses on the other. Also on the table were a couple of baguettes, a butter dish and a choice of various varieties of jam. 'It's like a hotel,' he remarked.

'Don't start saying things like that on a regular basis,' she remarked drily. 'I might just consider creating a price list!'

'And putting on a pinny perhaps? Have you seen Dad this morning?' he asked after a moment, changing the subject.

'Not yet,' she replied. 'You?'

His grunt sounded pretty negative too, and once more they became quiet. She put his cup and saucer down in front of him, and he grabbed a croissant and dunked it carelessly in the coffee. Then, having bitten off the soggy end, he put some butter and sweet orange jam on the dry bit, and bit into it again, and took a mouthful of coffee from the cup and sat back. *A couple more mouthfuls of coffee*, he thought, a*nd I might be awake enough to see Natalie without feeling intensely foolish.* At that moment in time, foolish was what he felt. He was far too old to have a teenage crush on a girl who was really little more than a teenager herself. *Well,* he thought, *she wasn't really a teenager any more, but in the right light she could be mistaken for one. Actually,* his mind continued, still silently, much to his relief, *in the right light she could be mistaken for heaven.*

'Penny for your thoughts,' said Michelle. As if! There was no way he was going to divulge those kind of thoughts, for any amount of money.

'Trying to put a day together,' he replied. 'I have to wander up to the town hall, and see what's going on. Either I or Natalie are going to have to contact the Examining Magistrate or Mrs Clermont perhaps, to see how far they are getting on with the identification of the body that we dug up yesterday.' He would probably phone them from his office in the town hall.

'Morning, Uncle Shammang,' was Bruno's greeting as he walked through the kitchen into the dining room.

'Good morning, sir,' the detective replied to his nephew. 'Did you sleep well?'

'Like a log,' he replied.

The next arrival was Truchaud Père, who appeared to still be wearing what he had been in when he had gone to his room the night before, complete with added moisture. The detective and his sister-in-law exchanged glances. 'Come on, Granddad,' she said, getting hold of him gently but firmly by the upper arm. 'Let's get you back upstairs and out of those mucky old clothes and into some clean ones. What do you say to that?'

'Must I?' said the old man, 'There's breakfast all laid out and everything.'

'And it will still be here when you come back, all cleaned and spruced up.'

'Promise?'

'Oh, I promise.' She rounded on the younger clan members sitting at the table. 'And so do those two, too.' She was making absolutely sure that there would be food still available for the old man when he finally ended up downstairs, scrubbed.

Just after they had disappeared outside, Truchaud's mobile phone went off. Bruno watched him pull it out of his pocket, look at its display for a moment, and then having pushed a button, put it to his ear. 'Yes?' he said. There was a pause and then he said, 'Hang on, I'll be right over.' He looked at the phone again, pushed another button on it, and standing up, dropped it into his pocket.

He turned to Bruno. 'That was the town hall, and apparently they need me there right away. Can you apologize to your mum, and promise her that I'll do the washing up at the next opportunity.' With that, he grabbed his trench coat from the stand by the door, pulled his keys out of his pocket, unlocked the wrought-iron gates to the domaine, and threw them wide open. He unlocked the BX by sticking the key into the door; it was far too old to have a remote control, climbed in, and headed off out.

Fauquet was most impressed with the speed Truchaud took to get to the town hall. 'I drove,' he replied, 'and really there wasn't any traffic. Now, where is this fellow?'

'That was him in the main office, reading a magazine.'

Truchaud adjusted himself behind his desk, and said, 'Send Mr Gauvre in, and let's see what this is all about.'

The man walked through the door: a squat middle-aged man in his middle fifties, with a face which looked as if he had consumed more wine during his life than was good for him. He also wore a rather angry expression. 'Where's the chief?' he asked gruffly.

'That would be me. Commander Truchaud at your service.'

'Where's the uniform?' Gauvre came back.

'Until three days ago I was in the civilian National Police.' He continued, not strictly truthfully. 'I am having a uniform made, but I'm afraid these things take time, even in France. What can I do for you?'

'I want to report a missing person, or at least that's the report I want to make, and yes, she's missing.'

'Would you like to go into a little more detail? Who exactly is missing?'

'That would be my daughter, Solange. We had an argument the night before last and she walked out. She hasn't come back yet.'

'How old is this girl?'

'Seventeen.' *Hmm*, thought Truchaud, *no longer a child, and not yet an adult.*

'Can you describe her? In fact, do you have a picture of her?'

The man fished about in his wallet and produced a photograph of a girl's face, only she couldn't have been more than seven or eight. She had wispy fair hair, even features and a slightly naughty grin. 'You don't have a more recent picture, do you?' he asked. 'I suspect she doesn't look a lot like this now. This must have been taken ten years ago.'

'Yes, that's about right,' he said, 'but it's how she should look, if she hadn't done all that piercing and hair-dying stuff.'

'So what colour is her hair now?' he asked.

'Jet-black.'

Truchaud sat back and looked over the table, 'Was that what the argument was all about? Her turning herself into a Goth?'

'Goth? What's that?'

'Dying her hair black with piercings and things. It's one of the things the kids of today seem to do to make themselves look different from their parents.' He softened his voice. 'Fairly horrid, isn't it?'

'You are so right,' he said. 'I put it down to that boyfriend of hers. I don't know why he wants her to look so repulsive. She was such a pretty girl until he got his hands on her. And anyway, how is her fiancé going to want to marry her when she looks like that?'

'Fiancé?' Truchaud asked.

'Yes, sometime in the future she's going to marry Jean Leduc's son, and they're going to live happily ever after.'

'Is that her decision?' said Truchaud. 'Or is that what you were arguing about?'

'She has always been going to marry Étienne Leduc, ever since they were children. Our families are business partners, and Étienne's father and I are lifelong friends, as well as very distant cousins. The kids played together, they laughed together. What else was going to happen? Of course, they're going to get married.'

'Does Leduc make wine too?' said Truchaud, making sense of the picture.

'How did you know I make wine? I don't think I ever mentioned that.'

'Mr Gauvre, you have a famous name among the wine fraternity here. Your Grands Crus are fairly legendary.'

'So you're one of *those* Truchauds!' he replied. 'That explains a lot. I didn't think you were allowed to do police work in the town of your birth.'

'I didn't think I was, either, but I'm here anyway, and there was a temporary vacancy, so it was a solution that was convenient to the town hall.' Truchaud offered Gauvre a coffee, which he thought about for a moment, then declined.

'Tell me a little more about Solange,' he said, 'What was the argument about the day before yesterday?'

'What is it always about? I haven't the faintest idea to be honest. We find something to disagree about, and neither of us seems willing to back down. We both just dig our heels in and it gets louder and louder. Her mother then slams a door, which nowadays, doesn't seem to have the same effect as it used to. A couple of years ago, it seemed to calm us both down, but not anymore. Do you have teenage kids?' he asked.

'No, I have a not-quite-teenage nephew, but we don't argue yet.' Truchaud thought for a moment about that. Were they going to start fighting in a couple of years? He really hoped not. 'Has Solange run off before?' he asked.

'Not without telling her mother or sister where she was going,' he replied.

'She has a sister?'

'Adèle; she's fifteen, and they couldn't be more different, and yet they seem to get on together okay. She hasn't punctured her face or dyed her hair, or anything like that.'

'Boyfriend?'

'No, she's not old enough for that yet. Nor is Solange really, but that doesn't seem to have stopped her.'

'Do you know where Solange's boyfriend lives?'

'Haven't the faintest idea: in a grubby squat in Dijon, I expect. Why should I want to know that?'

'Because, in all probability, that's where Solange is. Do you think Adèle might know where he lives?'

'Why should Adèle want to know that?'

'Because you've already said that she and her sister care about each other, and in all probability, it would have come up in a conversation between them, even if Solange didn't tell her she was going off the day before yesterday. Is Adèle at home at the moment?'

'I imagine so. She wasn't up when I left the house to come here this morning.'

'So she's a bit of a teenager too then?'

'You mean she doesn't get up first thing in the morning?'

'In a nutshell, yes.'

'I suppose you're right.'

'Right, here's a plan. Is your car outside?'

'No, I walked down.'

'Well mine is, so why don't we both get into my car, and go back to your home? We'll get your wife to wake Adèle up, and see if she knows where the boyfriend lives. If she knows the address, we copy it down, and go and pay this boyfriend a visit. How's that for a start?'

Gauvre looked at the Commandant for a moment. 'What if she doesn't know his address?'

'That's a bridge we will have to cross if we get to it.'

Briefing Fauquet as to where he was going to be, Truchaud dropped his mobile phone into a pocket and led Gauvre out to the car park, and walked over to his old BX. Gauvre looked at Truchaud's car slightly askance, as if he couldn't remember when he had last contaminated his clothing in such a ramshackle vehicle. He climbed into the passenger side and found it was comfortable enough, even though it had cloth seats. It took Truchaud five minutes to drive from the town hall to Gauvre's domaine. The gateway was much the same size as Truchaud's, but the courtyard behind the gates was considerably bigger. Truchaud pulled up next door to a large black

Mercedes 4x4, larger in every dimension than Truchaud's BX. Gauvre found the handle and let himself out and walked up to a large double door in the wall. Within the double door was a further door handle, and a door within a door.

'Come on through,' he said.

Truchaud followed him through the door and found himself in a large cool warehouse. Considering the ambient temperature outside, even though it was still quite early morning, he was suitably impressed with the temperature of the warehouse. Within the warehouse there were metal tanks, one of which he tapped as he walked past. It sounded empty. 'That's a fermentation tank,' said Gauvre, 'and it's not doing anything at the moment. In the autumn that will be working hard and we will be very careful making sure it doesn't get too hot.' He tapped the thermometer on the side of the tank.

Beyond the fermentation tanks were steel crates of bottles with French tax capsules already on the necks, and behind them were collapsed cardboard cartons. Truchaud raised an eyebrow. Gauvre pulled a bottle seemingly at random from a crate. Around the neck was a label with a date from eighteen months ago, and a smart Gevrey-Chambertin village wine label on the bottle. Gauvre's design was colourful and Truchaud was impressed. He returned the bottle to its owner, who then put it back in the crate from whence it came.

'If a tourist wants to buy some wine from us now, he can do so, and we crate it up how he likes. No one apart from a tourist will want to buy wine from this vintage, at this time of year, so we wait until the end of August and then we crate all this stuff up and bury it in the cellars, in preparation for sending it off to the dealers in cartons of dozens or half-dozens. A local might want to buy a bottle of a vintage that's ready to drink now. He'll take it home to be drunk that night with a friend he's trying to impress. I'm sure that happens at your domaine too. It means we will already have work for the casual workers to do while we wait for the harvest to start.' He led Truchaud through the crates to a door at the back of the warehouse, and they walked through it. The temperature immediately went up at least five degrees.

'The warehouse is air-conditioned?' asked Truchaud.

'Temperature and humidity controlled,' replied Gauvre, 'obviously.' He called out for his wife. Truchaud was somewhat surprised that that was exactly the word that he used. 'Wife!' he shouted. *Not a word he himself would have used as a term of endearment,* Truchaud thought, *even when he was married.* He thought about Bertin calling Michelle 'Wife' and wondered whether both of his eyes might have been blacked.

Mrs Gauvre was a squat busy woman who appeared from behind where the men were looking. He introduced her to Commander Truchaud.

'Oh, there are some winemakers in Nuits-Saint-Georges called Truchaud. Do you know them?'

Gauvre told her slightly testily that he was one of them, and asked if Adèle was up yet. She replied equally testily that she thought it was extremely unlikely, but that she would give her a shout. And that was exactly what she did: she planted her legs apart, put her hands on her hips, took in a very impressive lungful of air and bellowed Adèle's name, loud enough for it to be heard a dozen kilometres north in Gevrey-Chambertin. Not a sound was heard, so she repeated the performance, and added that she should get herself downstairs as her father wished to see her immediately. The venom she put into the word 'immediately' astonished Truchaud.

What astonished Truchaud even more was that the maternal bellow worked. From the top of the stairs emerged a very unkempt teenager, still in pyjamas, with her hair all over the place and a left arm stretching out and up, clenched like a Black Power athlete, with a right fist in front of her mouth. 'What?' she shouted back.

'We want to ask you something,' replied her father. Truchaud was beginning to understand why Solange and her father failed to communicate, even though he had yet to meet the girl in question. He moved back into the room finding a chair beside the kitchen table, and parked himself on it.

A girl appeared at the door. He had little idea of her build, as the pyjamas were large, considerably larger than the girl they contained, and could certainly have contained two Dagmars or Natalies easily, with room to spare. She had fair hair, which looked totally slept in. She wore no make-up, and there was still sleep in the corners of her eyes. 'What?' she asked yet again.

'The Police Commander here wants to ask you some questions,' said Mr Gauvre to his daughter. Truchaud thought that he shouldn't bring him into their family quarrel.

'Done nothing,' said the girl, still truculently, but probably still asleep. 'What?' she asked for a third time.

Truchaud thought he should probably calm the atmosphere. 'We weren't saying for a moment that you had. We wondered whether you might know where your sister's boyfriend might be.'

'What?' she said again, and Truchaud was beginning to wonder whether the girl might be somewhat thick. 'You mean Pierre?'

'If that's his name, yes,' Truchaud replied gently.

'He's probably round his place. Why?' *Well, it was a different question from 'what?' he thought, so that might constitute some sort of improvement.* Maybe she was waking up.

'You wouldn't happen to know the address of his place, would you?' asked Truchaud.

'Might do,' she replied, but as that was all she appeared to be about to say, her father erupted in a further volcano of invective. After a further moment of muttering, she produced an address in Chenôve; a southern suburb of Dijon.

'You see, you didn't have to make it so difficult, did you?' said her father. 'If you'd produced the answer in the first place, we could have avoided all the unpleasantness.' Truchaud felt very sorry for the girl, and realized that in order to have a more constructive visit to the boyfriend's flat, and assuming that the other girl was there, he needed to use a slightly different tack.

Chapter 22

Chenôve, Thursday morning

Gauvre got back into Truchaud's car, and as they drove out of the main gate, Truchaud told him that they were stopping off at his own domaine to collect his police sergeant. 'I think she might be useful in any questioning that we might want to do,' he explained. 'She's a highly trained investigator,' he continued, 'and fairly gentle to boot.'

He hoped Natalie would be up by the time they got back to the domaine, and fortunately she was, and had just put a second cup of coffee down. Dagmar was also back, though there was no sign of Simon Maréchale. Dagmar positively glowed, even more than Renate glowered at the dining room table. *Hmm*, Truchaud thought, *I know exactly what you've been up to, and moreover, so does Renate.* Maybe she wanted to be up to that too, but wasn't. 'Natalie, can we borrow you for a moment,' he asked.

'What had you in mind, *chef*?' she asked.

'I've got a missing person's case just come up, and we're going to visit a place where the girl in question might have gone to ground.'

'Lead on, *chef*,' she said. She burbled a few words in German at the two girls, who dropped their eyes fairly quickly, and returned to their respective breakfasts. Truchaud told them in English to stay at the domaine until he and Natalie got back, and doubted that they would be very long. As they left the house and returned to the car, he explained to her that the man sitting in his car was the missing girl's father, and that he wasn't a particularly amiable man. While he was telling her that, he made absolutely sure that his mouth wasn't in a position to be lip-read by the man in the car.

Natalie opened the back door of the car and climbed in. She put her arm between the front seats of the car and introduced herself as Sergeant Dutoit, Paris National Police.

'Delighted to meet you,' he replied, and probably wasn't being ironic Truchaud thought as he saw Gauvre's eyes giving her a quick up and down.

The day was warm and bright, *Good weather for the grapes*, Truchaud thought as they headed north up the Seventy-Four, through the villages. You would never have known as you drove through the simple little village of Vosne-Romanée that halfway up the unprepossessing hill behind the village was home to some of the most fabulous and expensive wine in the world. Through Vosne on the way north they came to a wall on the left side of the road, which announced the next village. The chateau of the Clos de Vougeot was visible over that wall, or if you weren't looking where you were going, you might see it through Maison Faiveley's own gate in the wall. There was a tight roundabout as the Seventy-Four now bypassed the village, but back in the day, the main road from Paris to Marseille would have gone through that narrow main street, not much wider than a tall man's arm span. Past the roundabout and back on the open Seventy-Four, looking left up the Côte you could see, climbing up its bank, the village of Chambolle-Musigny, and above that, the woods. Between the village and the road stood the village and Premiers Crus vines, some of which had gained an international reputation of their own. Among the vines were people at work, one of whom was leading a pony pulling a plough. There was also a big painted sign, which read, 'Nature, Chambolle-Musigny thank you.' The next village was also mostly up the hill too, but there were a couple of roadside cafés and a couple of vineyards had staggered down the hill to make rather disappointed contact with the edge of the road. That was Morey-Saint-Denis, and then there was a five kilometre stretch of open road until the Seventy-Four hit the small town of Gevrey-Chambertin, which must have been two-thirds the size of Nuits-Saint-Georges itself. There were a couple of junctions in the small town of Gevrey-Chambertin controlled by traffic lights, and Truchaud had never known them to be in sync with each other. Gauvre waved at a couple of people as they drove through the place. That would be an interesting conversation in the future:

'Who was that I saw you with in that tatty old Citroën the other day?'

'Oh, just some guys, you know.'

Truchaud was watching the road behaviour quite carefully. There were a number of tall blue tractors pottering along at fairly low speed on the Seventy-Four. Not everyone used ponies and ploughs, and drivers in 'Champs-Elysées Tractors' would be tempted to overtake them even if they weren't pre-pared to wait until the change in the double white line gave them permission. One large Merc pulled out and crossed the double white line to overtake the tractor.

'*Merde*!' said Gauvre, angrily.

'What?' asked Truchaud.

'You're going to turn around and chase him to give him a ticket, aren't you?'

'I thought about it.' He paused for a moment. 'Then I thought Sergeant Dutoit here was bound to remember the registration number and she'll jot it down for us to deal with later. Right?' Natalie replied from the back that she had,

'Got it, *chef*.'

It was a neat bit of by-play between the two of them, but it explained to Gauvre that the two of them weren't to be trifled with.

Beyond Gevrey, Brochon and Fixin, there was a little more countryside round Couchey, but this bit of countryside was populated with fruit trees rather than vines on the whole. Once the sign on the road said 'Marsannay-la-Côte,' Truchaud knew that they were on the road into Dijon's urban sprawl. Follow-ing the road which was now a dual carriageway interspersed with traffic lights there was a further sign with Marsannay-la-Côte and a red diagonal line through it, and a similar sized sign above it which read 'Chenôve'. There was little to tell between the two suburbs, but at the next set of traffic lights, Truchaud pulled into the outside lane and prepared to turn left and up the hill into the village itself.

'Where are you going?' asked Gauvre.

'Your daughter gave me an address, and that's where I'm heading. Is there a problem? Do you know a better way to get there?'

'No, sorry. I was obviously distracted.'

Truchaud didn't say anything, but chuckled internally. 'Look out for number 163. It should be on the right,' he said to Natalie and Gauvre, both of whom were sitting on the right.

'There it is.' Truchaud was impressed that Gauvre spotted it, or at least announced that he had spotted it before Natalie. *Perhaps,* he thought, *Gauvre had been here before.* Outside there was enough space to be able to park a medium-sized car, for example, a BX. It did say that it was residential parking only, but if the local Dijon Municipal Police caught him, he was sure he could talk his way out of it.

The winemaker and the police got out of the car, and walked up to the door. There were a few bells with names beside them, but none of them were the surname that Adèle had given him for Pierre. At the bottom was a button with the word 'concierge' printed beside it. A crackly rather distorted voice came out of a speaker below the line of names. 'Yes?' it asked.

'Commander Truchaud, National Police,' said Truchaud brusquely, wondering whether he really should be announcing himself that way, when he was playing the role of the Chief of Nuits-Saint-Georges Municipal Police. He continued. 'We're looking for a girl called Solange Gauvre, and we have reason to believe she may be on your premises.'

The door opened a crack and a pair of rather wizened elderly eyes looked out. 'We haven't got anyone of that name registered here,' she said.

'Yes, but we understand she is staying with Pierre.'

'LeCaillou?' the old woman asked.

That would do, he thought, *it would get us through the door.* What a silly name to call a boy, if your name was already 'Pebble', then probably the worst choice of name for your son would be 'Peter, the stone'. Some people didn't deserve to be parents, but then Gauvre, on his right, was hardly a shining light himself.

'Where is he?' he asked.

The little old lady opened the door casting an eye over Truchaud's and Natalie's warrant cards as they passed her. She then poked Gauvre with a bony finger, 'Where's your card?' she asked.

Truchaud explained that he was the girl's father, and that he wouldn't be making any trouble. He then looked at the wine-maker and said, 'That is true, isn't it?'

'What?' Truchaud wondered whether he had taught Adèle how to speak; they had the same limited vocabulary.

'That you're not going to make any trouble?'

'If you say so,' Gauvre replied.

The old lady pointed them down an ill-lit ground-floor corridor, with intermittent doors off on both sides. The building was certainly deeper than it appeared from the road. He wondered whether the upper two floors comprised single maisonettes each. 'Third on the left,' said the concierge. It was apparent that she wasn't going to accompany them to the door.

Truchaud balled his fist and knocked three times on the door. 'Pierre LeCaillou?' he called, 'Police.'

'Huh?' came from within. 'Just a moment.' Pause. Then they heard an expletive, then a 'Coming'. The door creaked open a little but the chain was still on it. Truchaud waved his warrant card at the half-face he could see behind the chain. The face looked puzzled, but the door was pushed closed, and the sound came of the chain being removed. The door then opened fully and the half-dressed young man said politely but bewilderedly, 'Sorry, what's this all about?'

He was just wearing a pair of trousers, but had no shoes or socks on, nor was he wearing a shirt. His long ginger hair looked as if he had been wrestling with it, and he had at least three days' growth of stubble.

'That's him,' came from Gauvre behind Truchaud. 'Here, you, what have you done with my daughter?'

'Oh fuck!' said the youth, glaring balefully at Truchaud. 'What did you bring him here for?' Without waiting for an answer, he shouted deeper into the flat, 'It's your old man, and he's brought the fucking filth with him.'

The flat, such as it was, had a door off either side: one into a kitchenette, and on the other side, into what looked like it could be a bathroom. Straight ahead was a wider space behind an open doorway, which had a table with a laptop on it under a rather large but tatty window. Truchaud and Natalie followed the youth quickly as he bolted down the corridor into the room. Through the door on the right was a fairly large bed, and in it was a raven-haired girl with studs round her mouth. She was covered by a duvet, which she had pulled up to her chin, her hands tipped with black-painted nails. Her hair was a matching black as was the lipstick she wore. There were small gold, or was it gilt, rings through her upper lip, and a similar sized ring through her nose. She had one further sharp gilt rod poking out through the middle of her left cheek, which seemed much paler than the colour of her hands. Truchaud was already fairly convinced that the sum total of her apparel was the metalwork, the bed and its duvet.

'What are you doing in there, you slut?' snarled Gauvre at the girl.

'Mr Gauvre,' said Natalie softly. 'Please calm down. This isn't helping.'

'But that's my daughter he's got in that bed. Arrest him.'

'On what charges would you like me to arrest Mr LeCaillou?' Natalie asked still very gently and menacingly softly.

The boy was very nobly standing between the adults and the girl in the bed, who was hanging on very tightly to the bed-clothes. Gauvre moved forwards towards her, and nobody was quite sure what happened next, except presumably Natalie, as he was, a moment later, sitting on the floor with his back up against the radiator in front of the window.

'No, sir,' she said, returning to her previous relaxed position. 'I don't think we want to do that, sir, do we?'

'Here,' Gauvre bellowed from his position on the floor. 'Did you see what she just did to me?'

'No,' said a completely honest, but nonetheless impressed Truchaud. 'Actually, I didn't. I would need to watch the instant replay of that one. But I would advise you to remain exactly where you are. Everybody needs to calm down, right now.' It was now the Commander's turn to be assertive. He turned to Gauvre. 'Are you hurt?' he asked.

'No,' came the reply.

'Good. Now stay exactly where you are.' Next he turned to Natalie, 'Are you okay?' he asked.

'Fine,' she replied.

'Also good. Now,' he turned back to Gauvre, 'explain to me exactly why you want this young man arrested.'

'Because he's fucked my daughter, and she's still a child.'

'Dad, I'm seven-fucking-teen,' came straight back from the girl in the bed.

'Do you agree with that statement, Mr Gauvre?' asked Natalie; 'that she's seventeen?' she continued without the expletive.

'Yes,' he said, 'and that still makes her a child.'

'Not by the French law of consent,' she replied. 'She may not be allowed to vote, drink alcoholic liquor in bars without the presence of her guardians, or bear firearms in French Military uniform, but she is old enough to consent to have sexual relations, and has, in fact, been old enough to give such consent for the past two years. However, there is no evidence yet that any sexual act has, in fact, taken place.'

'But she's in that bed, and he's half-naked too,' Gauvre started to whine.

'What do you want me to say?' asked the girl, 'All right then, we've just been fucking ourselves silly. Is that what you want me to say?'

'Oh!' Gauvre moaned again. 'How do you think Étienne's going to feel when he hears about this? Do you think he's still going to want to marry you?'

'I sincerely hope not,' she replied, 'but it's always possible that the stupid prat still will, and we're going to have to think of something else. Maybe I'll have to try being a dyke.' She looked at LeCaillou for a moment, and almost smiled, 'Sorry, I mean bi.'

'Let me get this straight,' said Natalie. 'Do you, or do you not wish to be married to this man Étienne … whatever his surname is?'

'No.' There was absolute certainty in that monosyllable.

'And do you wish to marry this man Pierre LeCaillou?' She nodded at the boy standing next to the bed.

'Er, not right now either. It's quite fun and all, but I don't think either of us wants to get married or nothing. It's not like we've got any money. So how could we afford to do something like that? Huh?'

'You've got a fortune waiting for you, young woman, when you marry Étienne Leduc.'

'Yeah, but it won't be my money: it'll be your money, and that poor old sod Mr Leduc's money. It won't be anything to do with me.'

'You stupid young woman. What do you think this was all for? Your mother and I just want you and Adèle to be happy. That's what this has been about.'

'Well, maybe you should marry Adèle off to Étienne then,' she replied. 'Have you asked her whether she would like to? Oh sorry, I forgot, what we want has bugger all to do with any of it, does it? But she's said it's all right: even Adèle's old enough.' She added the last while jerking a thumb at Natalie, but still hanging on tightly to the duvet with the other hand.

It was beginning to come into Gauvre's head that he had lost this argument, and in all probability, lost this daughter for good as well. Truchaud could see that his eyes were beginning to become filmy. 'I think I had better just go,' he said.

'I think that's probably the right decision, yes,' Truchaud agreed with him, and helped him back to his feet from his position against the radiator. The two men walked out to the door, without another word.

Natalie stayed behind for a moment, fishing in her pocket for a card. 'Look,' she said, 'I really am sorry for the home invasion we have committed on you today,' she said. 'If you need to talk to me or my *chef*, or wish to make a complaint, just give us a call.'

'I don't think you were ever invading my home,' replied LeCaillou from her left shoulder. 'I think all you and your boss were trying to do was to show her old man where to get off.'

'You may well be right there,' she said.

'Look,' said Solange, pulling aside the duvet, showing she was completely clothed underneath the duvet, complete with jeans and even wearing laced-up boots. 'We saw you arrive, and knew what was going to go down. Pierre just had time to get his shoes and shirt off before you knocked on the door.'

Natalie grinned at both of them, 'You kids!' she said.

'Don't tell him that,' Solange replied with a grin. 'And don't tell him that I'm still a virgin neither.'

'Are you?' she asked, then smiled and turned on her heel. 'I wouldn't dream of it,' she chuckled sadly and followed the men out of the building.

Chapter 23

Nuits-Saint-Georges, later Thursday morning

Truchaud deposited a sad and rather deflated Gauvre at his main gate. It was rather like dumping a bag of potato peelings out of the car at the local rubbish tip. There hadn't been a word spoken on the return journey from Chenôve, and certainly Truchaud had felt no urge to break the silence. Natalie climbed into the front of the BX after acknowledging Gauvre's retreat having given him one of Duquesne's cards, in case he had wanted to get in touch with the local police again. Truchaud remarked how astounded he was that the inheritance laws could make such problems within families.

Natalie looked at him; she was obviously thinking about the other case. 'I think we need to wait until we've got the report back from the lab about our body,' she replied. 'If it does belong, as we are fairly sure, to Horst Witter, then the things that people may be driven to do by the inheritance laws may suddenly be pulled into sharper focus.'

Truchaud pulled up in the domaine and they both got out. He was in the mood for coffee, and Natalie needed little persuasion to join him. They looked out of the front window of the dining room, and could see the tops of two heads, nodding in conversation, through the windscreen of the camper, so the girls were safe too, and talking to each other again. The breakfast table had been cleared so presumably Dad had been fed, though there was little evidence as to where he and the rest of the family had got to. The coffee machine was fairly rapid and it took little time to generate two cups of hot creamy coffee.

'Well,' said Truchaud as he stirred his cup, 'what did you think of all that?'

'A very sad, disintegrating family being driven apart by money. I don't think Gauvre is a bad man, just a rather stupid man, who, sadly, doesn't place a higher value on either of his daughters than that of a basic commodity. And at least one of those daughters is aware of that, and is rebelling.'

'Do you think that she loves Pierre?' he asked.

'I doubt it, but at least she has found an ally in her war against her father. I think the question that is more relevant is whether Pierre loves her.'

'Why do you ask that?'

'Well, I think he probably does, which is why he is willing to let her use him in her mind games with her father.' She told him about the last words that she and Solange had exchanged, and how totally insensitive to Pierre's feelings they had been. Even if Pierre wasn't devoted to her, the fact that, in their own little theatre piece, they had been playing the parts of rampantly sexually active teenagers, Pierre's self-respect would have taken a nose-dive if it became public knowledge that they hadn't actually done the deed, even once.

'She wasn't going to let us arrest him.'

'She knew damn well that we hadn't got any grounds to arrest him. Statutory rape was not something we could arrest him for. She was old enough to legally consent to having sex and she knew it. It wasn't necessary for her to actually have sex to win that round. It merely required her father to think she had. It was only fair that she made it absolutely certain we had nothing else to arrest him for. It was the nicest and most inno-cent-smelling student's flat I have ever visited. There wasn't even the aroma of fruity male socks.' She stirred her cup. 'It was almost as if the whole thing was a set-up.' Truchaud thought about the smells of the flat in Dijon that he had visited a couple of months ago, and the various scents that had pervaded that. He chuckled as he thought of the mixed reek of male hormones and cannabis that was 'Hairy Eddie'. He then thought, rather sadly, about Suzette, and thought that sometime that day he would have to brief her family of their need to fight for Simon, if they wanted to hang on to him. That was, of course, always assuming he was not involved in Horst's disappearance.

'So,' he mused to himself rather than particularly expecting an answer, 'where do they go from there.'

'Well,' Natalie replied anyway. 'She's thrown away her family and her home, hasn't she? She may still be a virgin now, but I doubt she will be by the end of the week. She's got nowhere else to go, so she will stay there with him, whatever she really wants to do. Tied in a relationship, with a pleasant enough lad, who, however, she doesn't love, she'll be pregnant by the autumn … and then?'

Both of them shuddered and Truchaud felt he needed a change of subject. He picked up the phone and dialled Captain Duquesne. 'Hello,' he said, 'any news from the Dijon crime lab yet?'

'Nothing so far,' he replied amiably. 'If you feel like popping round for a coffee some time, all you have to do is turn up.'

Truchaud felt guilty looking at the hot steaming cup on the table in front of him. An image rose up in front of him of an old friend he had forgotten, and his need for coffee and companionship: a friend he had replaced with a different chum, but the same drug. In his middle age he was reliving the parable of adolescence. He looked at Natalie for a moment, and then said, down the phone, 'See you soon.'

'What?' she asked.

'I was just asking if he had heard anything from the lab.'

'No, I heard that. I was just wondering what that look was all about?'

'What look?'

They locked eyes for a moment, then she gave in. 'Oh never mind.' Both pairs of eyes dropped back to the coffee cups, Truchaud's for one, with relief rather than anything else. One thing he was now certain of: she was certainly aware that he was looking at her, as that was the second time in twenty-four hours that she had commented on it. He would have to stop even glancing at her, like the moment just past. She was aware of even those.

He poured the rest of the coffee down his throat – it was still a little warm to do that comfortably – and without looking at her he told her he was going out. He climbed into his BX and drove out through the wrought-iron gates. That brought Dagmar and Renate out of the camper and face to face with Natalie at the front of the house. 'Who was that going out?' asked Dagmar.

'Only Truchaud,' replied Natalie. 'He has things to do.'

'Any specific things?' asked Dagmar, still playfully.

'We'll have to ask him when he comes back, won't we?' she replied, apparently nonchalantly, though Renate, for one, wasn't convinced.

Meanwhile, Truchaud was saving it till he was outside the gates before he actually thought about where he was going to go. It would have been fairly well known that he was currently surrounded by 'a bevy of beauteous female youth', so he would have felt that he stood out fairly obviously if he, a Frenchman, parked himself on his own outside the Café du Centre. Anyway he had just had a cup of coffee, and it was too early for lunch. He thought about swinging by his new office again to see if anything else had come in since his departure on his adventure with Gauvre. If he had thought about it for any longer, he would have realized his car had ideas of its own anyway, and that it was taking him into the eastern side of town, down into the smart modern housing, where for example, a local doctor's family might live.

The car pulled up beside the pavement and its door opened, depositing its driver on the pavement. There was no doubt in Truchaud's mind that all the decision-making had been the BX's, and that it had had nothing to do with him. But as he was now here, he might as well go in and say 'hi' to Geneviève.

She was obviously pleased to see him. Yes, her husband was at work with the sick and needy of Nuits-Saint-Georges and its environs. Yes, her daughter was still in Dijon, putting the finishing touches to her dissertation. Yes, it was her daughter that Truchaud wanted to talk to her about.

'Oh?' said Geneviève, 'she's not in trouble, is she?'

'Not directly,' said Truchaud, getting control of a conversation for the first time in about an hour, 'but she is in danger of losing Maréchale's interest.'

'What?' said the one woman that Truchaud had failed to fight for and had therefore got away. Was that why he was here: because he had let Suzette's mother get away because he had never had the bottle to fight for her?

'There is an extremely attractive young woman who has recently arrived in Nuits-Saint-Georges, and Simon is very aware of her,' he said.

'What, you mean that police sergeant you brought down with you?' Geneviève giggled almost like the teenager she really wasn't. 'I thought it was you who had his eyes on her,' she added. *God, really?* Truchaud thought. *Is it that obvious?*

'My dear old stick,' he said redirecting her thoughts for a moment, 'the only person I still have eyes for is you.' *Not bad*, he thought, *sadly no longer true, but a reasonable performance*. The sooner everyone stopped thinking the truth, then at least he would still be able to continue working with Natalie, and 'with Natalie' really meant 'in Paris'.

'Oh, you!' she said still chuckling. 'So, who are we talking about then?'

'There's a girl from East Germany called Dagmar Witter, who is a distant relation of the Laforges, and has recently arrived in town. She appears to have caught Simon's eye.'

'How distant?' asked Geneviève, catching on to the implications immediately.

'Close enough,' replied Truchaud.

'Would you know whether she might be interested in him?'

'I haven't known her long enough to know whether her current interest is one of those ephemeral things that will vanish by the end of the week, or whether it is something that we ought to be watching out for.'

'And we have to ask ourselves what your interest is in all this?'

'I had rather you hadn't asked that question, though I was afraid you might. My own personal financial interests, I suppose, would have to side with Dagmar.'

'Oh?'

'As you know, Marie-Claire and Michelle, who are the active members of our respective families, are intent on bringing the Laforges and the Truchauds together into a formal partnership. Neither of them, however, is particularly skilled as a winemaker, though I have a feeling that the boys will be when they grow up. Until then, they need a lead winemaker, probably for at least the next ten years, and that is where Simon would fit in. Marrying him into one of the families would be a very elegant solution, and apart from Michelle, there aren't any girls in our family. And don't think that idea hadn't occurred to your brother, Jean, even though he says he's vehemently against arranged marriages.'

'Oh!' she said, as if the idea had only just occurred to her. 'I tell you something,' she said, 'I think you need Simon more than we do.'

'I certainly agree with that, up to a point. Right now, if we find after a while that we can't stand the man, we could always sack him. Once he is a signed up member of the family, it becomes altogether a different kettle of fish.'

'There is, of course, one other solution to your family's problem.'

'Oh yes? What might that be?'

'You could always marry Marie-Claire. That would really bind the two families together as a single unit.'

Truchaud shuddered. 'God forbid!' he said. He was aware that very successful arranged marriages had been organized between people who knew each other far less than he and Marie-Claire. What was okay for the Bourbons dynasty did not appeal to him now. He continued, after recomposing himself, 'Anyway, something inside me told me that I should put you in the picture. Perhaps also, because I actually rather like Suzette, and I would hate for her to think that the Truchauds had betrayed her just for the sake of a few euros.'

'On the other hand, she would respect you for looking out for Bruno, who has already lost so much, and must be worried about his grandfather as well. You need to be looking out for your family first and foremost, Charlie.'

'Suppose so,' he said glumly. 'I think all I wanted to do was to absolve myself of any responsibility in this. Commander Truchaud goes cluck!'

'Like a chicken?'

'Got it in one! Now what would be really convenient is for my mobile phone to go off, to summon me back to the town hall for an emergency.'

'Don't you like it here?' she asked.

'No, I suddenly feel uncomfortable discussing these sort of affairs with you.'

'You mean affairs of the bedchamber? When we were kids we talked about everything, all the time. It's really only very recently that anyone, apart from the lowliest peasant, was allowed to fall in love. That was their reward for being a serf. Most of those with any social standing at all had to marry according to their status, to preserve, and if anything to *enhance* the family's wealth. We were really the first generation to have had that choice, and maybe even we didn't really.'

'Do you really think we talked about everything all the time when we were kids?' he asked. 'I seem to remember one topic that we never touched with a bargepole.'

'Oh really? What was that?'

'Us.'

The two middle-aged people looked at each other properly for the first time in quarter of a century, and were now saying the things to each other that they should have said then. It was too late now. Her green eyes opened wide, reminding him how she used to look all those years ago. All she needed to do was go slightly out of focus, and the lines would vanish, and yes, from her perspective, for him to get more colour in more hair. He thought about it for a moment. For someone who had never really pulled any sort of relationship together his whole life, he was having an awful lot of relationship thoughts at the moment. Maybe he was going into the male menopause, and his system was telling him that if he didn't get on with it now, it would soon be too late. But then with Jenny, it had been too late for years, and he knew it.

'This isn't fair on anyone,' she said. 'You came here telling me that my daughter's relationship is under threat, and then you start trying to re-awaken old feelings in her mother. What are you playing at, Charlie?'

'To be honest, I don't know. One thing I am certain of is that I wasn't trying to stir up an old romance between you and me. Certainly, when I arrived, all I wanted to do was warn you that there's a Dagmar on the patch.'

'And probably not to tell anyone that it was you who'd told me.' She completed the sentence just like they always had when they were together.

'I suppose something like that, yes.'

'I accept that and I'll pass it on to Suzette when I next speak to her.'

'Today, please,' insisted Truchaud.

'Well, of course, today; she's my daughter. We speak to each other every day.' She looked at him surprised. Wasn't that how all kids related to their parents? Truchaud doubted that the Gauvres spoke to each other for days on end, even when they were under the same roof.

Truchaud didn't stay much longer. He had done what his car had told him to do, and there wasn't anything else that either of them wanted to talk about, although they could no doubt have found something. However, what he really wanted to do was talk to the forensics lab in Dijon, and that would have been singularly inappropriate for him to do from a private house unrelated to the case. As his phone resolutely refused to go off of its own volition, he made his excuses and said that he had an appointment in ten minutes at the town hall, and that he'd better get there now. He could have walked there from Château Girand within those ten minutes, but his car was sitting outside, wagging its rear windscreen wiper, expecting him to take it for a walk, so he climbed in and drove off.

Chapter 24

Nuits-Saint-Georges, Thursday, midday

Truchaud pulled up in the car park and climbed out of his battered old car. The town hall seemed quiet as he walked in, and even the adenoidal girl behind the reception desk only looked up momentarily, just to check that it was actually the man she expected it to be who'd just walked past her wearing a trench coat at the height of summer.

He walked up the stairs to the office, and, as the door was locked, he took out the key that he had been allocated. He hoped that there was no alarm behind the door, as nobody had given him any codes to type in, nor, come to think about it, had he been shown the location of a keypad. He held his breath, imagining for a moment the look on the adenoidal girl's face downstairs when the alarm went off. But the longer he waited, the longer nothing happened, and finally, he shut the door and walked through into his inner office.

He picked up the phone and dialled. 'Is Mr Castaigne there?' he asked, 'the Investigating Magistrate?'

'Hold on a moment,' came the reply. There was a click or two, and then, 'De Castaigne. Who's this?'

'Truchaud here, Nuits-Saint-Georges Municipal Police, phoning to see if you've heard anything from the blood test yet.'

'The body in the woods …'

'Just west of the vineyards, yes,' Truchaud completed. It was almost like two secret agents passing a secret code between each other.

'I was talking to one of the technicians just before they went off for lunch,' Castaigne replied. 'And they haven't found any

213

reason yet to prove that the body and the donor of the sample aren't related.'

'That means?' Truchaud pushed.

'I think it means that they're seventy-five per cent convinced that the two are blood relatives. There are no major gene markers that are different, aside from the obvious.'

'The obvious?'

'The X and Y chromosomes. The donor was an XX whereas the corpse was XY. You know, male and female.'

'Well, we knew that anyway, and it doesn't prove anything.'

'Yes, it does. It proves that the two samples did not come from the same person. That would formally need to be proven in court.'

'Well, we know that anyway,' replied Truchaud, slightly cross.

'But the lab didn't. That was something we didn't tell them: all they got from us were two samples, and we told them we were looking for a match. The first thing they came back with, very quickly, was that they did not come from the same person. We said, yes we knew that, but could the samples come from two people who were closely related? They are now in the process of answering that question, and at this moment in time I am informed that it looks promising that they will. To be absolutely definite about that, I'm afraid that we're going to have to wait a little longer. They have to do more tests.'

'Would you have any objection to us investigating further, on the assumption that it will come back as a positive match?'

'As long as you don't have a major temper tantrum with us if I come back and say, "actually, very sorry, but there was no such match".'

'I don't do tantrums,' Truchaud replied.

'I'm very glad to hear it,' replied the magistrate. 'So, where are you thinking of going next?'

'I was going to call a meeting with the local Captain of Gendarmes, the National Police Sergeant you met, and myself. It might also involve a spot of food.'

'Haven't you had lunch yet?'

'Not yet, no.'

'Go forth and be nourished, Commander; it's good for the brain.'

'Will do. Speak to you soon.'

The next two calls were to Duquesne and Natalie, suggesting that they meet at the Café du Centre in five minutes, with a view to lunch and conversation.

And in five minutes time someone sitting outside the café might have spotted walking down the street from the north, a middle-aged man of medium height in a trench coat. Walking in from the east, past the post office, was a stocky man marching in a smart blue uniform, and just turning onto the street from the south was a very pretty blonde woman in slacks, who looked rather younger than either of the two men. Whether that person sitting outside the café would have realized, before they all sat down at the same table that they were well known to each other, we shall have to ask him, once we find out who he is.

Truchaud explained the nature of the conversation he had just had with de Castaigne. 'So that's it? We assume that the body is Witter's?' said Duquesne. 'It's fair enough. It wasn't as if it was likely to be anyone else's. We really don't get many missing people in Nuits-Saint-Georges.'

Natalie chuckled, and remarked that she and her *chef* had already solved the case of a different missing person that very morning.

'Oh?' said Duquesne. 'I didn't hear anything about that.'

'If there had been anything for you to hear,' replied Truchaud, 'I can assure you that you'd have heard of it. I think it really did fall within the Municipal Police's brief, especially bearing in mind that it landed on my desk.' He explained the Gauvre story and its denouement. Natalie added her concerns for the future, so that if it all kicked off again later, after she and Truchaud were back in Paris, then at least the Gendarmerie was briefed. Natalie also promised to write it up quickly so that there would be some paperwork on file. In exchange,

Duquesne promised that the Gendarmerie would maintain a watching brief only on the case.

'So where do we go now with the Witter case?'

'Well, that was what I wanted to talk to you about,' replied Truchaud as Christine's son wandered over with a handful of menus and bade them all good day. Was Natalie going to do the tourist thing and order a plate full of snails, and if so, were the men going to keep her company? They all went for a rather light option despite the morning that the two civilian police had had: liver pâté followed by sea bass, just accompanied by a carafe of water, *Château Municipale*. Somehow, none of them felt like wine: in Duquesne's case that was because in his uniform he stood out like a sore thumb, and it was bad public relations for a gendarme to be seen with a drink in his hand.

'And you look very like a policeman who's on duty in that trench coat too, Truchaud,' he remarked. 'So guzzle away, mademoiselle. You couldn't possibly be on duty, unless you've just been arrested by these two policemen, but they are both so hungry that despite your criminal activities, they have just had to stop for lunch.'

'Or I could be Mata Hari, the spy, and I'm working on you to give up your secrets,' she replied. They all chuckled at that, especially Truchaud, as he knew that it was all quite possible, as far as he was concerned. He redirected the conversation.

'Anyway, on the assumption that the body is the one we're looking for, we need to decide how he got there and why. The only person we know who shoots, or rather shot people in the back of the head, was the late unlamented Molleau. The question is why Inspector Molleau would have shot Witter in the head.'

'Well, Commander,' replied Natalie, 'he also tried to shoot you. We rather assumed that that was to keep you quiet, as you had got rather too close to what he was getting up to.'

'But we didn't know of the existence of Witter at that time. If he was going to silence someone about Witter at that point, he should have nuked the Gendarmerie,' remarked Duquesne drily.

'I assumed that I was the target to silence my thoughts about Jérome Laforge. Suzette and I found his body similarly executed in his office. He took out Laforge in the spring, which must have been at least three months after he took Witter out.'

'Okay, so that's the time span. Was he active before Witter in the winter? Is there anyone else we should be looking for?'

All three of them looked at each other and none of them could think of a positive answer to that one. Natalie paused and then said slowly, 'Unless …' she started, then stopped as the pâté was arriving. A side plate was put in front of each of them with a portion of butter wrapped in foil, and a couple of slices of toast. The centrepiece of the plate was a slice of smooth-textured brown pâté whose aroma certainly made Truchaud salivate. Truchaud thought it would go particularly well with a sweet white wine. Traditionally, foie gras, which this wasn't, but could be, was served with Sauternes or Monbazillac, but as neither of them were on the wine list anyway, as they came from the other side of France, they weren't an option.

'They don't make a sweet wine in Burgundy,' Truchaud had observed when he was holding forth about wine in Paris to anyone who might listen. Now he wondered whether that was something he might get Maréchale to do, as an experiment with some grapes from the wrong side of the Seventy-Four sometime.

'Pâté's good,' said Natalie, crunching happily on a piece of toast spread with pâté.

'You were about to say?' said both men simultaneously, as they emptied their mouths.

'Well, I was just thinking, suppose someone already knew about his skills as an executioner?'

'You mean both these killings were contract killings?'

'Yes, that's it. Certainly, if you want to kill someone, and don't think you're up to doing the deed yourself, or perhaps you're afraid of getting caught, what better way than hiring a hit man to do the deed for you?'

'That would probably be an expensive way of going about it,' remarked Truchaud, looking around to make sure no one was eavesdropping on their conversation.

'It might have been the cheaper of two evils,' remarked Natalie drily. 'Look at it this way: what was Horst Witter about to do?'

'We think he was about to claim part ownership of Domaine Laforge.'

'Assuming he was claiming his grandfather's share, he was claiming fifty per cent of Domaine Laforge.'

'But hang on,' chipped in Duquesne, 'do we know that's what he was up to?'

'Well, we do know that the whole of last year he kept coming back to Nuits-Saint-Georges, and spent the whole of last harvest working at Laforge's. He would have got to know the ins and outs of the business quite well by then. He may well have gone back to Boppard and got to work with his little pocket calculator, and the sums would have given him an enormous number of noughts. What would you do if you realized you had inherited a half-share of a domaine like Laforge's, captain?'

'Right back at you, Commander, as the reality is that you do,' said the captain.

'Ah yes, but it is my family, and while Bruno wants to make wine from Domaine Truchaud, it is worth more to me as a going concern. But to Witter that might not have been the case. Supposing he had said, "Half of this is mine, and I want to cash it in. I'll take my half and sell it on to the Chinese, and go and buy myself a *Schloss* somewhere in Germany with the proceeds?" That's a statement that would have rocked Laforge back on his heels. Look at it this way. If a total stranger appeared out of the blue, and told you that he was going to inherit half of your domaine, what would you do?'

'Well, surely Domaine Truchaud is only worth the annual product,' replied Duquesne.

'Not exactly,' said Natalie. 'There're the house and the vineyards. And Simon said that the most valuable of all the vineyards he works is your parcel in the Clos de Vougeot, which is worth more than the Laforge's plot in the Echézeaux. They're both Grands Crus, and I hate to think what they would be worth on the open market, even more to the owners of the plots next door, especially as they would expand the sizes of their own parcels.'

Truchaud looked at his hands: he really had no idea at all how much those plots would fetch on the open market. 'I have no idea,' he said.

'But I bet Laforge did, probably down to the nearest penny. I bet he also worked out the cost of hiring Molleau as a contract killer. That option worked out cheaper.'

At that moment in time Madame Tournier herself arrived with three steaming plates of fish, potatoes lightly dusted with fresh parsley and haricot beans. 'And how are my favourite police today?' she asked cheerfully.

'Is it good for the image of the place for the police to be eating here?' asked Duquesne.

'Well, I haven't noticed a drop-off in sales when you eat here, so I suppose it must be.'

'Or do the organized crime capos in Nuits-Saint-Georges eat somewhere else?' Natalie remarked drily.

All three of them looked at her with a slightly shocked expression. 'Well, that's one possible explanation,' she said.

Mrs Tournier walked off with the side plates on which the pâté had been served. The three police removed the paper hats from the dishes, and tucked into the delicately poached fish underneath. Truchaud immediately thought of Domaine de la Vougeraie's white Clos Blanc de Vougeot, for which he had a very soft spot, and would have been a very good accompaniment to this fish dish. He restarted the conversation about Jérome Laforge. 'At that point in time he struck lucky,' Truchaud remarked sadly.

'How so?'

'My dad appeared on his doorstep with an offer he couldn't refuse.'

'Huh?'

'The whole stock of last year's Vosne-Romanée.'

'Would that have paid for the cost of a contract killer?'

'It would if you had labelled it Richebourg, and sold it off abroad.'

'But it would have taken him years to convert that into cash.'

'And that was his problem, and perhaps that wasn't what Molleau was willing to do, which was possibly why Laforge went back to my dad to negotiate a long-term partnership. Maybe he was trying to take over the Vougeot vineyard.'

'Your brother would never have stood for that.'

'I know. Convenient he wasn't there. I wonder if any of them knew I was still around, at least in spirit?'

'I rather think they probably didn't. May I ask you, *chef*, what would have happened within your family if he had succeeded in killing you?'

'Well, there would have just been Dad, Michelle and Bruno left. Within a short time that count would have been down to just Michelle and Bruno. In order to make the business viable, I suspect that she would have put the whole shebang on the market, and moved what was left of the family out of the area to the seaside or somewhere where you go skiing or something else, I don't know.'

'Quite, and that would have been the end of Domaine Truchaud. Have you any idea who might have bought it? Did Molleau perhaps own a share of Domaine Laforge? Was that his pay-off? If that's the case, do any of the survivors know about that?' Natalie was flying high. 'All this leaves us with the current problem: where does that put Dagmar? I suspect her life is seriously in danger at the moment.'

'I think that is what we have to work out next. Do we know what everyone feels about Dagmar being a family member, and come to think about it, what does she feel about the family? We do know that Old Mr Laforge appears to have taken quite a shine to her. Does Maréchale know she's the boss's great-niece? What does Marie-Claire think? What does Jacquot think? The three of them looked at each other.

'May I suggest a plan,' said Truchaud. 'Natalie, your project is Dagmar. You and she speak to each other best. Would you rather pick her up first, with you taking the lead, or should we go and see the Laforges first, with me taking the lead?'

She looked at him and shrugged. 'I'm easy either way,' she said.

No, you're not, he thought but didn't voice that statement. He turned to Duquesne. 'Captain, may I request that you are available with your lads in case either of us runs into trouble? How does that look?'

One of the girls arrived at the table and asked if they had considered a dessert, which all three of them declined. 'Coffee?' she asked. There was no way Captain Duquesne ever refused coffee, so the general consensus was that was fine. She cleared the table around them and wandered off with the used crockery and cutlery. 'Can we have the bill at the same time?' asked Duquesne.

'Together?' she asked.

'All in one would be fine,' he replied.

All three of them waited for the coffee thinking about their plans for the afternoon, and when it arrived, they stirred their coffee. 'I think that fits the bill,' said Duquesne, picking it up from the table.

Truchaud took it from him. 'Municipal expense,' he said smiling, knowing full well that particular bill would never make its way into the town hall.

Chapter 25

Nuits-Saint-Georges, Thursday afternoon

Natalie walked back to the town hall with Truchaud to pick up his car. A quick walk through the office revealed nothing that Fauquet couldn't do, though if something cropped up, he had Truchaud's number. 'Is it interesting, *chef*?' he asked, aware that his new boss and his old sidekick were working a case.

'I'll tell you about it when it breaks,' said Truchaud with a smile, and with that, he and Natalie left the building and collected his BX downstairs, and drove into the back streets.

They walked into Laforge's shop, and to Truchaud's surprise, it was Suzette behind the counter. 'I thought you were still in Dijon, working on your thesis,' he said.

'I handed it in this morning,' she said. 'Thought I'd best get back to work this afternoon,' she paused, and then added, 'and get some money in my pocket again.' Whether she had talked to her mother over lunch, she wasn't letting on, certainly not yet.

'Is Marie-Claire in the house?' he asked her.

Looking at Natalie for a moment she said, 'Yes, I think she's in the back office. Do you want to go on through?' She knew now who Truchaud was and how he related to the business. She was working out where she had seen Natalie before: that dinner during the spring. She had been the Paris police officer who had taken Truchaud back to the Capital from Nuits-Saint-Georges; but it had been very civilised, she had waited till after dinner.

Marie-Claire was indeed in the back office, as was Celestine, hammering away at a keyboard. Truchaud momentarily recalled the sound of a typing pool from his days as a young policeman, all those years ago, and thought that the absence of that infernal racket was one advance that the arrival of the computer age had made.

'Any chance of a moment?' he asked Marie-Claire, as if he was giving her an option.

She saw through him in an instant. 'Do you want to come on through to the back?' she asked.

'Would you like coffee?' Celestine chirped up as they walked through.

'Nothing for us, thank you,' said Truchaud. 'We've just had one.'

'Not for me either,' said Marie-Claire. 'Thank you, Celestine.'

Celestine's shoulders slumped as she went back to her terminal. Not only was her input not wanted in this supposedly interesting meeting, but she wasn't even required to help. There were moments when life just wasn't fair.

They parked in the sitting room of the private part of Laforge's domaine. Marie-Claire looked expectantly at the two police officers, realizing instinctively that this wasn't a domestic reprise of the visit the night before.

Truchaud explained that they thought they had found Horst. 'Dead,' he added rather melodramatically.

Marie-Claire looked at them and simply asked, 'How?' None of the histrionic, 'Oh, how awfuls' came from Marie-Claire.

'We dug him up,' he explained, equally tersely. 'The body is in the path lab in Dijon, undergoing tests to formally identify him, but we're fairly sure it's him.'

'Surely Dagmar would be able to identify him. He is her brother.'

'It's not that simple. He'd been buried for quite a while, and the body really isn't fresh enough for visual identification purposes.'

'This is beginning to sound quite gruesome. What are they going to use? Dental records? That's what they do on the telly.' *She didn't appear to know anything about the case,* mused Truchaud, feeling rather relieved.

224

'Not that easy either,' said Natalie. 'To use dental records the victim has to have visited a dentist prior to his demise.'

'And he had a perfect set of teeth?'

'In one,' Natalie replied.

Truchaud took over. He was determined to have one conversation of which he remained in control, despite Natalie's presence. She wasn't wearing any scent, but hers was a powerful presence in the atmosphere around her.

'At this moment, we are gathering information about him, as we know he is missing, and we think the body we found may be his remains. Were you aware he was your cousin?'

'Well, I am now.'

'When did you first become aware he was?'

'The day before yesterday, when you first brought Dagmar round. Once I understood that, I realized Horst must have been my cousin too.'

'What were your feelings about that?' Truchaud asked.

She looked at him slightly askance, then replied, 'Probably that she was lucky not to have found us when she was younger and my uncle was still alive. She might well have been to his taste when she was fourteen. No, that's unfair, although probably true. I don't know.' She looked uncomfortably at Truchaud.

'And your thoughts about the inheritance laws and how she fits in?'

'What? You mean that technically she might own a bit of Domaine Laforge?'

'In a word ... half.'

Her eyebrows rose in surprise. 'Explain it to me. How does that work?'

'Well, look back to the mid-fifties. There would have been the three Laforge adults: your grandfather; his brother, who wasn't dead, although all France thought he was; and your great-aunt who was in Indochina. All of them technically inherited a third share of Domaine Laforge when their father died. Then your great-aunt died without having either married or procreated, so her share reverted half and half to her two brothers. Your great-uncle was poorly, but recovering in

Germany, and had fathered a daughter. So, let's call his fifty per cent entitlement in the domaine *the German Share*. On his demise that share passed down to the daughter, and on her death, would have been shared equally between her two children: Horst and Dagmar. Horst has subsequently passed on without heirs as well, so that share rests entirely in Dagmar's hands. Under French law, at this moment in time, the domaine is owned half by Dagmar, and half by your grandfather, who owns the French Share, unless there are any documents you may have, which tell us otherwise.'

'Right,' she said. 'And when Granddad passes on?'

'Presumably the French Share will go to you, and therefore, you and Dagmar will be equal owners.'

'That seems simple enough. I suppose, therefore, that the young lady and I need to have a real heart-to-heart, don't we? I suppose the bottom line is, what does she want to do with the German Share?'

'When Horst was alive, of course, he was only entitled to half the German Share, as it was already split two ways between him and his sister, even though she didn't know anything about it.'

'So where does that leave me?' she asked.

'Exactly where you were before all this began. At the moment, you own nothing, but the owners – and there are now two of them: Dagmar and your grandfather – pay you an income from their business in recompense for the work you put into it.'

'Does Dagmar know this?'

'I doubt it, unless Horst told her. As far as we understand, she knew absolutely nothing about Horst's link with Nuits-Saint-Georges until a couple of days ago.'

'I wonder why he didn't tell her what he was working on,' Marie-Claire mused, glancing vaguely at Natalie who had remained very still and silent.

'It's a pretty huge thing to tell your sister, isn't it, especially when you realize their past. They're East Germans and not from oligarch or bureaucratic stock, just the proletariat, and here he was, finding out that he might be worth something, without having worked for it. If it was me in that position, I would have probably made damn sure it was all true and above board, before I started putting my sister's hopes up.'

'If it were me,' Truchaud added, 'I would have waited until I had decided what I wanted to do with my share, and then worked out how that would fit with my sister. My immediate thought is that his interests would have involved joining the family firm; he had, after all, spent a lot of time last year working with you.'

Marie-Claire laughed grimly. 'He might, of course, have told Uncle Jérome that he would have to go. He might have found out about his interest in young girls, and that there was no way the new owner was going to allow him to be in the same room as his sister.' Truchaud was interested how she kept coming back to her uncle's abusive nature. He wasn't aware Natalie knew about it from Marie-Claire. He looked at Natalie and then wondered how anyone could not trust that face.

'Of course,' said Natalie, 'there is one other thought. What happens if Dagmar were to die now? Who would inherit her share?' Truchaud and Marie-Claire looked at her carefully. 'Old Mr Laforge, that's who, as he's her nearest living blood relative, which would reunite the French and German shares. Now let's go back six months and put ourselves in your uncle's shoes, sitting in his office talking to this young German, who has just come in to tell him that he has incontrovertible proof that he is your uncle's cousin. Even if he didn't tell your uncle that he had a sister, he would be telling your uncle that his father did not own the domaine outright.

'I don't think that that matters yet,' Natalie continued. 'Even if Horst told him that he was going to come and live in Nuits-Saint-Georges, and learn to be a winemaker from the ground up for the total benefit of the firm, the bottom line remained that he was there, and half the show was now his. His very presence was a threat. We already suspect that your uncle was involved in some shady enough business already. It was, after all, around that time that the *chef's* father turned up offering to give him the complete stock of last year's Village Vosne, and he nearly bit his hand off. His father may or may not have suspected it, but with Horst now on the scene, any decisions about the domaine would have to have been made with Horst. Now Horst may not have known much about wine, but he would have known from a first mouthful that there was nothing rubbish about the Truchaud Vosne. So, whatever Horst wanted to do with the business, and however benign and amiable Horst may have been as a person, Horst had to go.'

'And probably the sooner the better, before he had any inkling that he was in serious danger.' Marie-Claire completed Natalie's sentence for her.

Truchaud agreed with that summary of the case, and said so. 'So, still sitting in Uncle Jérome's shoes, who do we know who might be able to help us get rid of this annoying German, in such a way that no one would be aware that he had ever existed?'

'But at the same time, if it turned out that it did become common knowledge that Horst did exist, then there must have been proof that could become available that he did exist, but doesn't now!' *Natalie was on fire*, Truchaud thought. 'The body could possibly be dug up and *found* at a later date.'

'So who do we know who could do all this in a skilful and *professional* way?'

'Interesting that it appears that Uncle Jérome thought that this was beyond him, whereas he was not averse to committing all sorts of sexual peccadilloes,' remarked Marie-Claire drily.

'All of us draw a line somewhere. He obviously couldn't face killing someone.'

'Which is an interesting observation,' remarked Natalie, 'bearing in mind his associations during the 1970s.'

'Oh?' said Marie-Claire, surprised, and probably not knowing anything about it.

'Your uncle in the seventies was involved with the Baader-Meinhof faction.'

'What?' she expostulated. 'Really?'

'But,' continued Truchaud, 'we never found any evidence that linked him directly with any actual killing. There was some suggestion that whenever killing was being done, Jérome was always somewhere else.'

'I didn't know anything about that,' said Marie-Claire.

'Then when your father had his accident, your grandfather summoned your uncle back to Nuits-Saint-Georges, telling him to grow up and do some proper work at last.'

'But obviously your uncle didn't sever all his ties from those days. Did we ever find out how Molleau got the job in the Municipal Police here?' Truchaud tossed that one carelessly at Natalie.

She threw an explosive smile at him, and Truchaud felt quite uncomfortable in the middle of his chest for a moment. Surely that wasn't how angina felt? He took a deep breath.

'The paperwork was nowhere to be found in the filing system. It's almost as obscure as how the current incumbent got the job. That one appears to be the result of shooting his predecessor and then stepping into the dead man's shoes.'

Truchaud smiled at Marie-Claire. 'And that comes from the mouth of the only one of the three of us who wasn't actually there at the time.'

'So Jérome calls in his mate Molleau and asks him to dispose of Horst?'

'How do we know it was Molleau?' asked Marie-Claire.

'Well, we know Horst was killed the same way that he tried to kill me, and the way that he killed Jérome: a slow bullet to the back of the head. We do know from ballistics that the bullet that killed Jérome was fired from the same gun with which he attempted to kill me, and I recognised it as the gun he had been playing with in the town hall earlier. Ballistics has, in its possession, the bullet that killed the person that we think is probably Horst, and their preliminary report states that it was fired by the same gun that nearly killed me. I suppose it is possible that someone else could have fired a different gun into the back of the skull that might not actually belong to Horst.' Truchaud shrugged.

'So this whole conversation is conjecture?' asked Marie-Claire. 'Why are we talking about it yet?'

'Really to work out if Dagmar is still in danger,' said Truchaud openly.

Marie-Claire stopped and turned round slowly to look at him. 'You mean you were trying to work out if I was involved in the killing too?'

Truchaud looked her straight back in the eye. 'Not exactly. I was trying to prove to myself to my own satisfaction that you were *not* involved, and thus constituted no threat to Dagmar. I know that doesn't really help, but there it is. The next thing we have to work out is where does your grandfather, and in particular, where does Simon fit in? You have in your shop outside, a rather charming young thing, who thinks she has a boyfriend, who we think spent last night with Dagmar.'

Marie-Claire said nothing, which rather confirmed that that's where she thought Dagmar had spent the previous night too. Everybody was silent for a moment or so, and finally Natalie chuckled quietly. The other two looked at her. 'What?' they asked in unison.

'I was just thinking how the survival of both your little domaines might depend on Simon Maréchale's choice of bed mate.'

'What do you mean?'

'Well, if he goes off and marries Suzette, then sooner or later he will end up working for Parnault's, but if Dagmar snares him, then he'll stay here, and, *chef*, you did say that your hope for the future of your family's domaine required the presence of a wine master for at least the next ten years. Dagmar's activities last night could just about have saved everything, provided she sticks with it.'

'What an appalling thought,' mused Truchaud. He thought quietly about Maréchale for a moment. What did he actually know about the man? 'I know we looked for paperwork about Simon's past three months ago and found nothing. Did you ever find his references?' he asked Marie-Claire.

'Once you appeared to have solved that case, I think we all stopped looking. I have talked to him since from time to time about his past. From what I understand, he grew up in Provence, and then moved to a fairly major chateau in the Pomerol, and was working as a sort of senior apprentice under their chief winemaker, when he applied for this job and got it.'

'That would have been an interesting correspondence,' mused the Commander, 'between a Burgundian and a Bordelais winemaker. I wonder how your uncle worked out whether the man in Bordeaux was just trying to get rid of a labourer, who was useless. Where better than to unload him but onto a Burgundian! Do you know what particularly attracted your uncle?'

'Well, you understand that Burgundy is a pure single-variety wine?'

'Pinot noir for the red, and Chardonnay for the whites, yes?' asked Truchaud, implying that she should go on.

'Well, most of the Bordeaux wines are blends of different grapes, and each different chateau has their own signature blend of different grape varieties. Hence each different claret has a slightly different taste. The left-bank wines, which include what they call *Médoc*, are predominantly made from Cabernet Sauvignon grapes, with some Merlot added in various proportions. The right-bankers, such as Pomerol and Saint Émilion, tend to be dominated by the Merlot grape, with small proportions of Cabernet Sauvignon. Pretty much all of them add a splash of a third variety: the Cabernet Franc.'

'You seem to know quite a lot about it,' remarked Truchaud.

'I have listened to Simon hold forth on occasions. One of the things he learned during his two-year apprenticeship in Bordeaux was the blending of the Grand Vin, the chateau's number one wine, and its second wine, which isn't quite as good as the first wine, but is more modestly priced. The quantity of the second wine available depends on how many grapes get harvested in a particular year.'

'I think I could listen to this for ages, but it isn't really what we need to talk about at the moment. Just running off at a tangent, did you ever taste any of the Pomerol stuff he was involved with?'

'Actually, yes. He brought a couple of bottles to the interview.'

'That he had made himself?'

'Er, no. The wine he made himself probably won't be really ready for another ten years. If you think Burgundy takes a while to open up, well, good Bordeaux takes at least double that time.'

'So how did he get the job through providing a couple of bottles he had nothing to do with?'

'The bottles were brought to demonstrate to my uncle and grandfather that the man whose references Simon was relying on, knew what he was talking about. After the interview, when Simon went back to Bordeaux, he took a couple of bottles of our Échezeaux, as a thank you.'

'So as long as eighteen months ago, Uncle Jérome was thinking about blending Burgundy, and brought in someone who knew about blending grapes.' Truchaud thought for a while. 'He had to be careful. There have been any number of scandals over the years about people bringing some wine up from the Rhône valley, and mixing it in with their Burgundy to give it body.'

'Not only Rhône, but in the past people brought up nice cheap wine from Provence, or even shipped stuff over from Algeria to perk up their wine. I like to think they all got caught, but they probably didn't.'

'What did you think of your uncle going into the blending game then?' asked Truchaud.

'You'll be glad to know that we had a big family meeting to discuss that,' Marie-Claire replied, and added, 'before Simon even arrived. You know we get your red from the east side of the Seventy-Four?'

'Yes, you've been doing that for a long time.'

'Well, you probably know that we generally feel that your grapes from the other side make significantly better wine than other basic Bourgogne wine, although we aren't allowed to call it anything different than the stuff from Ladoix, south of Nuits-Saint-Georges. One thing that my uncle found was that if he added Ladoix wine to your wrong-sided Vosne wine, he ended up with a mixture that was better than the Ladoix on its own, but less good than your Vosne: a simple addition sum. His idea was to find a blend that was more than the sum of its parts, hence the recruitment of Simon. It was all just to make a better basic Bourgogne, at least to start with. Does that make sense?'

'Completely. And it was somewhat later, therefore, that your uncle came up with including Grand Cru wines in the blend.' Truchaud added drily. 'I was just reassuring ourselves that Simon wasn't also recruited as a hatchet man.'

'No, I seriously doubt it. I am sure that Simon has wine in his blood, and at this moment in time, he assures us that he prefers Bourgogne to the Bordelais, although he has a little corner in the cellar for his own bottles, and there is a little claret in it.' There was a little chuckle in Marie-Claire's voice.

'The bottom line is,' said Natalie, 'that Simon was recruited simply to make wine, and nothing else. I can go along with that. He is also an attractive young man, who, in his time here, has attracted a Parnault girl and your cousin.'

'I doubt that my uncle had any intention of recruiting a winemaker for the Parnault family,' she said ruefully, 'so let's hope that he keeps Dagmar here, and thus both of them in our winery.'

'May I say "aye" to that,' said Truchaud. 'Perhaps the thing we have to do next is to go back to our domaine, and see what the girls are getting up to. Natalie, are you all tuned up to speak lots of difficult East German?'

Chapter 26

Nuits-Saint-Georges and Ladoix-Serrigny, later Thursday afternoon

Truchaud and Natalie climbed back into the car and pottered back round to the Truchaud domaine. The first thing they noticed was Gretel the Škoda's absence from the courtyard. Both of them headed for the kitchen at the double. Through the kitchen they hurtled where they found Michelle seated at the dining table surrounded by papers. She looked up on their entrance.

'Where is she?' Truchaud asked breathlessly.

'Who? Dagmar or Renate?' she asked innocently.

'Either … er, both … Dagmar,' said Truchaud flustered.

'They both took Bruno off in the car to look at the vineyards,' said Michelle. 'What's all the panic about?'

'Was it just Bruno they went with?' he answered.

'Well, no. Simon came round too, as he has to wander round and check over the vines. He may not need to do anything, but it's still the flowering season, and we need to make sure that mildew or mould doesn't sneak in via the back door.'

'Simon?' Michelle wasn't sure that the winemaker's name, as spoken at that moment by her brother-in-law, would have required a question mark or an exclamation mark after it, had it been written down on paper. It did come out, however, accompanied by an undignified quantity of spittle.

'I think you two had better sit down and tell me what's worrying you. It is my son that they're all out with.' So they sat down and told her about the conversation they had just had with Marie-Claire. 'It doesn't sound like anything to worry about, provided you're not Suzette, and I think it might even fill Bruno with renewed hope.'

'I'm not talking about Bruno's silly little crush on a girl who's far too old to notice him. I'm worried that Simon Maréchale might have had something to do with Horst's death, and if so, might have similar plans for Dagmar.'

'You really aren't in any way romantic, are you, Shammang? I would have thought that wholesale slaughter was positively the last thing that Simon has in mind for Dagmar.' Michelle was obviously getting a lot of amusement out of her brother-in-law's anxiety. 'What do you think, Natalie?' she asked the Detective Sergeant, who sat silently on the other side of the table from the Truchauds.

'I am inclined to think the same as you,' she said cautiously, 'but at the same time that is only a guess, and it isn't our job to make guesses. We do need to get it right. If we have guessed wrong and Simon was involved in Horst's murder, then that does put Dagmar in danger.'

'And therefore isn't she fortunate to have Bruno and Renate along with her. If all three find themselves dead, then the only way that Simon isn't the prime suspect is that if he's lying alongside them, as dead as they are.' That was an odd way for a mother to look at it, and both police officers looked at her slightly askance.

'If Simon is lying beside them equally dead,' remarked Truchaud drily, 'I think he would still be on the list of suspects, though possibly we might consider him to be slightly less competent than before. Do you know which way they went?'

'I think they went south first. The Laforges' southernmost parcel is in Ladoix-Serrigny, halfway up the north side of Corton Hill. That's where I heard Simon tell Bruno they were going to start. I think the girls are quite keen to see the extent of the vineyard holdings that we have.'

'Well, that's the direction we go in then,' said Truchaud. 'Coming?'

They were in the process of walking out into the courtyard when Truchaud's phone went off again in his pocket. He looked at the mobile and it told him it was a Dijon number. He wondered who that might be, but on the assumption it might be the path lab or perhaps the Investigating Magistrate, he accepted the call. There were times when he frightened himself.

'De Castaigne here. Are you busy?'

'Fairly,' Truchaud replied cautiously, not giving anything away.

'I've got a report back from ballistics. It appears that the bullet was fired from the same gun that you handed in in May. Are you doing anything now? I would like to talk to you about that.'

'Hang on,' he said, and turning to Natalie, he told her that the Investigating Magistrate wanted to see him. Would she mind borrowing a gendarme from Duquesne to accompany her to Ladoix?

'Provided it isn't Lenoir and he wants to drive,' she said with a shudder. It alarmed Truchaud to realize how attractive he found her even when she was expressing alarm or dismay.

'I'll make sure. Hang on.' He returned to his phone. 'I'm in Nuits at the moment. I'll be with you in a quarter of an hour or so.' Castaigne assented and said he would be in the mortuary and did Truchaud know where that was. Truchaud said he did, rang off and then redialed Duquesne. 'Truchaud here. Can I send Natalie round to borrow one of your gendarmes to accompany her? She's going down to Ladoix-Serrigny to find the German girls. We think they're there, with Simon Maréchale. At this moment Simon is only on the suspect list, and probably not very high up it, but we need to be reassured they're safe.'

'Who would you like?' Duquesne asked.

'Mac Montbard would be less likely to want to drive and thus scare the lunch out of Natalie,' Truchaud suggested.

'He's never wrecked a car, you know,' said Duquesne, knowing exactly who they were both talking about.

'Maybe, but Natalie would rather not be present at the scene the first time he does,' returned Truchaud's dry reply.

'Fair enough. She's in the office, so tell Natalie to pop round and she'll be ready for her.'

Thus they went their separate ways: Truchaud in his BX headed north to Dijon, and Natalie woke up her Mégane and set off for the Gendarmerie, somewhat relieved she had been allocated someone who knew their way around. She was not certain that once off the Seventy-Four she would not have got lost. Anyone would have told her that it was almost impossible to get lost on the cote. Above the vineyards to the west was dense woodland, and down the slope to the east was the Seventy-Four running north to south, and beyond that there was the motorway a short distance further to the east, also running north to south, and back again. The distance between the woodland and the motorway was never more than a kilometre. If you missed either of them driving east west, then there was an argument that said you shouldn't be driving at all.

Truchaud, meanwhile, drove straight out to the motorway, and headed north in the Metz direction. The first junction off was towards the Rocade, the Dijon by-pass. He slotted a couple of coins into the machine and pressed the button to get a printed receipt. Someone had obviously been refilling them with paper, as it obligingly printed one out for him. He would decide later on which police department would actually have the pleasure of reimbursing him. He reckoned that would finally depend on the outcome of the case. He pulled off the Rocade at the Quétigny turning and headed into town.

Provided you weren't a corpse, Truchaud couldn't help thinking that there weren't many pleasantly cooler places to be in the height of the summer than the mortuary. He thought perhaps if you had access to one of the underground cellars in Nuits-Saint-Georges that would run it pretty close. Like the cellars, it was cool; there weren't many people about; and it was quiet. But the cellars could be dusty, and the mortuary was always scrupulously clean. On the other hand, the smell in the cellars beat any other aroma Truchaud knew.

De Castaigne met him at the door and took him round to an office. Whether it was his, Truchaud couldn't and de Castaigne didn't say. He fished around in a drawer and found the ballistics report. Sitting himself down, he flicked the report across the desk. Truchaud picked it up and read it. The experts seemed satisfied that the bullet had come from Molleau's gun.

'Can you explain exactly how you came to be in the possession of this weapon?'

'It was pointed in my direction, and I was convinced that it was about to be discharged at me, so I exchanged fire with the man holding it in self-defence,' he replied.

'And you hit him?'

'Obviously I hit him; it's me standing here talking to you.'

'Lucky?'

'You have no idea how lucky. I am not the world's best shot.'

'And the person who was about to shoot you was Inspector Molleau, at that time the Chief of the Nuits-Saint-Georges Municipal Police?'

'Yes.'

'Chief of the Municipal Police? Not really a job that requires the holder to be a crack shot with a pistol.'

'I couldn't agree with you more, but I had been led to believe that Molleau was handy in the use of a pistol.'

'How so?'

'The first time I met him formally was in his office in the town hall. He made quite a play of dismantling and then reassembling that pistol in the drawer of his desk, without looking at what he was doing even once. I imagine he had had some firearms training in the past, and that was what he was telling me. At the time I had no idea why he was telling me that. Actually, I'm still not sure. I never saw him actually fire the pistol, of course, so I had no idea how accurate he was with it. He wasn't standing that far away, so neither of us had to be much good.'

'Did you know he was firing low-velocity rounds?'

'No. At that point we knew that it was a low-velocity round that had killed Jérome Laforge, but we didn't know who had fired it until ballistics came up with a match with Molleau's pistol, after I had handed it in. I must confess to being a little thrown by that.'

'And that Mr Laforge's killer was already dead. How did you feel about that?'

'Somewhat unfulfilled, I suppose. I have always separated my role from that of the judiciary, and I felt distinctly uncomfortable being the judge, jury and executioner all in the blink of an eye.'

'I can understand what you mean.' The magistrate looked at the detective in front of him. 'I suppose that this also seems to further point to the body belonging to Horst Witter, though we'll still have to wait for the DNA tests to come through to be absolutely sure.'

'Well, if it wasn't Horst in that hole, then we'll have opened up a whole new can of worms to find out why Molleau executed John Doe, and at the same time, we will need to be asking all over again, "Where is Horst Witter?"'

The two men both shrugged. What could they do but wait? 'Needless to say,' de Castaigne said to Truchaud, 'stay around.'

'I'm not going anywhere,' he replied.

Meanwhile, just on the west side of a village not far north of Beaune, climbing up the hill on foot were two policewomen: one in mufti and the other in uniform. They had spotted the group of people they were looking for, so they had parked the car where the village buildings gave way to the vineyards at the base of Corton Hill. Natalie waved at them, a gesture of which she wasn't sure Truchaud would have approved, but as she'd got Montbard in uniform as company, it was fairly obvious at a distance who they were. All four of them waved back, so they didn't rush to climb the hill to reach them. It was a warm day, and in the late afternoon, it was becoming quite close and sticky.

Simon greeted them both, and in particular Montbard. 'Are you on duty?' he asked. Looking her up and down.

'Oh yes. A gendarme in uniform is always on duty.'

'So when you come off duty ...?' he asked playfully.

'I take my clothes off,' she replied in kind. Natalie glared at the pair of them.

'What duty brings you up here then?' he asked, still making the conversation with Montbard.

'She came here with me,' Natalie explained fairly forcefully. Now was not the time for the gendarme to be flirting with a suspect. 'The Commander was called away on other business, and I thought I would like to find you all, so I borrowed Mac to keep me company, and show me round. It's remarkable how supportive the Gendarmerie is down here compared with Paris.'

'So the gendarme on duty came to support you, which presumably means you're on duty too, and I have to ask you the same question: why are you here on duty?'

Natalie shook her head slowly. 'At this moment in time I just need to know where everyone is and that they're safe. As I didn't know where Dagmar and Renate were, I needed to come and find them.'

'Michelle would have told you they were with me, how else would you have found me?'

'I'm a bit of a tourist as far as Burgundy is concerned, and I'd never heard of Ladoix-Serrigny before.' She thought about it for a moment. 'So somewhere round here there must be a vineyard called Le Serrigny. Does it make red or white wine?'

Maréchale was already smiling, 'Ah well, you see, every rule in Burgundy is created just to be broken. There is no vineyard called Serrigny.'

'I don't understand.'

'The village of Ladoix-Serrigny was created by joining two hamlets of Serrigny and Ladoix together. I don't know exactly where the joins are now. Between them and Nuits-Saint-Georges you will have driven through Corgoloin and Comblanchien to get here.'

'And nearly got wiped out by a lorry coming out of the quarry. What are they digging for up there?'

'Marble. Comblanchien marble is one of the most highly desirable stones in the whole of France. The stone is also an important component in the terroir as a whole, as it's quite hard and dense and is pretty impervious to water so it stays in the topsoil, but in those two villages there is so much stone it takes priority over the grapes.'

'The wine isn't anything particularly special either,' added Bruno. 'There are no Grands Crus or Premiers Crus, and the best village cru is called a Côtes de Nuits Villages, much to the annoyance of Brochon, the next village north from Gevrey-Chambertin, whose best appellation is also Côtes de Nuits Villages, and you have to know whose wine you are buying to know whether the wine you're buying is from Comblanchien or from Brochon.'

'Yes,' added Simon. 'It's hardly satisfactory for the casual buyer. Anyway, what can we do for you, officers?'

'Did you know Dagmar's brother last autumn?'

'Yes, I suppose I did, but I didn't know anything about his family, or that he had a sister.' He instantly translated the question and answer into English for Dagmar's benefit. She grabbed his arm nearest her and cuddled it.

'Did you know he came back to Nuits-Saint-Georges in November?'

'Yes, I did hear that he was back, but I don't think I saw him. Why?'

'How did you hear he was back?'

'I think Young Mr Laforge probably told me. Funny thing that, you know. I seem to remember that Young Mr Laforge wasn't that happy about it.'

'What do you mean?'

'Well, I seem to remember him asking me if I would help him out by ridding him of this "pestilent priest"; you know, the Thomas Beckett line.'

'What did you say to that?'

'As far as I can remember I laughed and wandered off. I had things to do.' A moment of realization passed in front of his eyes. 'You don't mean that Young Mister Laforge actually wanted to kill him, do you?' He had stopped translating into English at this point. 'Why would he want to do that? As far as I can remember he was an okay worker during the vintage.'

242

'Ah well,' said Natalie, 'it wasn't his work ethic that worried Mr Laforge, it was his bloodline.'

'Huh? I don't understand what you're talking about.'

'Did Dagmar tell you where she was yesterday?'

Maréchale looked slightly sideways at her, then at Dagmar. 'You mean, apart from having dinner with us?'

'Before that,' Natalie said, and the winemaker looked slightly relieved.

'Go on.'

'She was having a blood sample taken in the forensics lab in Dijon.'

'Why would she want to do that?' asked Maréchale, nonplussed.

'Commander Truchaud and I found a body up in the woods on the west side of Nuits-Saint-Georges yesterday morning, and we think it might belong to Dagmar's brother.'

'Does she know this?'

'She is aware who we think it *might* be. That's why she was willing to have the blood test taken for DNA matching.'

Maréchale looked at Dagmar for a moment and his face nearly collapsed. 'Oh, the poor little sausage,' he said and threw his arms round her.

Dagmar's eyes widened and she mouthed the word, 'What?' in German over Maréchale's shoulder at Natalie.

'I think he's just found out for the first time what we think happened to your brother.'

Dagmar looked at the detective alarmed. 'You don't think he had anything to do with that, do you?'

'Considerably less so over the past thirty seconds,' she replied.

'So, why would you think that someone at Laforge's killed her brother?' Maréchale asked in English, totally by mistake, especially as Dagmar would have understood, but Natalie, not really.

'We're going down to the bottom to find a glass of something refreshing,' interrupted Bruno tactfully, and explained that to Renate at the same time, almost pulling her with him by the wrist.

'What a good idea,' said Natalie. 'Why don't we all go?' She turned to Maréchale, 'Something cold and wet?'

And so they all walked back down to the village with Maréchale casting a close eye over the vines for which he was responsible as he walked past them. On a couple of occasions he stopped and lifted a leaf on a vine and looked underneath it. With an expressive 'fine' he let it drop again and kept walking. Once they were out of the Laforge parcel, he took no further interest in the vines. There would be another day when he would cast a close eye on his neighbours' vines, to make sure they had nothing contagious to spread onto his parcel, but right now, he had to sort out what on earth this detective was on about: that and this new girl, who kept knocking the skids out from under him.

Seated in the little café in the village, most of them were drinking cold soft drinks. And, in a three-language conversation, which must have been very bizarre to the French folk in the room, Natalie first cleared with Dagmar that it was okay to discuss with Simon her blood relationship with the Laforges, to which she agreed, perhaps in the hope of learning more herself. Then she explained to Simon the identity of the girl with whom he had spent the previous night.

Well, she thought, *either he really didn't know any of this, or he's a damn good actor*. It was particularly handy having Montbard with them, as she expressed surprise at the same moments as the winemaker did. Meanwhile, Renate looked sadder and sadder. She was becoming abundantly aware that fate was driving a 900-kilometre wedge between her and her best friend. Bruno was trying in his best German to be sympathetic, but she wasn't really listening.

Chapter 27

Nuits-Saint-Georges, Thursday evening

Truchaud sat in his room contemplating his nails. In the background, Jerry Garcia was playing a guitar solo over an alternating rhythm from the rest of the band, which intentionally never quite let the listener settle. However his thoughts were more on the case than on the music, though he would never have admitted that to anyone else.

His mobile phone interrupted the band's performance, and apologising to Jerry for turning him down, he did so and looked at the number on the face of his mobile. It was a very similar Dijon number to the one he had answered before, perhaps even identical. 'Mr de Castaigne?' he asked.

'How did you know?' came the reply.

'Lucky guess,' he said. 'Who else has been phoning me regularly this week from Dijon? Even my father's Guardianship Magistrate doesn't phone back this often.' *Actually*, he thought, *he hasn't phoned back at all; I must chase that up.*

'The DNA lab has come back with some more information.'

'Go on.'

'Firstly, they are satisfied that the DNA of the body you found and the DNA of Dagmar Witter show a sibling match.'

'Translated into normal French, it means that they are indeed brother and sister, and thus the body we found was indeed that of Horst Witter.'

'Correct.'

'As I'm going to need to be able to explain that to Dagmar herself, can you just fill in how they came to that conclusion for me, please?'

'Well, it goes like this, the DNA is broken down into four unit blocks, called alleles. There are several different variants of each allele, and if you DNA test an individual against an

245

unknown sample, all the alleles have got to be the same before you can say that the sample left at the crime scene and the sample from the suspect match. So far so good?'

'I follow that so far, yes.'

'Now if the alleles are identical more often than is probable in two samples taken from the population at random, then the samples are considered to come from related donors: cousins or whatever - although I suppose they could come from the Indian subcontinent.'

'Huh? What's that all about?'

'There was a volcanic super eruption just off the island of Sumatra about 70,000 years ago, which practically wiped out the population of the Indian subcontinent, which was repopulated by the descendants of the few survivors there were, whereas mainland Europe suffered no such catastrophe. Therefore there is a much wider gene pool among the population of Europe as a whole, especially considering the general migration of people since the Middle Ages. Anyway, getting back to our matches. To declare that two individuals are, in fact, siblings, there have got to be a good number of matched alleles, which would be beyond the realms of even related matches, but not quite all the same, because if they were, they would belong to identical twins, and these two siblings aren't that close.'

'One was male and the other was female.'

'Quite. But those different samples were very closely matched, and the lab is convinced that they come from siblings, who share both parents. There were a good many alleles that were identical.'

'Thank you for that.'

'Before you go, there is one other thing I think you might be interested in that the database threw up.'

'Go on.'

'Well, they put a sample of the late Jérome Laforge's DNA on the database, after his post-mortem was performed.'

'Why did they do that?'

'Well, they had no idea really why he was killed, and there

was some suggestion that he had been involved with the Red Brigade once upon a time. If he had been involved in urban terrorism in the 1980s, then there are still a number of cold cases from back then that they are still trying to sort out.'

'Was he involved?'

'It doesn't appear so, so far, but it did produce something; he appears to have been quite closely related to the Witters.'

'So he was right,' said Truchaud.

'What do you mean?' asked de Castaigne.

'Well, we're working the case on the assumption that Laforge arranged for the killing of Horst Witter because he was the grandson of his own father's brother, and thus, owing to the inheritance laws, he would own half of the domaine.'

'Up to a point that's true: he would have owned half of the domaine that existed at the time of the death of Jérome's grandfather. If Jérome's father, or indeed Jérome himself, had added more parcels to the domaine after his father had died, then those items could just have remained with that side of the family, if a conflict arose.'

'I can see that would make things more complicated. Let's just hope that that doesn't come up in conversation.'

'Oh quite.'

Truchaud sighed. At least this case appeared to have reached a solution, and much to his relief, it appeared it would not end with a court appearance, apart from the formal inquest. 'It appears, Commander Truchaud, that you have already executed the murderer guilty of the death of Horst Witter.'

'It appears I did, though at that time it wasn't my intention.'

'I'm not making any accusations, especially down the telephone.' Truchaud could hear the smile on the magistrate's face. 'Stay in touch,' he said. 'We'll need to set a date for the inquest.'

'Well, you know my official telephone number at the town hall, and you've got my mobile number.' And with that, they disconnected. Truchaud went back to the record player and turned it up to audible again. Even knowing that record as well as he did, it took him a moment or so to work out where he was in the concert. He lay back on the bed and let the music wash

247

over him.

He must have been at least half-asleep when there came a soft tap on his door. He stretched and in his most schoolmasterish voice, he shouted, 'Come!'

'Uncle Shammang, supper's nearly ready,' came Bruno's voice through the crack between the door and the frame.

'I'll be right down,' he replied, and walked over to his player and ejecting his precious Grateful Dead CD, he put it back in its 'jewel box', and then turned the machine off. Turning the light out, he followed his nephew down the stairs.

At the bottom of the stairs he ran into Dagmar, and asked her, in English, if he could have a word with her. They went outside into the courtyard and he explained to her the content of his recent conversation with de Castaigne. She looked at him sadly, and replied, in French, 'So he's definitely dead then?'

'I'm afraid so,' the detective replied.

'I had thought he was, even before we ever came to France,' she said, 'You know how you sometimes feel these things?'

Truchaud could see here eyes glisten for a moment, and he wondered whether she was going to cry and collapse in his arms. What she actually did was clear her throat, and say that his sister-in-law had cooked them dinner, and it was ready, so they should go in before she threw it at them.

Michelle had cooked rabbit with mustard seed and olives, and served it with sliced potatoes baked in a cheese sauce, Dauphinois style. 'Rabbit's one of those things my mother always liked serving up to the English in her little eatery,' she said. Michelle had grown up above a little café in Normandy. He didn't actually know quite how she and his brother had hooked up for the first time. When the question had been on his mind, it had seemed inappropriate to ask at the time; and when it might have been appropriate, well, he just wasn't thinking of it. 'It's probably the thing that separates the French and the English even more than the Channel.' Simon translated that into English for the amusement of Dagmar and Renate.

Dagmar came back with a little French asking why that was. She was already beginning to show that she was cottoning on to what was going on around her.

'Well, we French regard animals with four legs, wings or fins as potential food first and foremost. The English first ask whether they can use the animals for labour, or as something soft and fluffy to be cuddled, and to go "ooh" at, before they then ask if they are edible. There are animals that we simply don't eat like cats or dogs.'

'As a matter of interest, why not?' Dagmar asked, interested. She was aware they didn't eat cats or dogs in Germany either.

'Well, they're carnivorous animals. We don't eat carnivorous animals.'

'Why not?'

'Presumably they don't taste very good,' was Simon's explanation.

'How would we know that if we've never tried them?'

Michelle looked distinctly uncomfortable and her brother-in-law piled in to help her out. 'I think it's simply a little too close to home,' he said. 'They say that human meat tastes quite like pork, but I've no intention of getting involved in a plane wreck in the Andes to try that out.' He cleared his throat and continued, 'I've never quite worked out why they can't be both at differing times in their lives. The English also get really squeamish about eating horse meat. Why is that? The horse pulls a plough for as long as it is capable, and when it is no longer capable to do that, stewing it up in a *pot-au-feu* is an efficient method of recycling the protein.'

Dagmar didn't follow that so Simon translated for her. She thought for a moment about Truchaud's justification for cannibalism, and then replied in English that she and her brother used to trap rabbits in the woods out beyond Chemnitz when they were children. Their mother used to stew them, but it wasn't like this, she continued. The mustard seeds were just a wonderful addition as were the sliced black olives. She liked the wine too; what was this wine? She had spotted the bottle that Bruno had brought up from the cellar had no label on it.

Truchaud grinned at her. 'This is a rival product,' he said. 'My father here made this in 2003, the year of the heatwave. A

249

fair number of people died of heatstroke that summer, and in the wineries it was a difficult year too.'

'Yes, I heard about that,' said Maréchale. 'It wasn't an easy year for anybody.'

'It was the first year that the vintage started in August for over a century. I like to think we did okay. This has settled down nicely in the bottles, but I understand that other peoples' wine is still, even after all this time, struggling for balance, and some of it has just given up in despair.'

'I think that's just being polite. I think there's a lot of wine out there from good vineyards, belonging to good domaines, whose future is simply in the stew pot, some of ours included. Well done, Mr Truchaud.'

'What?' said Dad from his end of the table.

'Mr Maréchale likes your Nuits-Saint-Georges.'

'Oh, this is mine, is it?' He took a further sniff at it and then a mouthful. He nodded at the glass. 'Nice full nose and not too sharp in the mouth. Is there a lot more of this in the cellar?' he asked.

'I doubt it. I think we sold most of it a long time ago.'

'I hope we got a reasonable price for it.'

'Do you want me to go and check?' asked Michelle.

'No, no point,' said the policeman. 'What we got is what we got, but if anybody wants to bring a bottle back for a refund after all these years, then we have proof that it is his cellaring rather than our viticulture that's at fault.'

'Do people bring bottles back?' asked Renate in surprise, as the three-language conversation moved around the table.

'Occasionally,' said Michelle.

'So what happens then?' she asked.

'Depends on how important they are as a customer,' she replied. 'We might give them a bottle of something else in exchange, I suppose, but generally, we smile sweetly and sympathize, and that's about it. I like to think that we've weeded out all the duff bottles before they go on the market, and if a particular bottle is corked, then we generally work out that every half-case contains a free bottle for that eventuality. If

250

there isn't a corked bottle in a case then the buyers are the lucky ones.'

'Corked?'

'Sometimes the corks go off over time in the bottle, and there is a rather unpleasant corky smell left in the glass that just won't go away. I have no idea why that happens.' Bruno had joined in the conversation at this point, 'but it does occasionally. We do replace those, don't we, Uncle Shammang?'

'If somebody's got the face to come back with a bottle just because it's corked, we probably would. But can you imagine it: someone's preparing to serve dinner to his friends, so he pulls the cork of the bottle he has carefully chosen, and tastes the wine, but it's corked! He can't serve that one to his friends. It's going to be a difficult enough logistical problem to nip down to the cellar to get another bottle and get it up to room temperature before dinner, without thinking of digging up the passport, and diving into the car and driving all the way to the airport, even if there is a direct flight to Dijon Longvic airport. Then it's a taxi here to get another bottle from us, and the return journey all the way back in time for dinner. He would need the use of a star ship in that enterprise,' he quipped.

'Uncle Shammang, not all our bottles go abroad,' Bruno laughed.

'Yes, if it was the butcher down the road, I'm sure we would sort him out to his approval. We would hate him to be selling us duff meat in revenge. This rabbit, incidentally, is excellent: beautifully tender; it just falls off the bone.'

'That,' said Michelle drily, 'is the skill of the chef, and has nothing to do with the butcher.'

'Of course, *Maman*,' said Bruno instinctively, ducking his mother's displeasure.

At the end of the meal, over a brandy or marc, depending on the individual's choice, Truchaud explained to all the conversations he had had with de Castaigne and Dagmar before they had sat down to dinner. He had waited till then to avoid taking the attention away from Michelle's cooking, and also ensured that everyone would be in a mellow mood. Even Dagmar wasn't particularly surprised.

'I thought that something must have happened to him when we got to Boppard, and found no trace of him. From there on, I think we both knew we wouldn't see him again. The tragedy is that he didn't live to see what he had found.' She turned to Simon. 'Tell me, would he have made a half-decent winemaker?'

'Well, when he was working with us, he always seemed to take on board what we asked him to do very quickly. Certainly when I asked him to do something, I had no worries that it wouldn't get done. Does that make sense?'

'Yes. So at least he died doing what he wanted to do, and the fact that he came back so soon after the harvest tells me that he wanted to become part of the family.'

'It's very sad that Jérome didn't take it that way,' agreed Maréchale. 'So what are you going to do?' he asked the girl, looking her straight in the eyes.

'Well, you know I'm a primary school teacher in Chemnitz, so there's no immediate hurry for me to get back and start teaching kids again. I know this sounds very selfish, especially to you, hon,' she said, looking directly at Renate, 'but what I would really like to do is to stay here and learn to speak French properly. During that time I will make my decision as to whether I want to stay, and see whether I am going to make something out of Horst's legacy.'

'Well, I have to go back to Chemnitz next week,' said Renate. 'I have a job that expects me to be ready, willing and able on Monday.' She didn't sound at all happy about Dagmar's decision. 'What about the car and the flat?'

'You take Gretel back with you and hang on to the flat. If anybody asks, I'm on extended leave here in France, which is true. By the time term starts, I will have made my decision as to what I'm going to do in the future.' She smiled gently at Maréchale. 'Are you happy with that?'

He nodded thoughtfully. 'You will need to have at least one long conversation with Old Mr Laforge and Marie-Claire, and I think that will need to start tomorrow.'

'Do you know a good tutor of French as a foreign language?'

'I can think of one,' he grinned, 'but I suspect you will need some formal training as well, and I'm sure you'll find someone either in Beaune or Dijon. Beaune might be better, if there is one, as then you would be able to enrol into the college and learn some theoretical viticulture too.'

'It's back to school all over again,' she said, and turned to Natalie, who was sitting quietly next to Michelle. 'Do you think I'm making the right decision?'

'I think you've chosen not to make a decision until you have to, and to my way of thinking that's the right way to go about it. Michelle?' she tossed the last at the woman sitting next to her.

'Yes, I think you're right. Once you can speak French fluently, please feel free to come round and talk wine at any time with my father-in-law and me. It may be instructive to all concerned.'

'Where will you stay?' asked Renate, continuing to be dismayed.

'Well, I've got my brother's camper. Is there any reason I can't continue to keep parking it here?' she asked Michelle.

Maréchale wouldn't hear of it. There was room in his flat for two, and it would surely be appropriate for her to park the camper in the Laforge yard. After all, she was a Laforge now. He looked at Renate. 'I have a spare bedroom: it's a little full of clutter at the moment, but there'll always be room for any friend of yours to stay.'

Truchaud looked at them all. Maréchale and this girl had known each other for merely a couple of days, and already they were planning on moving in together. He wondered what a love of that consuming force felt like? He didn't have the face to even mention his feelings to Natalie, and yet those two were taking the plunge already. He looked momentarily at the sergeant's gold-framed face, took a deep breath and said nothing.

'If you decide to come back, how will you get back?' asked Renate.

'I tell you what. Shall we get that camper fit for a long run?'

Maréchale replied. 'That way you will feel comfortable that whatever happens between me and Dagmar, you will know she always has some means of escape? Would that make you feel happier?'

'You would do that?' Dagmar asked Simon, at least part playfully, and all in French. She snuggled into the crook of his left arm for a moment, then, catching her friend's eye, disconnected herself. 'Look,' she said, 'I tell you what. Why don't I stay here with you in the camper tonight, and tomorrow morning, we'll walk round to Simon's and you can see where it is and what it's all about. Is that okay with you too?' she asked Simon.

He looked slightly crestfallen – he was obviously rather hoping to spend that night as well in the arms of this girl – but he could be patient too. 'Of course,' he said.

'I'll get some schnitzel from the butcher and we'll cook you a German supper tomorrow night, and we'll have one of Horst's bottles with it.'

'Horst's bottles?' asked Maréchale.

'Oh yes, one of Horst's friends gave me a couple of bottles of the local Boppard wine for him. It might be very interesting to try one.'

'You mean, you've never actually opened one?'

She shook her head, 'Nope,' she said.

'This is one very brave girl moving in with a winemaker, and toasting the event with a bottle of wine she has never even tried. Well, I shall be wandering off now, and I'll see you both tomorrow.' He stood up and Dagmar wrapped herself around his neck for a few moments, then let him go, and sat back down with her friend.

There was a silence in the dining room that no one particularly wanted to break after Simon had left. In the end it was Natalie who did so. 'Well, as I'm returning to Paris tomorrow, I think I had better get some sleep. See you all for breakfast in the morning,' and she got up and left the room.

Michelle hissed into her brother-in-law's ear, 'Do something, you silly fool. I think she's just given you an ultimatum.'

Chapter 28

Nuits-Saint-Georges, Friday morning

There was no cockerel to crow that morning, nor had there been one any morning for that matter, but Truchaud really missed it that day. He felt like someone had taken his favourite capon and put it in the coq au vin. He showered, dressed and went downstairs.

Where was she? She hadn't left already surely, not without at least an '*à bientôt, chef*'. He poured himself some strong coffee from the cafetière on the sideboard, and added a dollop of cream from the jug. It was just like staying in a hotel, he thought guiltily, and taking a slurp, he walked out into the courtyard. There she was, with the boot of her Mégane up, presumably loading her bag into it. 'Do you want coffee?' he shouted at her.

'Yes, please,' she replied. 'Be with you in a minute. Don't eat all the croissants.'

The butterflies in his stomach settled. Now he had to work out a plan to make her stay, or at the very least, come back very soon. On his other shoulder sat a severe looking angel in a white kaftan, wagging an admonishing index finger: God Almighty on a zebra crossing! Was he listening to himself? This wasn't the thought process of someone even a third his age. Where was he coming from? 'You're her senior officer, for heaven's sake! It is singularly inappropriate behaviour for someone in the position of power you have, to feel that way towards her. Thoughts like that are tantamount to rape. She's half your age, man. How on earth do you think it's possible for a beautiful young woman as young as she is to even think the same way about you? Grow up, and don't make a fool of yourself.'

He poured her coffee, while listening to the argument going on between the cherubs in his head. He decided to let her make the first move. If she really cared about him, then surely she would make it. 'Yes that's right, take the coward's way out. You're going to lose; you know that don't you?' said the cherub in the red suit on his other shoulder.

Why had his imagination painted the cherub on his side like the devil? But he was right, wasn't he? Even at that moment in time he knew Natalie was leaving and going back up to Paris and out of his life, perhaps forever. A great well of sadness and loss welled up inside him, and he had no idea how to get rid of it. Catch a crook? Piece of cake. He could do that any old day. Catch a ray of happiness? Not a chance; never even got close.

She walked in and picked up the cup and joined him at the table. She helped herself to a croissant and some butter and jam. Smiling gently at him, she munched down on the croissant.

'Now this is something I'll miss,' she said. 'We never get croissants like this anywhere in Paris.'

'You could always stay,' he said hopefully, looking upwards and to the left at her.

'But I've got work to do, and staying just for the five-star croissants wouldn't stretch my credibility with the Old Man. They told me yesterday that he's missing me, and he's gone into a bit of a decline.' Truchaud tried to imagine the Divisional Commander in a 'bit of a decline', but his imagination wasn't up to it, certainly not that morning anyway.

'You have that effect on people,' he said glumly.

'I expect I do,' she said gaily. 'Are you going to go into a bit of a decline after I've gone?' she asked.

'I expect so,' he said, staying in the glum mode; but somehow she didn't believe him, or at least didn't appear to. Michelle had got it all wrong; it was as simple as that. He pushed a mouthful of croissant into his mouth with jam on it and chewed for a moment. It was followed down with a mouthful of coffee.

'While you're here, will you keep an eye on Dagmar? She's a nice kid and I would hate for this all to blow up in her face.'

'You can count on me keeping an eye on her. After all, the two businesses are partners, so I'll probably see her most days. At least I will keep an eye on her until I too get back to Paris.'

'You will be coming back then?'

'That is my intention, but it probably won't happen while my father is still alive,' he said ruefully. He found himself sitting in the prosecuting counsel's chair, accusing himself of wishing his father dead so he could get back to the girl. *Oh go! Natalie, just get in your damn car and get on the road. You don't feel like I do; you have made that abundantly clear. Now just get out of here and go and play in the mean streets of Paris, and have done with it.* Of course he didn't say any of that out loud. Maybe he should have, he thought.

She patted her mouth with a tissue. 'Well,' she said, 'I must be on my way.' She stood up and they embraced in the French way, kissing the air about three inches laterally of each ear. 'I'll see you at the inquest, *chef*,' she said and climbed into her car, started the engine, and drove sedately out between the stone courtyard gates out into her future.

Truchaud walked slowly and sadly back to the dining room and sat down with his head in his hands, inhaling the strong roasted aroma of his coffee.

'Has she gone?' said Michelle's voice from somewhere. He hadn't realized she was still in the house until she spoke. He hadn't really thought about her at all until that moment in fact. 'You let her go,' she said accusingly. 'Sometimes, Charlemagne Truchaud, I fail to make any sense of you at all. I was obviously labouring under the misapprehension that that girl actually meant something to you. For reasons I completely fail to understand, you mean an impossible amount to her.'

'How do you work that one out?' he asked her, feeling a little bit riled at this point. It didn't suit him at all for his sister-in-law to nag him for no obviously good reason.

'Well, she said so: pure and simple.'

'I don't understand you. What exactly did she say?'

'Three very simple words: "I" and then "love" followed by "him".'

'It's a bloody shame that neither of us had the bottle to say it to each other face to face, and also a bit of a shame that someone, who's supposed to be on our side, didn't actually help it get said, so to speak. Perhaps when she comes back down for the inquest, you'll try to facilitate that.' He changed the subject. 'Have you seen the German girls?'

'They went off with Bruno to Maréchale's place in the campervan.' Truchaud looked through the window, and realized that it also wasn't in the courtyard, which now had a very strange rather alien uncluttered look, which it had always used to have, but he'd got rather used to it looking like a walled car park in the town centre.

'I think I'll go off to the town hall and see if they have anything they want me to do,' he said. 'I'm sure we'll have some planning for Bastille Day that they'll want to discuss. It's not that far off, you know.' He stood up and washed his and Natalie's crockery by hand in the kitchen sink, thinking of how a teenager might leave her cup unwashed. He gave it an extra scrub to make sure she was all gone, and then dried it to a shine. He gave his sister-in-law a wan smile and he too left the building.

He took his BX with him this time, as he took a rather circuitous route to the town hall, driving straight past it and on to Vougeot. From there he turned left at the roundabout, through the village, and then up past the clos itself into the narrow convoluted streets of Chambolle-Musigny. He slowly drove out on the famous Route of the Grands Crus and pulled in on the side of the road, just for a moment to watch a pony being led between the rows of vines of the Bonnes Mares Grand Cru. He took a deep breath and took a small track between the vines back down to the Seventy-Four, and feeling properly awake at last, headed back to Nuits-Saint-Georges and the office.

Coda

Later that day, back at the domaine

'Uncle Charlie?' came a little voice from behind his left shoulder. He looked round from his glass, which he was simply watching rather than making any serious attempt to drink from. Suzette was standing there, sad-faced beneath her tawny bob. 'I think we both lost that one, didn't we?' she added.

'Yes, I think we did,' he replied grimly.

'Can I thank you for siding with me against your own personal interests?' she said after a while.

'I'm not sure that I did anything really.'

'You tried to warn me, and you didn't need to, you know.'

'Yes, I think I did. I would never have forgiven myself if I had any active role in whatever came out. I needed to know that whatever happened was simply due to happenstance, and that I had no role in it.'

'Well, thank you anyway.'

'Don't mention it. Do you want a cuppa, or would you prefer to join me in a marc?'

'I think I'd prefer the marc if it's any good.'

He took a sip from his glass and thought for a moment, and then swirled it round his mouth. 'It'll do,' he said once the fiery liquor had given him his breath back.

'Then I'll join you in a marc,' she said and pulled up a chair.

Truchaud went to the sideboard and got out another glass, not in any way feeling guilty about feeding neat spirit to someone young enough to be his daughter. Dammit, had fate had its own way back in the day, she would have been his kid anyway. He poured her a couple of fingers into the glass. She picked it up and took a good pull from the glass. She shuddered for a moment as the alcohol hit her system, sighed and then said in

259

a rather rasping voice, 'I agree, it'll do.' They both nursed their liquor for a moment, and then she asked, 'Do you think she'll come back?'

'Who? Natalie?'

'Who else would I have been talking about? Yes, Natalie, of course.'

'I doubt it. Why should she want to? She's got the job she's always wanted, at the centre of the universe. Why should she want to hang around in a backwater like Nuits-Saint-Georges? What else do we do here apart from make wine well, and park badly?'

'So what will you do?'

'Remember I mentioned parking badly? Well, that will be my job for the time being: making sure it doesn't get any worse; that and looking after my father. What will you do?'

'Well, I shall go back to university next term, and try to keep Hairy Eddie out of trouble, always assuming that he doesn't get into any over the summer holidays, while I'm not there to watch. Meanwhile, Uncle Jean has given me a job over the break in his own domaine. I don't think I could cope with working at Laforge's any longer.'

'No, I understand that. I'm sorry about what happened.'

'I don't see why you should shoulder any of the blame, or really anyone for that matter. It just happened.'

'So, why are you here, not that I'm in any way not enjoying your company?'

'I couldn't think of anywhere else to be. I understand about you and mum.'

'That was a very long time ago.'

'Maybe, but I think it was very important to both of you, and therefore I'm sort of part of all that.'

'Well, thank you, Suzette, I appreciate that. I hope you'll always feel you can just drop in on me and say hello.'

She took another mouthful of the marc, and spluttered for a moment. She then said, 'Provided, of course, you keep up the steady supply of alcohol!'

'Not a problem, provided your mother doesn't object!' And for the first time since she had arrived, they both smiled at each other.

'You know something? I think I'd prefer you to play the role of my dissipated uncle than that of a clean-living godparent.'

'Provided you aren't planning to drive home after we've delivered a further grievous injury to that bottle, I'd be happy to play the role of your dissipated uncle.'

Truchaud's father appeared across the courtyard, and looked at them slightly crossly. He harrumphed at them, 'I assume you both know whose bottle that is … or rather was,' he said.

'Yours?' asked his son innocently.

'Damn right,' he replied, parking himself at the table. 'Now get me a glass, and get out the cards.' He looked at Suzette's face, adding, 'As the pretty one's here already, I think a few hands of Tarot are in order, don't you?' Truchaud got another glass from the sideboard and the cards. He put the glass on the table in front of his father and pushed the bottle towards him. His father poured a couple of fingers of marc into his glass and took a sniff, thought about it for a moment, and then put the glass down again. He put his hand out, palm upwards towards his son. 'The cards?' he said. Then he shouted up the stairs, 'Bruno? Are you coming down?'

Truchaud looked at his father puzzled, 'Bruno's here?'

The boy came downstairs looking rather bored, though he brightened up considerably when he saw Suzette sitting at the table.

'Tarot?' she smiled almost unscrupulously, knowing the effect that her smile would have on the boy's blood pressure.

'Why not?' he said, pulling up a chair at the table and parking on it.

'I would have thought you would have been with Jacquot in the vineyards somewhere, or out doing something,' Truchaud asked his nephew.

'Jacquot's busy,' came the terse reply.

'Oh?'

'Jacquot's got a girlfriend, and he now spends most of his time with her.'

'Oh? Anyone I know?'

'I doubt it. She's called Adèle.'

Truchaud wondered whether she was the Adèle he had met the other day. He would find out soon enough if it became important. He pulled the cards from the box and after having given them a good shuffle, he cut the pack, and passed it to his father, who started dealing, correctly in the tradition of Tarot, three at a time, counterclockwise, creating a six-card dog as he dealt.

About the author

R.M. Cartmel has been a writer one way and another since being a medical student at Oxford. After a long career as a successful and much sought-after GP, R.M. Cartmel decided to retire from practice and dedicate himself full-time to the creation of crime fiction. This is his second novel.

Also by R.M. Cartmel:

The Richebourg Affair

'R.M. Cartmel's *The Richebourg Affair* is a well-crafted treasure of unforgettable characters, eloquent yet whimsical language, intrigues burrowed into the ways of classic French wine making, and vintage murder mystery writing. I felt so comfortable in Cartmel's hands as a storyteller that I couldn't believe it's a debut novel.'

Jeffrey Siger, best-selling author of *Murder in Mykonos*

'Whether you are a lover of detective novels, the great wines of Burgundy, or, like me, both, *The Richebourg Affair* is a gripping read that will have you turning the pages from beginning to end.'

Chris Pollington, Private Account Manager – Berry Bros. & Rudd, Wines and Spirits Merchants, London

Other titles from Crime Scene Books you might enjoy:

The Tsar's Banker

By: Stephen Davis

A pacy, exciting story, which might, just might, be true…

The Romanovs, the last Russian Imperial family, were fabulously wealthy – and not all their wealth fell into the hands of the Bolshevik revolutionaries. A fortune in fabulous jewels and money, it is said, was brought to the United Kingdom, and into the safekeeping of the Bank of England. Yet as recently as 1960 Sir Edward Peacock, then Director of the Bank of England, stated: 'I am pretty sure there was never any money of the Imperial Family of Russia in the Bank of England, nor in any other bank in England. Of course, it is difficult to say "never".'

This is the starting point for Stephen Davis' immaculately researched story of romance, revolution and acts of desperate heroism, as Philip Cummings, charged with bringing a precious container of the Romanov jewels out of Russia, must abandon his orderly life at the Bank of England to save not only the jewels, but also a beautiful Countess and her badly wounded brother.

- Will Philip manage to win through, and keep his beloved Countess out of the hands of the revolutionaries?

- Why does a sinister figure keep watch from afar?

- Who betrayed Philip, and will they prevail?

- Do the Romanov jewels really still reside in the vaults of the Bank of England?

'A thrilling novel painted in glorious period and geographic detail with the real life conspiracy theory of Dan Brown and the glamour of Ian Fleming at his best. It compels you to turn the pages to find out how Philip Cummings and the British Empire are embroiled in the destiny of Tsarist Russia. I loved it.'

Caspar Berry, Poker Advisor on the blockbusting movie *Casino Royale*

Coming in October 2015, a dark story of people trafficking, murder and abuse: *50 Miles from Anywhere* by Michael Cayzer.

The Romanée Vintage, the final volume of RM Cartmel's trilogy set in Burgundy over a winemaking year, will be out in Spring 2016.

All CSB titles available to order from
www.crime-scene-books.com